ROYAL OUTCASTS:
THE CORONATION

SEAN DAVIS

BALBOA.PRESS
A DIVISION OF HAY HOUSE

Balboa Press books may be ordered through booksellers or by contacting:

Balboa Press
A Division of Hay House
1663 Liberty Drive
Bloomington, IN 47403
www.balboapress.com
1 (877) 407-4847

Because of the dynamic nature of the Internet, any web addresses or
links contained in this book may have changed since publication and
may no longer be valid. The views expressed in this work are solely those
of the author and do not necessarily reflect the views of the publisher,
and the publisher hereby disclaims any responsibility for them.

The author of this book does not dispense medical advice or prescribe the use
of any technique as a form of treatment for physical, emotional, or medical
problems without the advice of a physician, either directly or indirectly. The
intent of the author is only to offer information of a general nature to help
you in your quest for emotional and spiritual well-being. In the event you use
any of the information in this book for yourself, which is your constitutional
right, the author and the publisher assume no responsibility for your actions.

Any people depicted in stock imagery provided by Getty Images are
models, and such images are being used for illustrative purposes only.
Certain stock imagery © Getty Images.

Print information available on the last page.

ISBN: 978-1-9822-5031-7 (sc)
ISBN: 978-1-9822-5032-4 (e)

Balboa Press rev. date: 07/07/2020

CONTENTS

CHAPTER ONE

HAVE YOU EVER wanted to punch a customer in the throat? Well try being a server on game day in Tuscaloosa Alabama. This town gets some of the biggest jerks from both sides when we play a home game, but then again, it's also one of the most exciting and fun events this town has to offer. Now I'm not a sports fan but who am I to tell someone not to enjoy something because I think it's boring? Just another day working my ass off for half the pay I should be bringing home and another day leaving at almost two am. Not to mention I'm the last one leaving the restaurant... again. Who else is going to clean up if I don't?

Anyway, I can't bitch too much I suppose. At least it's a beautiful night tonight. The sky is clear and full of stars and the fall air is clean and crisp. Now I just have to remember where I parked my car. The parking situation in this town on a home game is just pathetic. We can't seem to keep up with the increasing number of people that come to the games every year. It's the curse of living in a college town where the football team is always winning, I suppose. My feet feel like they are each one big ass blister. Just a few more painful steps later and I reach the parking deck. Tuscaloosa has been on a building boom the past few years and this is one of the many parking decks the mayor seems to think we had to build. It looks less like a parking deck and more like a refurbished warehouse, but that's the trend now to make municipal buildings look all historic so they blend. I hate this parking deck on game days, it's either so full you have to drive around for days to find a parking space or so empty you think you're being stalked by a creeper. Tonight the feeling of being watched is ridiculous, it's just little ole me and my paranoia to keep me company while I try to remember where I parked my damn car. Everyone else is either at a bar getting wasted or at a house party puking on each other while doing the nasty.

Walking through the parking deck I notice it's darker than usual. Giving it further inspection I notice that someone got a bit smashy with the lighting. I try not to think too much of it and tell myself the college kids and fans are drunk tonight and neither tend to make the best decisions when that happens. Finally, my car decides to make an appearance, and it seems to have company.

"Hey there." I say to the stranger standing next to my car while giving him my usual dude nod. He returns my nod with a smile. This guy doesn't seem all that right. He shouldn't be scary to me. He's an attractive well put together dude after all. Come to think of it, he's very attractive. Built perfectly, well-groomed, dressed to impress with that form fitting black suit. The kind of guy you want to get up close to just to see what he smells like. I've seen hot guys, but none have had this kind of effect on me before. So why is a hot guy like this one making me freak out so much? Could it be that we are the only two people here, or could it be that freaky ass smile on his beautiful face?

He finally responds with "You're out late aren't you little one?"

I can't help but give him a confused look. "Little one? I'm pretty sure we are about the same height." He responds with a chuckle and walks a few steps closer, I grip my keys between my fingers inside my pocket. If he thinks I'm going down without a fight he'll find out I'm not when my keys are stuck in his eye sockets. Why do I think he's going to hurt me?

"You seem to be afraid, why is that?' I give one of those pathetic laughs that sound like a cough and say "I'm not afraid, it's just been a long night. Just ready to get home." and smile like a dork. He steps closer, close enough for me to smell. Dear God, his scent alone makes the hairs on my arms stand up. It's like his scent is electric.

"Can, um... do you need a ride or something?" the frick? Did I just offer him a ride? I've never done that before in my life. I don't trust people in general because of the suck factor most of them have. His smile grows. "No, just out for a walk. I got a bit hungry and decided to see what this town had to offer." His voice is like butter. I give him a smile back and say "Well I hate to tell ya but at this hour there isn't much open. Maybe a bar, or fast food if you're into that." He reaches out and puts his hand on my shoulder. Holy shit, did my shoulder just have an orgasm?!

He finally says "No little one, that isn't my thing." Then that freaky ass smile comes back, but this time his face isn't so beautiful. Where did those pointy teeth come from? The next thing I know is his mouth is on my throat. Holy shit it hurts! I can't move! Why can't I move? He's not even holding me down. This isn't right, I should be able to move. Stop, I must make him stop. My finger.....My hand is still in my pocket. I can feel the keys but I can't move my arm. Shit shit shit! I'm not letting this freak take me out like this. If I'm going down I'm damn well making sure he remembers me for a long time. My face is close enough to smell his neck. He still smells amazing. I feel dizzy, shit I have to do something. His neck is so close, why not show him what it feels like. I open my mouth and try to bite him back. Why is it so hard to open my mouth? Slowly I manage to open it as far as I can, my tongue lands on his neck and he jumps slightly like he didn't expect me to fight back. I can't let this freak get away, I use all the willpower I can muster and clamp down with my teeth.

I had no idea how hard it is to break the skin with your teeth but I freaking did it. Blood comes flowing hard and fast, so fast it flows down my throat before I could stop it. I've tasted blood before as we all have like after a nosebleed or a fist fight, so I expected the same salty metallic flavor. As I'm guzzling his blood I ask myself three questions. Number one- Why the hell does his blood taste so amazing? Number two- Why the hell am I drinking it down like I'm dying of thirst. And number three- Why am I flying through the air upside down towards a car? Oh, I guess I pissed him off.

Well I guess this is it. I hope at least I left a scar on that pretty perfect neck of his. Looking at him it seems he's not feeling too well either. Guess I didn't agree with him, good. He's puking his guts out. Drunk ass must have had some serious bath salts or something. After he's done dry heaving I see him hit the ground. Looking closer I don't think he's breathing, the color in his face is so pale he doesn't seem real. He looks like he's carved out of ivory or something. I notice his clothes start to smoke for some reason. Is...is he on fire? Everything is going dark now. At least it doesn't hurt anymore. At least nothing else will ever hurt anymore.

I feel... Pain? Wait, I'm not supposed to hurt anymore am I? Why is it so loud?

"He's lost a lot of blood, what kind of knife could have done this type of damage? It's a mess." Why is there a lady with her hand on my neck? I'm so sleepy, just a small nap. Yeah just a small one.

Floating is fun. Is that me? Who is that lady and why is she jumping up and down on my chest? The frick am I in the hospital for? Oh yeah, crazy dude on bath salts. Oh shit...I'm dead aren't I?

Where am I now? It's so foggy. "My child" that voice...Why does she sound so familiar? I respond with sadness and a pathetic tone. "Hello?" I hate it, but I'm terrified and attempt to run from her. Nothing happens, my legs aren't responding to me. "Don't be afraid child" I can see her now. Not very well but it's her. "Am I dead? I'm really scared." Why would I let her know I'm scared? I wouldn't do that normally. She moves closer to me.

"Yes dear, you are dead. But do not fear, it's temporary and just the beginning." She finally comes into view. I can see her smiling. It's the most amazing thing I've ever seen. Her smile is so bright it could light up an entire planet. She's so beautiful. Her hair is the blackest of black, weightless like it's floating underwater. Her eyes are the deepest shade of blue, a color so intense that you can actually drown in it.

Her stare can stop an army with just a gaze, and her body is perfect. Not that fake ass version of perfection everyone tries to acquire, but curvy and made to impress. She walks closer with the most beautiful smile and lays her hand on my cheek, the warmest most perfect feeling comes over me. I'm not afraid anymore, I'm happy. It's like I'm home.

"Oh, my sweet boy, I wish you could stay longer but it's not your time just yet. But do not fear, we will see each other again soon enough. Just remember, if you can, when you return, you are the chosen. You are my child. You are royalty, and you are the very first of your kind." Then she smiles the most beautiful smile in existence while she brushes my cheek. "And you are perfect." And then after hearing her beautiful voice....More freaking pain.

God, my neck hurts so bad. My chest feels like it's on fire. Is someone crying? I try and see, and there he is. Sloan King. Poor guy, he looks like he's been crying for a while. I guess that's what you do when your husband gets killed.... Wait. Is that right? Did I die? I try to speak but choke instead. It hurts so bad as I cough. "Oh, my god! Brandon, he's awake! Nurse!" Seems I didn't die. Well that's good, I guess. I try and talk but it's not easy. "Hey there baby, sorry I didn't call." I say in a pathetic tone as he looks down at me and smiles.

"Shh, it's ok baby. Try not to talk. Everything's ok now. You are alright and that's all that matters." He looks back at the door. "Where's that fricking nurse?" He looks back at me and I can't help but smile at him. "I love you so much"

Sloan, the first and only person I've ever truly loved and the best person I know. Standing there in all his might with his salt and pepper hair and those beautiful dark brown eyes of his. He may not look it at first sight, but he has an extremely commanding personality. To top it off, he's brilliant and a borderline genius. If he was IQ tested I'm sure he would score off the charts. He's the kind of guy that if you dare approach him with an argument you better damn well come prepared. People have a misconception about gay people. I'm always hearing (gay people can't stay in a relationship because it's just not natural.) Well, we proved them wrong. Going on twenty years now. That's right. Suck it people. I do feel sorry for that nurse though, he's going to put her through hell.

The hospital food here isn't half bad, I just don't really have an appetite. I guess having a crazy dude try to eat you will do that to a guy. Sloan is finally asleep in the chair across from me. Poor guy has been worrying about me probably for days. He's sleeping so hard, I wish there was another bed here for him here in this room. He can't be comfortable sleeping in a chair contorted the way he is. Having your husband almost die can take it out of you I guess.

I shove the tray away and sit back and try to sleep myself, with no luck. I don't think I've ever been this awake before. Honestly, I feel like I could run a marathon and not miss a beat. Hmmmmm, So, this is what adrenaline is like? I could definitely get used to this. If there were only an easier way to get this awesome feeling going by myself. I'm not sure that being attacked and almost kicking the bucket is a fair trade off. Staring at the television infomercial about how much better it would be to cook your eggs in a granite pan than it would be in a non stick pan for the seventh time tonight, I hear a knock at the door.

"Sir, you have visitors" Before I can help myself I let out a groan. Oh look, the cops are here, goody. "Hello, You are Brandon King, correct?" I look up to the good ole boy speaking and give them both a smile. The talkative one seems a bit tired, like he hasn't had a day off in a while. Or a bath for that matter.

"Yes sir, that's me." The look on the one male cop's face makes me think he's annoyed that he has to be here. He gives me a nod. "We are here to investigate your attack. It says here you said a man tried to eat you?"

I give a shy chuckle. "I'm sorry about my statement earlier, I was kind of out of it ya know with all that happened to me To be honest I'm not sure what happened. Here I was minding my own business walking to my car and Some guy just walked up to me and clamped down on my neck and tried to take a chunk out of me. I think he was on something"

Mr. Could Care Less Policeman nods with an uninterested look. "That's ok sir, we kind of figured you weren't in your right mind when you gave your statement earlier. You say he was on something, can you describe his behavior?" I try and remember if Mr. Facebiter acted like he was high on something but thinking back I honestly can't say he was. I can't help but frown. "To be honest, he didn't seem like he was on anything at all. He seemed weirdly calm for what he was doing to me in that parking garage."

"We searched the surrounding area and didn't find anyone, who um, exactly matches your description. I'm sorry to say it seems the cameras were smashed so catching anything on video is out. One thing that was interesting at the scene was a pile of ashes right across from where you claim you were attacked. Can you explain that?"

I flinch when he reminds me of the burnt pile of asshat "Yes! Holy shit, I thought I dreamed that or something. OMG he was on fire when I passed out."

Apparently that answer upset Mr. Could Care Less Policeman a bit. Holy shit he seems really angry now.

He responds with a sarcastic and aggravated tone, "Sir, it's impossible for a man to burn that completely without being cremated." Oh goody, mister officer is a dick. "Well! I guess bleeding out because someone tried to make you their midnight snack will make your eyes go all wonky." I say back with my pissed off look rolling my eyes so hard they almost get stuck in my brain. "I'm sorry sir, I didn't mean it that way." The officer snorts back at me waking Sloan up in the process. Now he's done it. Poor Mister Officer Man has woken the beast that I love.

"Look, we are just frustrated because we have nothing to go on at this point to find out who did this to you. We will keep investigating but right now we can't do much." He hands me his business card." Call me if you remember anything at all." I nod and they both walk out.

Frustrated and more than a little pissed off, I lean back in the uncomfortable ass hospital bed. "Well that was a damn waste of time." Sloan jumps up reaching into his front pants pocket grabbing his cell phone. "Don't worry baby, as soon as they get a call from our attorney they will do their freaking job." I look over and smile at the man that I love, fuming and ready to strike, I reach my hand out to stop him from dialing.

"Baby, Calm down, it's ok. I was there. It looked like he was on fire but maybe my eyes were playing tricks on me, I mean I was being killed after all. With all that going on in my brain, and ya know almost being murdered, he had plenty of time to get away without me seeing him. I'm sure the police are doing all they can with what they have. Anyway, the crazy asshole won't forget me. He should scar quite nicely." I say with an evil grin puffing out my chest.

Sloan comes over to the bed and looks at me shocked. "Wait, you didn't tell me you hurt him. Why didn't you say anything? What did you do?" I look down at my hands. "Well, I'm worried that I might have caught something from the freak. I mean I, um, kind of...bit him back. Hard." Sloan looks back at me completely confused. "Wait, you what?" I hate to freak him out any more than he already is with all this new info.

"Sloan. I thought I was going to die and there was no way in hell I was going to let that asshat take me out without leaving him something to remember me by." He belts out his beautiful laugh trying his best to convince me that he is ok with all this shit. "I wouldn't expect anything less from you baby. Don't worry, the doctors are checking your blood for any, um, cooties. If you caught anything we will deal with it together baby. Besides, I'm sure everything is going to be fine." He's so cute when he lies. He's never been good at it.

I finally close my eyes and get some real sleep. No dreams, I guess that's a good thing. You would think I would be waking up in cold sweats screaming bloody murder, but nah. I look up to my door opening with two people walking into my room

The woman is a beautiful and flawless redhead with the cutest little pixie cut. Not many ladies can pull off that shit but her face was made for it. Her body is fairly lean and curvy all at the same time. Pixie cut is wearing cherry red stiletto heels, a black micro mini skirt and a short jacket with a dark frilly pink shirt. Imagine if a stripper conquered Wall Street. All in all she's pretty short compared to the guy part of the duo. This guy is massive! Chiseled features, scruffy facial hair, s Platinum blonde luscious locks cut short just off the ears with a slight curl. Mr. Universe is Wearing practically painted on jeans and a tight fitting black t-shirt.

Think Viking god gorgeous.

Pixie cut looks at me and smiles. "Well hello Brandon." I looked up with a frustrated look on my face. "So, I guess knocking isn't a thing anymore." She giggles at my frustration and it matches her look perfectly. "I'm sorry about that hun, but we are in kind of a hurry. My name is Lilly and this is Daniel." I frown a bit. "A pleasure. What exactly can I do for you?" She looks at mister Viking and back to me with a smile. "We are with Tuscaloosa parking security and we're just here to get some information if you don't mind." I chuckle at that. "Would have been nice to have the big guy there last night." Mister Viking grins at me

I lean back in the bed and look at them both and sarcastically say with a shy smile "Umm I hate to say it but your security kinda sucks." Pixi frowns a bit. "Yes, Brandon, I'm sad to say you are correct about that and we are truly sorry about what happened to you. So, Can you tell us what exactly happened last night in the parking garage from start to finish?"

I give her a confused look. "Shouldn't you just get my statement from the police? I told them everything that I know, even if they didn't exactly believe me." Mister Viking finally speaks up." We don't totally trust those reports. It's best to get the statement from the victim personally so we don't miss anything." Damn, his voice is so deep he even sounds like a Viking god, without the accent of course

The nurse comes barging in the door like she owns the place. You know the type. The kind of nurse who thinks polite bedside manor is just a suggestion. She loudly says to my visitors from the parking security, "HEY, You two aren't supposed to be in here." Mister Viking turns toward her and flashes his pearly whites...hot damn. I think the nurse just about fainted and I don't blame her.

"I'm sorry ma'am we won't be long, we just need to ask this gentleman a few questions about his attack. We are with parking security." From the look on her face I think he could have told her that they were there to eat all the babies and she would be totally fine with it. Hell I didn't think she even knew how to smile. It doesn't seem like she does it very often

"That's totally fine." She says with a smile. "Just here to check his stitches, it won't take long." The frick? What's with these two? She should be kicking their asses out.

"Hold still hun, I'm just going to check this really quick." She pulls the bandage back half way and looks shocked. "Wow, you seem to be healing very well. You probably won't even have a scar. Guess it wasn't as bad as the doctor thought."

The two-pretty people give each other a serious glance and then look back in my direction. The nurse wraps me back up and walks out grinning at Mister Viking the whole time oblivious to everything but him almost running face first into the door. Pixi turns from that train wreck and gives me a smile. "We have taken up enough of your time Brandon. We can just get the report from the police. Sorry to disturb you. Get some rest." They both smile and leave. The hell? I'm pretty sure they aren't with any security agency.

Pulling up to our townhouse it's a sight for my tired eyes. It's so good to finally be home. As I open the door, two fur balls jump at me and almost knock me to the ground. My pups seem to have missed me. Nothing like a fur baby to make you feel loved. Sloan drops the bags on the floor in the foyer and closes the door quietly behind me.

"What do you want for dinner my love?" I look back at Sloan and think about it.

"I'm not really hungry but you go ahead and pick." He frowns at me like always. He knows as well as I do that two Libras can't make a decision.

"You have hardly eaten anything in the last few days. You need to eat something." He's not wrong, I've just not been that hungry. "I'll eat, I promise. Just pick something, it doesn't matter to me." As he grabs his phone to order I head upstairs to unpack. As I am taking my clothes out of the bag, I realize that I feel gross so I decide to take a shower. Pulling the bandage off completely sucked. What did that bitch nurse use to put this bandage on, duct tape? Holy shit, should I be healed this much? The wound, It's totally closed up. I'm pretty sure Mr. Facebiter took a chunk out of me. It sure did feel like it anyway. I suds up, rinse off, jump out of the shower and throw on a T-Shirt and some jeans. There's a knock on the door as I reach the bottom of the stairs.

"That's probably the food!" Sloan yells. I grab my wallet and pay for the pizza. As I close the door I notice a car I don't recognize in the parking lot of the neighborhood. Who would spend that much money on a car. You know the ones I am talking about. Big black Mercedes Benz that costs more than a house. I half expect one of those real housewives of somewhere to get out all dressed in Gucci and carrying a little dog in her purse. I stare out from the door it starts up and slowly drives away. Now that I think about it, I'm pretty friggin sure that was Pixi cut.

It's not easy going to sleep anymore, but I guess that's to be expected after almost being murdered. Should I still be so hyper? Not wanting to keep Sloan awake after what he's been through, I decide to just sneak out and go for a walk to calm myself down. Sliding out of bed isn't at all easy. Sloan is holding me so tight I'm surprised I can breathe. No need to wake him, he hasn't slept well in days. As soon as the night air hits my face I feel amazing. Better than I have in days, years even.

I get about half way down the complex parking lot when my stomach starts to have a full blown conversation with me. I'm so hungry. I remember we have some leftover pizza at the house but it doesn't sound good to me at all. Why don't I want it? I friggin love pizza, the greasier the better. It doesn't make me sick to think about eating it exactly, but I just don't want it. As usual there are plenty of night joggers out getting their cardio in. Not exactly my thing. I'm not into socializing with the neighbors much so I don't know anyone who lives around here personally. Guess that makes me a bad neighbor. Oh well, I like my privacy. Besides that's really more Sloan's thing. He's the social butterfly not me, but I guess that's what makes us work.

I continue my walk when I take notice of a guy stretching out his legs on the walkway. I stop suddenly. It's his scent, what the hell? He smells amazing. He's stretching his legs in a squat in loose fit jogging shorts and tank top, and of course he's in amazing shape. Every muscle on his body is basically perfect and he has to have like zero percent body fat. Pretty much everyone in this complex stays in good shape. Kinda gives me a complex.

I get closer to him and he looks up at me and nods. "How's it going?" I nod back. "Not bad, you?" "Pretty good." He says with a smile. I notice him looking at my neck where the freak tried to eat me. "Damn man, you're the guy that got attacked, aren't you?

I heard you lived around here, I just didn't figure you would be out and about so soon. You ok?"

I smile and nod. "Yeah, just a bit restless tonight I guess." He gives my neck a closer look. "It looks like it wasn't that bad, you mind if I look a bit closer? Not a weirdo I swear, just a med student." I smile, it's kinda weird I guess but I'm pretty sure he wouldn't try and kill me in the middle of an apartment complex.

"Yeah, it's ok. Go ahead." It's dark so he pulls his phone out to use the flashlight. He leans in to get a closer look after peeling back the bandage. "Looks like you will heal without a scar." I can't explain it, but I seem to not be able to keep my eyes off his neck...what the actual hell? He looks up at me and seems to freeze almost as if he's looking at me in adoration. "Wow." he whispers "your eyes...they're so beautiful."

Why am I smelling his neck? Damn he smells so good. I open my mouth and lean in toward his absolutely stunning throat. I start to feel an ache in the front of my gums for a split second and then a feeling of relief when I hear a small pop and feel teeth emerging. I feel them over with my tongue and for some reason it feels very natural. What else that feels natural is me leaning in to him and feeling them slide into his throat. What's weird is that there is no struggle from him at all. He seems to love it almost as if this is the most natural thing for us to do. Two small holes open up on the roof of my mouth and I feel his blood come rushing into my body like my new little syringes are drawing it out of him automatically. He hugs me tight, like he can't get close enough. He tastes so amazing! So warm and full of life. The flavor is like blood but not. It's like I can taste his life. It's like swallowing pure joy.

Suddenly I hear a very loud and powerful female voice say, "That's enough!" Wait. Who was that? Was that voice in my head? She sounds so familiar like I have known her all my life somehow. I pull my teeth from the delicious neck I have been enjoying and then lick the area where they punctured. Can't waste a drop of that deliciousness. The holes that my new pointy teeth made in his neck are closed now like it never even happened. Wait. Did it happen? With my tongue I feel the two new members of my face. Two small fangs. What the hell? Where did these come from? OMG am I high? With further exploration I can feel a small hole on the back of each fang towards the bottom. The best I can figure is that the blood just traveled through them and exited through the roof of my mouth for me to swallow down. I look up at him and feel them sliding effortlessly back into my gums. Holy crap that's a weird feeling. Oh wow He's smiling at me. Finally he blinks twice and nods like he is rebooting or something.

"Thanks for letting me take a look at your wound, hope I didn't freak you out. You seem to be healing very well. Ok so Stay safe buddy." He stretches out his hand to shake mine and then He just jogs off. What the shit? What the actual hell just happened? Did I just hallucinate? And why the hell is everything glowing?

CHAPTER TWO

EVERYTHING SEEMS NOW to have its own color and glow. It's hard to explain, hell it's hard for me to even understand. The thing is that it's not exactly a glow, but more of a mist coming off of everything, kinda like when you get out of a hot shower and step outside in the cold bathroom and steam comes off your body. The grass and trees all around me have this amazing golden shimmery mist emanating off them. I notice that the damn cat that likes to nap on top of my car is glowing bright yellow, almost like sunlight.

As I am getting used to all these new freaky sights, I look up and see a girl walking her dog coming towards me. The cute little pup is glowing gold just like the cat on my car. Oh wow, the girl is glowing a brilliant snow white color. I look around at the cars and buildings and they don't seem to emanate any of this new freaky light. It would appear only living things have the ability to glow. I rub my eyes to make sure I'm not totally tripping balls. I thought some of that stuff the nurse gave me was a bit strong, but this has to be real, right?

To my left I notice a leaf falling from a tree and can see every detail as it falls. It's as if it's right in front of my face and then I realize I'm looking at a leaf that's across the street. Holy shit...it's across the fricking street. I can even hear the wind coming from the leaf as it falls. What's that crunching noise? I look closer, it's a damn bug eating the falling leaf. I can see a bug eating a leaf falling off a tree across the street and hear every sound it makes as it falls. Holy shit, I must be high.

The wind starts to pick up and I start to smell things. I can smell, everything. The girl that passed by with her dog a minute ago, still lingers here. She smells…Delicious? Shit. I try to get my mind off how delicious she smells by looking around. I look across to the woods behind my townhouse to see what I can see. The trees are glowing. I can see sunshine colors radiating off the little critters sleeping in the trees. As I scan this new and colorful alien landscape I see something different. A blue color that is in the shape of a person hiding behind a tree in the brush. That's when I freeze.

The figure behind the tree isn't moving. I don't want to draw its attention so I start walking away. Just looking at my feet trying to be as normal as I can. As I am trying to be as inconspicuous as I can walking away I look at my arm and I notice, well me. I have a color as well. My color is blue not the white like the delicious girl. A deep blue that's just like the deep blue ocean you see when you are on a cruise ship. I look around to see more people to compare. They are all white. Every person I see glows the same snow white. Approaching the door to my townhouse I see someone walking towards me in the darkness. It's a large man with that same shade of blue as me. I stop in my tracks with my heart beating so hard I know it's about to explode out of my chest.

"You're going to need a permit to hunt here." Mister Viking says with a grin.

I stare him down with a cold glare." Did the cops not give you enough information?"

He chuckles "You gave us all the information we needed." He nods towards my neck. "How's your neck feeling?" My hand automatically goes up to touch the wound from the attack. Where is it? It's totally gone. There aren't even any stitches remaining. I look back at him in a slight panic.

"What the shit is going on? Who the hell are you and why the hell are you following me?"

He runs his hand through his golden hair, smiling. "You have a way with words don't you kid."

Who the hell does he think he is calling me a kid?. His condescending tone absolutely rubs me the wrong way. I blurt out "Kid? Dude I'm pretty sure I'm older than you and you didn't answer my question. Who the frick are you really?' I glance behind him towards the woods wondering if that was him I saw hiding and spying. Much to my surprise the figure is still there hiding behind the tree.

"Also, who the frick do you have back there in the woods spying on me?" His eyes widen, he seems a bit shocked at the question. He looks back towards the trees and then back to me.

Amazed and with shock in his voice he asks, "You can see her?" He then looks back towards me "He knows you are here, come on over." He didn't yell, he just spoke in a regular conversation voice like before. I look towards the woods and I see the figure walking towards us.

There she is, little Miss Pixie herself coming out of the woods from her hiding place. "So, you two have been spying on us this whole time? That *was* you two in the car parked across from our house, wasn't it? I need answers and I need answers NOW! What the hell is going on here and I want the truth this time?" Pixi speaks up this time. Leaning into me close with a very soft tone as she says "Oh Brandon, you know what's going on. Use your head and answer your own questions. Its time to stop playing dumb and figure out what you know already. You just sucked the blood out of some random guy's neck. What do you think is happening?"

I stand there like a moron, frozen and blinking like I'm braindead trying to explain what happened logically to myself, trying to come up with any other explanation besides the obvious one.

Finally, I just say it." Vampires are a thing? Really?" I look at the ground, dumbfounded freaking out. I must be dreaming. That's it. That nurse gave me something in the hospital and its not out of my system yet. That has to be it. This is too weird for me not to be in a full ass dream.

"This has got to be some kind of a dream, that's right. I'm asleep and in the hospital still."

Suddenly I feel a sharp pain on my left cheek. "Ouch!" Did that bitch just slap me? "Did you just freaking slap me?" She giggles. "Did it hurt?" I give her my best death stare." Yea, bitch. It did."

She belts out a laugh. "Well then you are not dreaming. And forgive me for saying it but you have some balls kid." I stare back as the death stare fades from my face. "Why the hell do you guys keep calling me kid?"

Mister Viking shakes his head with a smile. "It's quite a bit to process I know. But there are some things that you need to know now instead of later. The truth is this Brandon. You have one week to process and come to terms with what you are." He pulls a card from his shirt pocket and hands it to me. "Here is how to reach us. You will need to call that number by the end of this week. If you do not call the number you will be hunted and killed. Trust me when I say there is nowhere you can hide kid so don't even try. You are one of us now whether you like it or not. There is no need for you to run from this, we can help you."

I look up at him in a panic, "What the hell do you mean, hunt me? You're actually going to kill me if I don't call this number before the end of the week?" He looks back at me with a cold and serious stare. His tone has changed and is now cold and very stern. "Yes Brandon, we will be forced to do just that. You need to understand something right here and now. You weren't supposed to happen. There are strict rules about turning someone. You need explicit permission to do so. If a vampire turns a human without that permission, then that newly turned vampire and the one who turned him is slated for execution."

I give him a panicked look. "But I didn't ask for this! That son of a bitch attacked me. He didn't ask me!" He looks back at me with pity in his eyes and with a much softer voice says. "I know Brandon, that's why we are talking to you like this and not killing you right now. You didn't ask for this, and to be honest, we are not sure why he turned you in the first place."

He looks out into space at nothing shaking his head. Almost as if he is having a conversation with his own brain he whispers, "And why would he ash himself after? It just doesn't make any sense" I start to say that he didn't ash himself, remembering how I bit into his neck and how he started puking all over the damn place before bursting into flames.

"Don't!" that voice in my head screams and I can't help but jump like I was hit by something. "What is it?" Pixie exclaims while looking around for whatever hidden danger is lurking.

"Nothing, I'm just a bit jumpy I guess."

She looks back at me with a frown. "I'm sorry Brandon, I know you didn't ask for this, but it happened nonetheless." She puts a hand gingerly up to my cheek, the same one that she slapped earlier. I flinch a little at her touch, but she just caresses my cheek anyway." I'm sorry for hitting you earlier. I know you are scared and I know you don't even know who we are but we are here for you. We want to help you get through this."

Viking dude nods "She's right Brandon, the card that I gave you has my personal number on it as well. You call me anytime ok? If you think you are in trouble or just need someone to talk to about this. You call me." With that, they turn quickly and walk away.

I look up at my door, I won't tear up...I will not tear up. This can't be real. Those two have got to be messing with me. Will they actually kill me? Will they kill Sloan? Oh shit, Sloan! What do I tell Sloan? I take one last deep breath and walk inside.

"Shit! I was about to call the cops Brandon! You had me scared shitless! Are you ok?" There he was in all his glory in full panic mode. Just wait. He doesn't know how stressed out he's about to be. "I'm fine baby. I just needed some air." He hugs me so hard I let out a cough.

"Please tell me when you are going for a walk next time."

He pulls back and looks me over, he freezes as his eyes lock in on the wound that was supposed to be on my neck. He stands there eyes wide open, blinking, shocked and with the cutest look of confusion on his face. "I think you need to sit down Sloan. I have a lot of explaining to do and I'm not sure you should be standing up for it.

After he realizes I'm talking to him he walks over to the sofa and sits down. The poor guy's face is full of fear. I notice that his glow seems to slowly change from snow white to a deep cherry red. I kneel down in front of him and take his hands in my hands trying to be as comforting as I can.

"First I need you to calm down, Sloan, ok? Just breath, I'm ok." He takes a few breaths but does not relax at all, but he tries his best to fake it for me I am sure.

"I'm not sure how to start, how do you explain….This." I look up and just rip the band aid off the situation.

"So, remember when I got attacked and I told you the dude burst into flames? Well now I know why." Sloan just sits there staring at me without saying a word." Apparently, he was what you would call, a Vampire." He starts to go for his phone "That's it! I'm calling your doctor."

I grab his hands tighter. "Stop and just listen for a second, look at me." He looks up in a huff. "Hurry up and finish so I can call the damn doctor. "I point to my neck." How the hell do you explain this?" He touches my neck like he's trying to wipe away some kind of makeup as if I'm trying to mess with him. "Vampires are just fiction Brandon. They aren't real, it's just fantasy."

I nod and chuckle at the same time. "If you asked me a few hours ago, I would have agreed with you."

I get up off my knee and sit down beside him on the sofa. "Look at me please baby. A few days ago, I was attacked by a crazy person and my throat was practically ripped out. I almost bled out, then I was thrown into a car and left for dead in that parking deck. And now...there isn't a scratch on me." I turn and show him my arms, legs, neck, lift my shirt. "See, look, nothing. How else would you explain it?" His eyes just about popped out of his head.

"Brandon."

I shake my head in frustration, "No, explain it."

He looks at me and points to my chest. "No, Brandon. Look." I look down.

What the fricking frick? I gasp. Now, just so you know, I have never been one for exercise. I have never been in horrible shape but I had gotten good at rocking the dad bod. That's why I am freaking out when I look down at myself. I have...abs. No kidding, actual abs. My body looks amazing.

I jump up and run to the bathroom mirror. "Holy shit!" I'm a freaking beefcake. It's like my body decided on its own to be the perfect version of itself. My face has always looked younger than it actually was because of chronic baby face, but now it's flawless. My close shaved dark brown hair shines. And hot damn, my grey eyes are like silver grey, glowing but not glowing. I mean I never liked to brag but I considered myself attractive with my dad bod, always said I would do me but now. Holy crap. I go back to Sloan who is sitting there on the sofa still scared shitless.

"I'm so sorry, please don't be scared. It's me. It's still me I promise."

He looks at me and starts to tear up. "Please don't freak out, I need you right now. I'm scared Sloan." I kneel in front of him again and look him in the eyes. "I need you to try and calm down. I know I've asked a lot of you the last few days but I really need you to be calm and collected right now."

He does his best to calm down, after he wipes the tears from his eyes he looks back at me.

"There has got to be some explanation for this. Vampires aren't real Brandon. Maybe it's some kind of drug you got in the hospital that speeds up your healing." I smile. "I'm pretty sure if that drug was invented they wouldn't use it on little ol me just to see if it works, especially at a hospital in Tuscaloosa of all places. Anyway, that wouldn't explain why I just bit the guy outside and drank his blood." oops...yep. Shouldn't have blurted that out.

"You did what?!" Damn... "Calm down. He's fine. He doesn't even remember. He's still good enough to finish his jog, so it's ok." He looks pissed now. "It's ok?! Are you serious? How is any of this ok?!" I can't help but be frustrated and a bit pissed knowing what Pixie and Mr. Viking just told me outside. "It's not! I didn't want this either, it just is! Do you think I asked for any of this?!" His face starts to calm and he shakes his head. "No, I know you didn't baby. This just doesn't seem like it can be real. None of this seems real or even logical."

I nod back at him with a sigh. "You're telling me."

That's when I tell him about meeting Little Miss Pixie Lily and Mister Viking Daniel and having a week to come to terms with who I am and what is to come. And no, he doesn't take it well. Sloan jumps up and heads to the bar cart in the dining room. "So, what does that mean exactly?" He asks me while taking a shot of tequila. It seems to be calming him down a bit. I notice that his color is slowly going back to snow white from the deep red it was.

"I'm not sure honestly. I guess it means that I'm supposed to accept what I am."

He nods as he slowly puts the bottle down. "So, how does this all work now anyway? Do you want to eat me right now or is this something you have to wait for a full moon?"

I can't help but chuckle at how cute he is asking me that. "No, it's not like the movies. I don't want to tear anyone's throat out. When I bit the jogger, I was just sort of hungry. Honesty I wasn't even thinking about it while I did it." He shrugs and gives me another concerned look. "Well you might want to make sure you don't do it again. I mean, what if someone out there noticed what you were doing."

He's right. Do I actually have control of when I bite someone? "I guess I need to call Daniel.

"You're totally right. I have to be careful." He nods and then shrugs again. "Or you can just bite me and test the theory." I looked shocked. "What if I hurt you Sloan? I can't live with myself if I did." He looks up at me with a smile. "Brandon, you just bit a total stranger in the street. He jogged off totally fine. What makes you think you would end up hurting me?" I look at him and am surprised he's being totally serious about this.

"I don't know. This is all new. I want to make sure before I even try ok. Let me call Daniel to get some pointers and make sure it's safe first." He looks a bit annoyed "Ok. Also, ask him when it's my turn." I look back at him confused. "Your turn for what?" He looks me dead in the eye. "To be turned, it's only fair if you are a vampire, then I will be too. Just so you and your new vampire buddies are clear on this, you are the one who's going to do it."

I'm not sure how to tell him the flaw in that plan, so I just give him the facts they gave me about needing permission and being executed without it. "That's easy, you will just have to get permission." He says matter of factly. "I don't even know what they are going to do with me yet Sloan. I promise as soon as I find out how all this works, I will. But Sloan, you don't even know what you are asking for yet? To be honest, I'm not even sure what all of this is exactly. I promise that as soon as I get all the facts you will be the first one to know."

He gives me the most sad and defeated look I have ever seen. "I just don't want to lose you. Promise me you won't let them take you from me." I can't help but hold him close. "I promise. I won't let that happen." He chuckles a bit in my arms." This new body of yours is nice"

I pull back with a grin." Wanna test it out?" and we head upstairs.

No people, I'm not going to kiss and tell. I don't ask my friends the details of their sex life. Maybe it is a southern thing but it's just not something we talk about around here. Just know everything works the same and it's all still fun.

The next day, I call Daniel.

"So, you want to know more about the feeding thing I take it?" Weird to answer the phone and have that the first thing that comes out of your mouth. "Not even a hello?" He laughs. "Hello Brandon. What can I help you with today?" I think about all the questions and realize I don't have two days to talk on the phone so I narrow it down just a bit.

"Yes, the feeding thing, let's start with that." He takes a deep breath and starts. "Well you will know when you need to feed when your body starts aching. You see, when you are low on blood your body starts feeding on itself. The longer you go without feeding, the more painful it will get. Now listen Brandon, do not ever force yourself to not feed. If you go too long you will become feral, you will feed on anyone or anything and you won't stop. You will drain that person dry in public, it doesn't matter, because you will have no control over your instincts at all. Trust me Brandon, you will regret it." With that last part, he sounded like he knows about that first hand.

"Holy shit. So, I guess the first feeding was a freebee then? I'm so not looking forward to feeding at all now." He was quiet. "What do you mean by freebee?" I shrug to myself. "I meant the pain thing. It must just have been an instinctual thing to teach me how to feed. I was just hungry when I fed on the jogger. No pain."

The silence is so thick I start to think we got disconnected. "You didn't feel any kind of pain at all?" I answer back. "No, none. What's wrong?" His voice changed back to his happy self. "Nothing, just getting as much info I can. I want to make sure I don't give you wrong information. What's your next question?" I take a breath. "So, here's the thing. As you know I'm married to Sloan." I can hear him adjust in his seat. "Yes, we know, and I know what your next question is and you need to know even if you got permission what you're asking for might in fact kill him." I freeze and feel like I'm about to start hyperventilating. "Brandon, we need to talk about this but not over the phone. I'm coming over." The phone clicks and I can't seem to move.

After I tell Sloan that Daniel is coming over, he goes into panic cleaning mode. Can't have a total vampire stranger see our dirty home. He gets the pups situated in the guest room upstairs and comes back down to hear a knock at the front door. Sloan stands in the foyer waiting for the vampire meeting. I open the door and I let Daniel inside.

"Well, I guess introductions are in order here. Daniel, this is Sloan." Sloan can't seem to stop staring at Daniel while he shakes his hand. Can't blame the guy. Mister Viking is hot.

"I can't stay too long but you two need to know this and it's best if I tell you in person."

I nod and am only just starting to freak out. "Brandon, most people like you, even with permission, don't survive the transition. To be honest, we are surprised how smooth it's going for you. It's usually not this easy for someone like you."

I just stare at him. "What do you mean like me?"

He runs his hand through his hair with an uncomfortable look on his face." Gay. Brandon, I mean Gay. The vampire gene does not work well with gay people." I give a nervous laugh. "So, you are saying vampire blood is homophobic?" He shrugs. "That's one way of putting it but yes. There are some gay vampires but they have some...defects." I can't stop myself from fidgeting. "Defects? Holy shit. Am I going to like, mutate or something?" He looks back "We don't think so. It always happens as soon as you transition. That's what's confusing us Brandon. One of the defects is feeding. Every gay person that successfully turns has a problem feeding. They are unable to stop. They are almost feral from the beginning"

I give a confused look back. "I stopped just fine, it was easy." He looks down to his hands. "Are you sure you are gay Brandon?" I can't stop myself from laughing. "Well the fact that I have never been physically attracted to girls and have only ever been attracted to dudes kinda makes me want to say yeah, I'm pretty damn sure. Not even a little bi. I'm one hundred percent gay." He looks back up. "Ok. that's why I want to do a small test on you. I brought a friend with me. Don't freak out." I snicker. "Freak out, that hilarious. It's all I'm able to do anymore. But go ahead."

He opens the door and calls in his friend. She's a good five foot totally gorgeous Asian woman with silver hair. I'm not kidding, totally silver hair. And it's beautiful on her. She's wearing a dress that leaves absolutely nothing to the imagination. Besides being low cut in the front, the dress hugs her curves as if it is just another layer of her skin.

"This is Kristen, she will be performing our little test today. It will be quick and easy but may make you uncomfortable. No matter what, just go with it, ok." I nod and look at her expecting the same shade of blue as a vampire or white as a human. I figure that my new vamp eyes show me colors so that I will be able to pick out my own kind. As I give her a closer look, I can tell she's not a vamp. She's not glowing white either. It's the same color as her hair. Maybe my eyes are glitching?

She looks at me and tilts her head a bit. "Let's get started, shall we?" She pulls Daniel over to stand next to her. She gives him a look and says "I'll go first." Then she reaches up and unties the dress straps that go up and around her neck. "Woah woman! What the hell are you doing?"

She smiles and says. "Calm down and just look at me." She kept her bra on at least. I give her a look over and blush a bit. She's put together pretty well.

"What am I looking for?" She smiles and seems to blush back at me then puts her top back on. "Ok it's your turn now." Then Daniel smiles and starts unbuttoning his shirt. As soon as he slides it off his impressive arms, my eyes can't stop looking at him. My eyes trace every inch of his perfectly formed pecs and abs. His arms are bulging in all the right places and you can tell he takes care of his body. He's perfect, his chest hair matches his head of hair perfectly. And you can tell he trims it up. Holy shit, are all vamps this beautiful? If so, it's not fair vamp blood doesn't like gay people. Damn...

"Ok that's enough Daniel." He puts his shirt back on and looks back to her.

"So, what's the verdict?" She smiles "Well he's one hundred percent homosexual. The way they both reacted to you proves it." Daniel shrugs. "Well, I guess that theory is out. Nothing we can do except keep an eye on you I guess." He starts walking towards the door. "So, Brandon, you need to take the next few weeks off. You will be staying with us for a few weeks at headquarters so we can get you registered and find out what kind of vampire you actually are." I belt out. "Whoa. What? No, I'm not moving ..." He cuts me off. "You're not moving, you are just staying with us for a few weeks. I know I don't have to tell you this, but you are absolutely forbidden to even try to turn Sloan, it could kill him. You don't even know if you are even able to yet. Not all of us have that ability." He looks back at Sloan.

"I'm sorry about all of this Sloan, your lives are going to change forever and there is nothing you can do but try and adapt. If you truly want to stay with him, you need to be strong and supportive." He turns back to me. "And I'm sure both of you know you shouldn't, but you cannot tell anybody about us. First of all, they will think you are nuts, Second thing, outing us to the public is punishable by death as well. Not just for you but for all parties involved. Just don't even try." He smiles and walks out the door while he says. "And stop freaking out so much. Stress isn't good for anyone."

CHAPTER THREE

IT WASN'T HARD to get time off from the restaurant. All of the football games are away the next few weeks anyway. To be honest I wish I could stay home and work because I am so nervous about going away with Daniel for a whole week. Sloan practically begged Daniel to let him go with us but Daniel told him that I need this time to learn and adjust to my new life and what all it entails. That part kind of scared the shit out of me, but also excited me at the same time. The drive with Daniel was quiet. I just couldn't think of anything to say really. It did however give me time to think about all that has happened and all that is to come. More like freak out honestly. What if Daniel was just taking me to be killed? What if they were lying to me the whole time and this was the easiest way to get me to a private location to see how big of a pile of ash I could make. That's what I would do if I were them. It's actually pretty damn smart, your victim wouldn't draw any attention to his situation at all because if he did he would be killed anyway. I look over to Daniel as we drive through the wilderness. Nothing on either side of the car but trees and nothingness. I am not even sure there are any animals out there.

Sheepishly I ask, "So, where is this place you are taking me? And what is it like?"

He slowly turns his head to look at me as his face grows into a big toothy grin "Well there are a lot of trees, and it's real quiet and secluded so no one can hear you scream." Now I'm not sure but I swear to God I think I turned white as a ghost and stopped breathing entirely.

He belts out a laugh. "Holy shit your face is priceless! Calm down Brandon. I'm not taking you to the woods to kill you if that's what you are thinking. You're just going to the agency to register and get some training on how to defend yourself and how to use your new abilities and what they actually are. You will meet the Master of Tuscaloosa and he will go over the rules and regulations that govern us. He's a great man but be careful when you speak to him, he is the Master so show some respect. And remember Brandon, you shouldn't be allowed to live, don't forget that fact. He has permitted you to continue to exist out of kindness about how you were created."

I give him a pained look. "You guys really would just have killed me just because I exist and it's outside the rules?" He looks me in the eyes with a cold expression that I haven't seen from him as of yet. "Yes Brandon, we would have because those are the rules we have lived by for centuries. You were not permitted to be created to begin with, but on top of that your creator was destroyed somehow. You have no master. That isn't supposed to be possible to begin with. So, consider yourself lucky that the Master of the City has decided to adopt you as his own."

The shocked look on my face could only have been described as some kind of cartoon character eyes bulging out of my skull. "He what? Wait? What do you mean it's not possible for someone created to not have a master?" Turning the car left onto the highway he sighs and shrugs his wide shoulders. "Basically what it comes down to is the blood inside us and how strong it is. When you are newly created, your master's connection is the only thing keeping your blood stable. When he or she dies the newly created vampire normally dies as well....Well usually, but then there's you

Brandon. You will learn all this soon enough. And yes, your new master is the Master of Tuscaloosa. Lucky, you!" he says with a big stupid smile.

After a long awkward silence in the car, the highway empties into the downtown area of Tuscaloosa where all the bars are. Being a city with three college campuses, bars are a real good business. Seems like a new one opens up just about every week. "Let me guess, secret base in a bar, right?" I laugh nervously in the seat next to my driver. He snickers at me, "You wish."

After a few more turns and the inevitable string of traffic lights, we turn into a municipal parking deck. The deck is 6 or 7 floors high and clad in brick and stone so it looks like one of the historic buildings in Tuscaloosa. He pulls up to the call box and enters a code. Shit...I start to breathe heavily and my palms are sweating. So this is what PTSD must feel like. I never knew it could be this bad. The mesh gate starts to go up and we pull into the deck.

"It's ok Brandon. I understand the fear you must be having right now but you are safe here."

I take a deep breath "Daniel can you promise me you aren't going to finish what that other guy started? I um, haven't had the best of luck in parking decks lately. He turns and gives me an annoyed look. "If we wanted you dead Brandon it would have been done a long time ago." We travel down a level underground and the feeling of anxiety sets in my body. Pulling into the parking space he shuts the car off and looks me dead in the eye. "And for your information kid, that other guy you are talking about wasn't trying to kill you."

I can't help but give him a panicked stare. "What the frick do you mean he wasn't trying to kill me?!" The look of anger on his face is making me want to jump out of the car and never look back. "How can you be this stupid?! Why would he try to kill you? He didn't even know you as far as we can tell, so why would he? He was feeding. We don't kill when we feed, well most of us don't anyway and he wasn't like..."

He cut himself off so I finished. "Me." I felt defeated as I realize I probably just killed an innocent man. What the hell did I do? Taking a deep breath he looks up at me with a calm look on his face and speaks in a much softer tone. "Look Brandon, there is a lot you don't know about vampires and this world, and there will be a lot of people who think you shouldn't be here. You are about to learn that you are in an extremely awkward situation now. One request from me is that you don't think everyone is out to get you because we're not. I was personally appointed by the Master of the City to be your guard. Just breathe man and try to calm your ass down."

I can't help but look up at him and smirk. "My guard? As in bodyguard?"

He gives me that big ass smile and winks. "Kinda yes. Now move your ass, if we are late you might be decapitated!" I freeze again and he roars laughing as he starts walking towards the elevator. The elevator is a typical parking garage elevator and to be honest I am not sure what might pop out of it at this point. We get to the doors as they open. There were two older men standing there waiting for us to walk on. Daniel puts his arm in front of me and says "No thanks we will wait on the next one." The guys on the elevator look kinda confused but shrug as the door closes.

"What the hell was that about?"

He says nothing just standing there with a cocksure smile on his face. When the doors open again it's empty and we walk on. When the doors close he starts to press the button on the floor we are on repeatedly. "Dude, that's the floor we are on. You ok?" He grins again as the light on the button flickers on and off as he presses it. Wait, is that Morse code? I watch in amazement as a small hollow clear tube pops out of one of the buttons. As the tube extends out toward Daniel, the end of the tube suddenly opens like a hinge and he sticks his finger inside. I see a small needle puncture his finger and draw blood which doesn't seem to phase Daniel at all. The tube retreats into the button again and

I hear a voice from the elevator speaker say in a decidedly British accent, "Sample verified, clearance accepted. Then the elevator starts going down, fast.

"Holy shit!" I say freaking out. Am I smiling like a crazy person? I've always loved a good roller coaster but this is a bit different. It almost feels like the elevator is being pulled down like a free fall and I am pretty sure I left my stomach way back up there. Daniel notices me smiling. "There you go buddy, just enjoy what you can when you can. This whole thing doesn't have to be so scary. You're a freakin vampire, think of what that means. Seriously man, you need to realize you aren't human anymore. You're not squishy anymore. Don't worry, you will understand everything soon enough. I'll show you, just trust me."

He reaches over and pats me on the back as the elevator slows. When the elevator stops that same British voice says through the speaker, "Administration Level." Then the door opens, and holy shit. I was expecting some kind of office setup but man I was wrong. It was a giant open area that seemed to be almost like a cave of some sort but massive and lit up like it was daylight. How can there be daylight if we are this far underground? My mind is racing but I try to pull it together and concentrate on what is in front of me. Looking down, There is a bridge connected to and leading from the elevator to a place across the deep void built to be a reception type area. It is all clean and perfect. Not dark and spooky at all. Think modern vampire cave with halls and rooms constructed perfectly and clean...so freakin clean.

"Holy shit..." I said to no one as I walked across the bridge to the desk. "Pretty cool huh." Daniel said with pride as we reached the desk. I look him dead in the eye. "I've been living on top of all this for years and had no idea? How the hell is this possible." He laughs and puts his hand on my shoulder "Think about it. It's not hard to be honest. Humans don't really pay all that much attention. Think about all the endless construction you see topside. Roads, new buildings, bridges in out of the way places for no reason, new sidewalks every other day not to mention the constant stadium construction on campus. Come on Brandon, how many parking decks does a city of this size really need?"

He stops and watches me try and piece it all together Holy shit. Tuscaloosa has had construction going on like forever. It's kind of become a joke to everyone that construction will never be complete because it takes years to finish one thing but before it's finished five more things pop up. I mean I can't believe that I just bought that it has taken them 3 years to just pave the roads through downtown Tuscaloosa. Sloan even said the other day, Tuscaloosa will be really nice one day if we ever get finished building it.

"Construction never ends here!" I say looking back at Daniel with amazement and a new enlightenment. "Now you're getting it. Brandon. But not exactly like you think. Most of the construction down here has been complete for ages. What you are seeing being constructed topside is just us making new ways to get around the city undetected if we wish. Now come on, let's introduce you to your new family."

We turn around and I see a peppy blond girl in a bright pink and green floral sundress smiling at us. I look closer and notice that she's human because she's totally glowing white. I say nothing to her but just smile back. "Hello there Daniel. So, I see you have our new member."

He gives her that charming smile of his. "Hello Lydia, looking beautiful as ever I see."

She gives him the cutest little giggle and blushes almost matching the bright pink of her dress. I can't help but be impressed at how damn good he is at that. "Yes beautiful, this is Brandon, our newest Member. Brandon this is Lydia, the most beautiful of our Guardians."

I look back at him inquisitively "Guardians?"

He nods. "Yes, Guardians, they are humans who wish to become like us. They serve as a connection to the human world and if they prove themselves worthy we give them the gift of eternal life." I nod back to him then turn to Lydia "It's a pleasure to meet you Lydia."

Her smile fades a bit but she says "I truly hope that you feel at home here Brandon."

I then realize that my being here must have slowed her progress to vamp hood. Shit, already making enemies. Go me. Daniel pats me on the shoulder and winks at Lidia "Now let's go get you registered."

We walk down the hall to a door marked registry. I know right, I was expecting some big flashy guards with swords and shit too. But to be honest it looks like the same boring kind of door to the same boring kind of office you would see in the average courthouse where you would get your driver's license.

"Here we are Brandon, the Vampire Registry for Tuscaloosa, Alabama. Now just do what they tell you to do and it will go smoothly. Oh, and one more thing, I don't recommend you trying to lie about anything in there. It won't work." Then he walks out leaving me all alone.

I look ahead and notice a familiar face...well familiar hair anyway. It's the silver haired lady that showed me her boobs. Well at least I sorta know someone. I give her a smile and walk over.

"Hello again, it's Kristin, isn't it?" She looks up with a smile. "Yes Brandon. It's good to see you again. How was the drive?" I shrug. "Long, so…you work here?" She spits out a chuckle "Yes sir. I'm the one who is going to register you." I give her a head tilt. "So you get all the fun paperwork huh." With a smile she shrugs. "Well not exactly, follow me."

She directs me down a long marble hallway lined with large gold framed pictures of historic events in Tuscaloosa, or as we call it T-Town's history. We walk through an open door into a room with just a table and two chairs and she closes the door behind her.

"Have a seat Brandon." I take a seat on the far side of the table and she sits across from me looking in my direction as she is pulling out some paperwork from a manilla folder. I kinda fidget in my chair waiting on what is to come and look back at her. I decided to have a closer look at her and to check and see if my eyes were malfunctioning the last time we met. Her color was still that same bright shimmering silver as before. Strange, but what do I know, I'm just a baby vamp after all.

She tilts her head as she looks at me just like she did the last time. "Brandon, what are you looking at?" I grin and say. "It's your hair, I've never seen that color on a person before. It's quite beautiful." She smiles running a hand through it. "Thank you Brandon, but you really shouldn't lie to me." I flinch at her honesty and reply "So you're a mind reader?" She shakes her head. "This isn't how this part is done sweetie. I ask the questions and you answer. Just be calm and answer truthfully. What are you looking at Brandon? "I take a breath and look closer at her color. I know this seems crazy and I certainly don't understand it myself but it seems that her color is stretching off her like a spider's webbing. What the hell? Oh wow, now it looks like it's coming closer to me. I look down at my own blue color and at how it compares to her silver color. My color kinda steams off my body as well but a little different. My color resembles thin blue tendrils almost like arms on a glowing blue octopus with no suction cups. I answer. "I'm not exactly sure how to explain what I am looking at to be honest Kristin." Her eyes grow big as I think she realizes what I'm looking at.

"You can see it, can't you?" I look up at her. "You can see it too?" Her mouth opens ever so slightly and she seems intrigued. Her webbing isn't stretching out to me anymore, it's retreating back to her. I follow her webbing with my eyes and then I notice she's watching my eyes follow. She seems amazed that I am able not only to see the color but follow the movement. I ask "What's going on? What Is this?" I hold up my hands knowing she can see my blue tendrils.

She shakes her head, "I have to say Brandon, you are quite the anomaly." I start to get frustrated. "Can you please answer me

Kristin? Is this normal? Am I mutating or something?" I notice the tendrils on my hands start flickering and jump a bit. I have never just watched my own color before like this. Why haven't I noticed how wiggly and freaky my color is before? "She notices me flinch and finally responds. "Brandon, calm down. You aren't mutating, you just seem to be especially gifted is all."

After I pick my jaw up off the floor and wipe the drool away I'm able to speak again. "What do you mean by gifted?" She looks at me and smiles like it's no big thing. "Here are the basics. When a vampire is created, some are granted a special gift of the blood. This is extremely rare. It seems you are one of the lucky ones" I can't help but stare blankly at her. "So, can you tell me what this gift is then? What does it do? How do I control it?" She smiles "Tell me what you are looking at Brandon."

I sigh. "You have a color kind of misting off you like a spider's webbing, and for a second I watched it stretch outwards from your body towards me. Why was it doing that?" I stare at her with my stern face. She flinches like she just got caught doing something she wasn't supposed to.

"When you were looking at yourself what did you see Brandon? Be as specific as you can be"

I roll my eyes. "OK so I was looking at my color to see what it was doing when you were trying to…Whatever you were trying to do." I lean up in my chair and lock eyes with her then continue, "You're not a vampire, you are also not a human. So, tell me Kristin, what are you exactly?"

That question was what did it. Her face was in total shock. She turned as pale as a goth girl can get and all she could do was blink at me. Total loss for words. She finally remembered how to speak. "How long have you been able to do this Brandon?" I hold my hand up defiantly. "Nope, I'll answer your questions but only after you answer mine." She gives me that confident smile again and sits back in her chair. "You're cute. Why tell you what I am when I can just show you?"

She sits up and the steam starts coming towards me again like a silver web. I jump up but I am not fast enough because it wraps around my arms quickly. I was expecting to feel pain but instead it felt more like warm and tingly energy working its way up my arms. I start to feel fuzzy and my vision starts to blur. I immediately look down and see her silver webbing merging with my blue mist. I think she's saying something to me but it seems like I am in a dream. I can't tell what's reality anymore.

"Why are you here Brandon?" She sounds so nice.

"Because my guard Daniel brought me here." I sound like I am drunk and start to giggle. "Guard, I have a bodyguard, how crazy is that. I'm a new vampire, isn't that cool?" I can't help but smile big when I say it. She grins. "Yes Brandon, it's very cool. Do you want to be a vampire?"

I frown a bit "I don't know. I'm scared, but excited at the same time. I don't think the other vampires will like me though. What if they want to kill me?" She gives me a knowing nod. "Why do you think the other vampires want to kill you Brandon?" I shrug "Because I'm gay. Vampires are a bunch of homophobes, remember."

She shakes her head. "No Brandon, not all vampires are homophobic. The blood is."

I can't stop looking at her webbing mixing with my blue tendrils. "Your little web thingies feel nice, you know that?" She blinks and looks slightly confused as she asks. "You can feel them?"

I nod petting my arm. "Yes." Then somehow, I move one of my tendril. Wow, I can move them? The webbing that's attached seems to please my little tendrils. It kind of...The only way to describe it is it tastes good. My blue likes the way her silver webbing tastes? I like the way it tastes. Yes that's it. The blue is a part of me. I start to pull the webbing inside me. I drink it down slowly. It tastes so good and I don't want to stop. I hear a voice screaming. "Brandon!" I blink and the webbing snaps back off me like a broken rubber band. Kristin jumps up out of her chair and is instantly across the room. She looks scared of me. Why is she so scared? And why do I feel so amazing?

CHAPTER FOUR

I HOLD MY hands up to Kristin like she has a gun pointed at me and I'm trying not to get shot in the face. "Holy shit Kristin, I'm so sorry. Did I hurt you? Oh my god I didn't mean to do that. Are you ok? Please say you're ok." Yep I was flipping the hell out.

Poor girl is in a heap on the floor holding herself and breathing heavily, her body shaking when she looks up at me. "I'm ok Brandon. Just give me a second. Sit down please." I sit down in my chair at the table and I literally can't stop saying I'm sorry. She gets up from the floor and walks back over to the table slowly and sits down in her chair. She runs a shaky hand through her hair, takes a deep breath and slowly then lets it out.

"Brandon, you need to be one hundred percent honest with me right now. Do you know what you just did?" I look at her right in the eye. "God no! I don't even know how I did it. What the hell was that?" Kristin lets out a sigh and she looks relieved with my answer for some reason. "Well Brandon, I'm going to be totally honest with you. What you just did was drain some of my power. Those things you called spider webs coming off me is the physical manifestation of my power. My life force if you want to get technical. You just absorbed part of my life force into yourself. You basically ate my power for lack of a better way to say it."

Holy shit! Now I do totally feel bad for her, but damn, I must say that's pretty freaking awesome. I did that? I look around the room trying to figure this out and notice something new I hadn't seen before. As if my new vamp eyes weren't awesome to begin with, now, after I gobbled up some of her power, I can see everything. I can see colors through the damn walls.

She snaps her fingers and it breaks me out of my own own trance.

"Brandon. Pay attention to me!" I flinch when she shocks me back into reality "I'm so sorry Kristin. I really am. Are you going to be ok? Does it still hurt?" She shakes her head. "I'm fine Brandon, I'll be fine. My power will come back in time but it's extremely important that we help you get a handle on yours. If you didn't stop you would have drained me to death.

And that's when my jaw hit the floor. Well shit.

She gives me a minute to get myself together. "How do you feel right now, I need you to describe everything no matter how small or insignificant you think it is. Is anything different than before that you can tell?" I nod "Yes, actually there is. For one, I feel pretty damn amazing. Like the biggest adrenaline rush ever. I feel…aware of everything." I lean in closer and whisper to her so no one but us can hear. "See Kristin the crazy thing is, I think I can see through the walls. Well sorta." Ok, now she's looking at me like I'm actually crazy. I lean back in my chair swelling with this new found bravado.

"I'm serious. You know how I can see the different colors coming off vamps and humans, and well whatever you are too? Well I can see the colors straight through the walls now." Well that seems to grab her attention. "Wow ok so now that's different.' She looks at the wall behind me studying it, then pulls out her phone and writes a text. After only a few seconds, she gets a response, she texts back something else and then looks at me.

"Brandon, I want you to look at the wall behind you and tell me how many people you can see through it." I can't help but get excited. I look back. And I can see two blue peeps and one white.

I then look back to her. "There are two vamps and one human in that room."

She just looks back down at her phone. "Well shit!" I guess my potty mouth is rubbing off on her. Yea me.

The next four hours started out fun but then turned really boring as we did the same thing over and over. Guess who's behind the wall. I felt like I was on a never ending bad game show. She called Daniel to be a witness to my new powers. He smiled the whole time like I was his or kid or something, and the school just called him in to tell him I'm a genius and don't have to go to highschool and I could just skip ahead and become the President and move into the White House next week. After four hours, we find out that all that new power stuff was just temporary.

It faded slowly and then just stopped all together.

So I guess I am back to being just a normal ass vamp again, so lame right? Kristin tells me she suspected these new powers potentially would be temporary. Kinda like eating a powerbar made of crack without all the shitty side effects like, wanting crack. I just felt normal again, well vamp normal I guess. My new normal. She finally gets all the info from me that she needs to get me registered.

Basically, from what Daniel tells me she's a walking living lie detector. She can see colors like I can too but she calls them auras. What makes us different is that she can only see silver, so she can't tell everyone apart like I can. Daniel lets me know that there are more things on this little planet of ours than just humans and vamps. I kind of figured if vampires existed there had to be other things out there that I can potentially see as well. He gives me the dollar rundown. Apparently, witches are a thing. Some people call them sorcerers. Kristin would be in that class. Their original name is Traveler. There are apparently other realities as well which is where they get their power from. Travelers can channel power from other realities and bring it into our own and shape it in different ways. Some more than others. Some can even

SEAN DAVIS

go to another reality. Hence the name Traveler. That's some cool shit huh. He stops there because apparently, we are late for my physical test.

I look kind of irritated. "Come on, why do I have to take a physical?"

He laughs. "Not a physical you doof, a physical test. It's time to show us what you're made of kid." Well frick. This is gonna suck. I hate running. "So, like track and sports-n-shit?"

He just about hit the floor. He was laughing so hard I thought he might poop himself. After he wipes his eyes and notices the pissed off look I'm giving him. "No Brandon. Like trying not to bleed too much." I just respond with a simple "Oh hell no!" He grabs me by the shoulder and pulls me into an empty room with mats and workout equipment. He has his serious face on now.

"Brandon, you are a vampire now. Stop thinking like a human. You're stronger, faster and better than any human on the planet. Physical combat is second nature to our kind. "He then takes a step back. "I'm going to hit you now Brandon." My eyes widen "The frick you are...."

He was so fast, I take his fist to the chest and I swear I flew back three feet. Trying to get my breath I stand up. He looks confused. "You were supposed to dodge!" I cough a few more times, "You ass face! That hurt!" His eyes grow cold, I hate it when they do that. "Brandon, you have to try harder! The people you will be fighting soon won't hold back. I'm serious, if you think this hurts you have no idea." He throws another punch. This time punching me in the face.

"Again!" He grabs me by the arm and throws me across the damn room. "You have to do better Brandon!"

I start to get a bit panicked. "Daniel..." and I get the worst feeling. "Daniel, what If this is my defect?" I say with total fear in my voice. He stops, stands up looking me over, then shakes his head with a sad look on his face. "I'm sorry to say if it is, it won't matter. It's gonna hurt, and gonna hurt bad."

42

After this failed combat, I clean myself up and put on some proper getting my ass kicked clothes. I put on a white karate style robe with a white belt to tie around my waist. Hmmm wonder who chose the white color. Seems like from the ass kicking I just got, red or black would be better colors to hide the blood. Daniel leads me to a room that looks like some kind of dojo. All kinds of fighting equipment line the walls. The floor is covered in mats so at least it will hurt less when I get slammed to the floor again. You know, the usual kind of room to train people to make things bleed and die kind of shit. I look around and there are a few more people in the room with me and Daniel. Three of the other people have the same color clothes as I do. I'm guessing they are the newbies just like me. I look to my left and I notice a set of twins. A guy and girl, both of them are strawberry blondes. Let's just call them southern sorority Ken and Barbie. Perfect hair, perfect teeth and not a blemish on their faces.

They are chatting away with some other sorority type brunette chick. As I walk into the room further all three notice me and give me a grin. Yup, you guessed it. One of those we are better than you grins. After looking over my competition, I notice a guy wearing all black come into the room and announce:

"For our first match, we have newcomer Jason". One of the newbs pops up with a smile. His red curly hair and his small build not to mention his face full of freckles makes him look so young, like he's twelve or something. "His opponent will be Janet." Announcer man points his hand towards the Barbie twin. She stands with full confidence staring at the newb and grinning like she's about to eat him alive. I kinda think she might. They walk onto the mat and the newb Jason takes one of those fighting stances like you see in action movies.

I'm pretty sure he has some type of formal martial arts training because to me he seems to know what he's doing. Barbie just stands there twirling her hair with her perfectly manicured finger and smiling right at Jason. I swear if she was chewing gum she would be blowing bubbles right now. Just looking at her I can tell that this bitch is evil. The guy in black stands with his hands in the air as the room fills with tension so much you can almost taste it around you. Finally he lowers his arms and yells. "And fight!"

Immediately Jason flies over with a kick towards Janet's head. She spins with a giggle as her left hand grabs his ankle while her right hand comes up for a full blown punch to his balls making him drop to the ground. I look up at the ref waiting for him to call foul but nope, he just stands there watching. Daniel looks over to me. "There is no such thing as a fair fight Brandon when you are fighting for your life."

Jason shakes his head a few times, gets up and looks pissed. He takes a stance and decides to go in for a few punches. Janet spins, dodges, and laughs every time he misses. She then spins up around and out of his way ending up completely behind him knocking him off balance. He turns around quickly. She then yawns, "You're boring." He then runs up and jumps trying to land a few flying kicks to her face. She dodges them with ease and when he lands he spins trying to land a backhand punch to her face. He fails, yet again.

Janet ends up grabbing his wrist tight with her left hand. I notice her looking right at me when that evil grin comes back across her face. She then crouches suddenly and comes back up with her right hand right on his elbow hard while at the same time pulling down his arm with her left hand.

The sound was horrible and sickening. First the unmistakable crack of his arm bending the wrong way and breaking, then him shrieking in pain. I was expecting her to be taken away but no. Instead a medical team comes out of one of the side doors behind a wall of mirrors to attend to Jason. While Janet is walking off the mat with a self important and superior smile the medics attempt to snap his arm back in place. I look over to Daniel in horror.

He does nothing but give me that sad face that I have seen way too many times lately. I can see the pity in his eyes when he says to me..."There is no such thing as a fair fight Brandon." The ref in black comes back up to the mat to make another announcement. "The next round we have the newcomer Brandon!"

I stand up looking over towards the twins. It's pretty cool because I can actually hear them from across the room as they smile and talk. Vamp hearing takes some getting used to but I am happy I have it now. "I'm going to make that faggot beg me to stop hurting him." Yep, so that's not the first time I've heard that said but never had a Barbie look alike talk about me like that.

Ref starts again. "His opponent will be Janet!"

I walk up to the mat trying to get my mind off all the pain I'm about to experience and make my stomach calm the hell down. The Ref looks down at me with a serious look. "You are not permitted to use your gift during this training session." Bitch Barbie looks shocked when she hears that. "Don't tell me this mo has a gift. What is it? Glitter bomb or something?" She actually laughs at herself.

I can't help but roll my eyes. "So, original Barbie. Seriously, how did you come up with it?" She stops mid-cackle. "Did you just freaking call me Barbie?" I look back." If the plastic vagina fits." oops...I think I made the vein on her forehead pop. I look back to Daniel and see him with his mouth open in surprise and total amusement at my response. I'm guessing the only thing going through his head right now is how many different ways that she's totally going to break me for that Barbie comment.

Ref's arm goes up. "Fight!" She doesn't waste time doing her cute little routine this time however, she's coming right at me full force. She gets halfway to me and then jumps up and tries to nail me in the face with her fist. The strangest thing happens then. You know the old saying when you think you're about to die the world slows down and you see your life flashing in front of you. Well it truly does but the weird thing is I think the world around me slowed down but I don't think I did at all.

I can see her pissed off face coming right at me and it's like I can just walk up to her in the air and have enough time to shave her head bald. I smile at that because it would be fun as shit. My face doesn't seem to be going at the same speed as my head though. My smile is coming in slow motion. I try to think fast. My body isn't moving as fast as my brain but she's getting closer. I must react fast. I tilt my body to the left a bit while bringing up my left hand to grab her wrist and at the same time using my right hand to grab her under her arm. Pulling her arm and using her own weight against her, I fling her over my shoulder as hard as I can.

So you remember when Daniel mentioned vampires are stronger, faster and better than any human on the planet? Well he wasn't kidding about being stronger. I flung that bitch like a wet towel. She flew across the room and landed on top of a punching dummy flat on her face. Time finally goes back to normal and the others in the room are gasping. I swear I heard Daniel whisper "Holy shit" from across the room. The twin brother screams "Janet, are you ok!" The ref stands there stunned at what he just saw an and after he was able to form words again, he calls the match.

Janet gets up and I've never seen a woman look so pissed. As she wipes the blood from her nose she spits blood in my direction. "This is far from over you insect!" I can't help but smile at her. "I hope not. That was awesome! Maybe next time when you try to fly you won't hit a wall."

Daniel grabs me by the shoulder. "Dude, although what you did was amazing and I'm sure, extremely satisfying, you need to reel it in. She's fully trained and is holding back. Don't make her any more pissed than she already is." I calm down and realize he just said she was holding back. Oops.

Afterwards, as everyone is leaving the room the twins and their little friend are glaring bloody murder at me the entire time. As the twin brother walked by, he mumbled at me.

"See you soon." I know right! I'm just making friends left and right around here. Loveable little me. Anyway. The only two people remaining in the room are me and my guard, Daniel.

Daniel gives me a very worried look. "Brandon you should be aware that guy is highly unstable. He makes his sister seem like a kitten. Be careful please." I can't help but look at him confused. "So, I gotta ask Daniel. Why the hell are people that are so bat shit crazy violent permitted to stay here at the headquarters? This has to be a security risk, right?" He shakes his head sadly. "They aren't staying here long term. Their master is here for a visit with the Master of the House. Their Master is the brunette that was with them in the training room. They are only here at headquarters for a few more days, so just stay away from all of them. They are under her protection and that means to attack them without provocation is a crime here. To destroy them is strictly forbidden by vampire law Brandon." He grabs my shoulders hard and looks me dead in the eye as serious as I've ever seen him. "To destroy a master's child is punishable by death." Here I am confused again. "What do you mean by child?" He lets me go and leans back with a smile. "You are a slow one aren't you." Letting out a sigh he says "A master can sire a child from his own blood." He looks at me and starts speaking to me like I'm a toddler "Or if he so wishes, he can adopt an unwanted or stray vampire." I look shocked. "Wait... you're saying I'm now the masters kid? Are you freaking kidding me?" Daniel turns and as we start walking down a long hallway to my what will be my new room, he keeps talking. "Here's the rundown. The master of the house had a, as you put it, kid." He stops suddenly. "Wait, you have already met him. His name was Jacob. He's the one that sired you in the parking deck before he was killed."

I about passed right the hell out right there in the middle of the hall. "That guy, was his kid?" My mouth immediately became so dry I was barely able to breathe. "Why?" I try and make sense of it all but I can't. "Why would he adopt me? I don't get it." Mr.

Jerkface thumps my forehead hard. "You really need to keep up Brandon. You're the bloodborne of his own bloodborne. His kid's kid. We don't call them kids just so you know. The proper name is bloodborne. Every sire is responsible for his bloodborne's actions, and when they are destroyed they inherit everything of theirs. That includes their bloodborne."

I nod to let him know I understand. But there is one problem. That problem is what the hell are they going to do to me if and when they find out I'm the reason dear ole daddy Jacob is dead. I eventually find out I get to my room, if you can call it that. Now I am not spoiled by any stretch of the imagination, but come on. We are the all powerful vampire crime fighting league or whatever and this is the best room they have? Pale gray blank walls, a tile floor and the only furniture is a twin bed and small 3 drawer dresser...lame.

Daniel seeing the obvious eye roll at my accommodations tells me I have free reign over the place. I can go explore if I want but that I need to get some rest. Seeing as though my mind is racing like a fat kid hearing the words free cake I'm going to look around the joint. I walk the hallways and look in all the open rooms. It's what you would expect to find in a large office complex, offices and the occasional break room. For some reason, I go back to the dojo. The weaponry hanging on the walls is very impressive. I go up and pull a katana off the wall and swing it like I am a five-year-old again. I've always had a fascination with blades ever since I was a kid.

"Careful, you might decapitate yourself boy." That familiar voice sent chills down my spine. I look back and the Barbie and Ken twins are standing there grinning like they got away with murder, or are about to. I give them a cocky smile and say "Well hello there, how's the jaw?" She snickers and walks with confidence to my right as the brother with his snotty I'm better than you attitude walks forward to my left. Now being a big video game and Tabletop Gaming Nerd and having been bullied all my

48

life, I know exactly what they're trying to do. Them flanking me gives me the hint that they are about to attempt to kick my ass.

It's not not like I already didn't expect it but come on, give a brother some time to prepare.

"So, I expected you to get your revenge eventually but couldn't you at least have given me a day?" The brother stops and gives me a nasty glare. He can pull off crazy eyes like nobody's business. "Nobody touches my sister and gets away with it, you disgusting freak!" No warning, none at all. He jumps and is on me like a spider monkey. I try and block him but he grabs my arm and slings me like a ragdoll toward the wall.

Time starts slowing down again, but this time not fast enough as I realize I'm flying through the air heading in Bitch Barbie's direction. I'm hyper aware of where I am in midair because of the state I'm in right now, so I'm able to quickly recover and get my bearings about me. I use my body's weight to flip myself over in midair so my feet are facing her head. Suddenly. I notice that she's smiling like she was expecting me to do that...shit. I realize that the blade is still in my hand and decide to change my tactics. Talk about your lucky shots. I think I might have overdone it a bit with how hard I threw the katana. Landing on my feet in a crouch I see the blade protruding from her right thigh. Time starts to suddenly speed up bringing me back to normal as I hear her screaming in pain and notice the blood pouring from her leg wound. I look back to try and get a location on brother boy. Finally I see him to my left side and boy does he look pissed. Really pissed.

Eventually I realize not only does he look pissed but his body shape actually starts to change. I realize in terror that his face is changing right before my eyes. I can hear bones cracking, and see his flesh molding itself like clay, forming what looks like scales. His hands extend, and his fingers start to elongate and at the tips. Out of each finger, long black sharp talons rip right through his flesh. That evil grin on his face is joined with two elongated fangs protruding from his gums.

Terrified, I suddenly find myself standing directly in front of some kind of massive snake human hybrid thing that is standing where Ken was standing before. What the frick? I barely have time to process what has just happened. In a blur of speed he launches himself at me giving me the pleasure of an up close and personal look at his newly formed face, and it's freaking horrifying. Also, why can't I breathe? Looking down I get the answer to my own question. His arm is actually inside my body. Just a heads up if you are ever wondering, the fastest way to a man's heart isn't through a good meal or his ribcage, you can get there much faster if you go through the soft tissue under the ribs and go straight up behind them. That's exactly what this psychopath just did to me. Looking back up from the arm in my chest, I have an excellent view of that horrendous evil altered grin of his. I give it a ten out of ten on the creepy and demonic scale.

With a hissing voice snake boy says, "I want you to tell me what it feels like to literally have your heart in someone else's hands." I look back down and am seeing a pool of my own blood forming at my feet, I can't move. I can actually feel his claw surrounding and inside my heart.

"Because you are new here freak, let me do you a favor and give you some basic education. You're a vampire so piercing your heart won't kill you, it can only paralyze you. But bleeding out like you are doing now, that will most definitely kill you." He looks down and smiles with pride at all the ever growing pool of blood that he created at my feet. Behind me I can hear his sister screaming. "Kevin! Stop! You can't kill him!" He looks me dead in the eyes with that horrible fanged grin. "Oh, but yes I can sister."

It's so cold now. I would shiver if I could actually move. Looking at fangboy's face I realize his evil grin starts to fade and for some reason he starts to shiver. I hear a voice behind him.

"You will remove your arm from my Bloodborne while leaving his heart intact, or you will spend the rest of your eternity without legs." He turns to look behind him slowly and I notice his legs are both completely frozen solid. That ominous voice speaks up again even louder as to certainly get the snake boys attention.

"You have a choice here, you can either release my bloodborne without any more harm, or I can shatter both your legs. The decision is yours." He turns back to face me and I see a very primal fear in his eyes as he is slowly pulling his arm from my body. The slurping sound that it made will forever haunt me for the rest of my vampire life. The only thing I can do is fall over on my side from the weakness and hit the floor hard. As I lay there in a half fetal position, I have a good view from the floor of snake boy so I get to watch as his legs start to rapidly thaw out.

He screams in agony as they go from frozen to thawed. "Just so you are aware child, that's only a very small taste of the pain you will experience if you ever venture to touch him again." In a panic, his sister rips the blade from her thigh, wincing in pain she makes her way over to her brother. She supports him as best she can considering they both have issues walking at the moment and they limp sadly out of the room.

My new savior rushes over and kneels down beside me trying to assess my condition. The look on his face tells me it's not good at all. Now that I am able to get a better look at him, I realize he's just magnificent. Dark black hair trimmed perfectly to his ears. His beautiful black beard and mustache are styled and trimmed to perfection over his impossibly perfect cheekbones His eyes are an amazing mix of silver and blue so vibrant set against the snow white background. So, this is my dear ol daddy. Man does it suck that I won't get to live to say hello to him properly.

He reaches out and puts his hand over the massive gaping wound that I got from snake boy in my chest and I begin to realize what he's actually doing. I feel the extreme cold as he freezes the hole in my chest. I'm sure if I had any blood left in my weak ass body It would hurt, but I feel absolutely nothing but cold.

He lays me down slowly and softly and I can see the panic building in his beautiful eyes. Softly and reassuringly he whispers, "Hold on Brandon. I swear I will not lose another child. I promise I'll be back soon." In a panic he lifts himself up and sprints out of the room leaving me alone, dying on the floor. Its kinda funny it would end this way. On the floor in a puddle of blood, broken and weak. Just like last time in the parking deck. That attack that brought me into this world and this attack is taking me out again.

As I lay there looking up at the punching dummies stupid ass face, I'm filled with a strange mix of sadness and fury. I had high hopes for this new life. It was going to be so amazing and exciting. Why couldn't it have been longer than a few weeks? It's just not fair! Killed by some homophobic asshat who's obsessed with his sister. Shit, I'll never get to see Sloan again. Shit, shit... Who's going to tell him? Oh, my God, what will he do? I don't know if he's even safe anymore because of all this crap. I'll never get to see the excited look on his face as we are flying upside down on the Rockin Roller Coaster at Disney World ever again, or hear his drunken laugh after a few shots of tequila while looking in his squinty eyes in Mexico. We were supposed to have eternity together and now I'll never see that smile again. I'll never get to see my pups again. My poor babies. My adorable rescue babies. I will never get to snuggle in that safe and warm puppy pile with my fur babies and Sloan ever again. Dammit! It's just not fair. All I can do now is patheticly lie here in self pity staring at the shadow of a stupid ass punching dummie and wait for the end, yet again. I would laugh at the irony of my situation if I could.

I notice the shadow growing darker. My breath is becoming so weak I may as well not even be breathing at all. My body has finally succumbed and becomes completely numb to all feeling. The shadow around me has become so dark now it's more like a pool of liquid black than a shadow at all and I realize it's starting to move towards me. I can do nothing but watch as it starts to pool under my body. The last thing I feel before I lose consciousness is the feeling of falling. Am I floating? It's so warm here. So black and so warm. Is this what vampire death is like? Dear god, I'll miss everyone so much. This is so not fair.

CHAPTER FIVE

HERE I AM, numb to all feeling and floating in nothingness. Is this just the fate of every vampire or is it the fate of every living thing? Hearing a faint noise I weakly open my tired eyes and look up to see an outline of a figure approaching me. As it floats closer towards me, I can see it's surrounded by a silvery blue glow. It's strange though as I've never seen that color before. All I can do is lower my head in defeat. I no longer have the strength to hold my own head up anyway.

"Oh child. My dear poor child. What have they done to you?"

The voice is so familiar. Is it her? I try to speak but don't have the breath anymore to form words. She strokes my cheek with her hand and I start to cry. "My sweet boy. This will not do." She lifts my face with her perfectly manicured finger. "It's time my child. It's time that I tell you everything that you need to know. I'm so sorry I wasn't able to tell you sooner but you had to come into your power on your own before I was able to give you the gift of this knowledge..." She smiles and I think that even though I am now dead, everything was somehow perfect.

She gives the most beautiful chuckle. "Dear child, no, you are not dead." Is she in my head?

"Yes Brandon. You do not have the ability to speak at the moment so this is how we will communicate for now." Of course, the first thing that goes through my mind is "Who are you?"

She gives me the most beautiful smile as she says, "My name Is Lilith and I am the first of my kind and mother to your bloodline. It is my blood that runs through the veins of every single vampire in your world. And you, my child, were the only human offspring left on Earth of my mortal bloodline." Her eyes lower to the massive hole in my stomach.

"But first before you actually do die let's take care of that nasty scratch shall we?" If I could breathe I would have laughed. I wouldn't call someone's arm ripping through your stomach to try and take your heart from your body a scratch. She lifts her hand and with her other hand she uses her nail to cut her palm. "With my blood you shall finally be complete my child." She tilts my head back to open my mouth and I can feel her blood running down my throat. The next thing I know, my body explodes in fire. I'm completely engulfed in a blaze of blue fire! Not fire exactly, but power. Pure, hot, exhilarating power. It's not burning me at all, but instead it's filling me, becoming a part of me. I realize the big ass hole in my stomach is now totally gone as if it was never there. Then the strangest thing happens. The darkness that was surrounding me starts to latch on to me, just like when Kristen used her webs on me. I let it in, I let it all in. I absorb every bit of darkness, and as soon I devour all of it, the nothingness around me explodes with form. My eyes go wide with amazement. Is this the dojo? Looking closely I realize it is, but then again it's not. It's so strange, it's like light and dark have switched roles. Lilith's beautiful face lights up with the most beautiful smile I've ever seen.

"Dear boy, look what you've done." I blink back at her. "What happened?"

She walks over and puts her hand on my cheek again. "My child, you have brought life to a dead reality." I can't help but to look like a moron trying to figure out what she just told me. Lilith looks around and walks touching the wall, the punching dummy, and the blades on the wall in amazement as if she's trying to feel something new or something she's lost and found again. "Brandon, this place you are in is called the Shade. It's one of the many other realities in existence. This one was destroyed some time ago however. For some reason I think its essence was drawn to you and then attached itself to you somehow. It seems that your very existence gives it form." She looks around in amazement.

"By the looks of it, the form you gave to the Shade was that of your own world." Her smile grows so big I can barely stand to look away. "So this is your completion. Your complete Tribus Sanguinem." The only thing I can do is stand and stare at her. She gives me a warm smile.

"Tribus Sanguinem, you are the first of your kind to have three gifts from the blood as it should have been in the beginning, and you will now be the last." She takes a few steps closer giving me an intense stare.

"Now child name your first two gifts." I look like a moron again for a bit longer, I'm getting really good at that by the way but then I finally say, "I can see colors from living things. Also somehow I can make my color absorb others." She grins. 'Yes, you are able to see the very life force of any living thing. It will grow with time. Take care with that one as it can be extremely dangerous. Now, name your next gift my child."

I think hard trying to come up with one but I don't remember doing anything special besides the one I already mentioned. She smiles running her fingers through her raven hair. "Brandon, when you fought that foul creature that tried to tear your heart from your body what happened?"

I look up and say." Well time slowed and I was able to react quickly but isn't that just a vampire thing?" She shakes her head. "No, my dear. Vampire reflexes are heightened and their speed is increased but not to the extent that yours has been. You essentially slowed time itself. As with your other gift it will grow as well." She looks around with a prideful look on her face.

"This my child is your final gift. The power over your own reality." She smiles at me with a prideful look, and I can't help but feel happy to make her proud of me. "You are truly of my bloodline Brandon. The Shade is a powerful reality and the way you have shaped it will indeed make you very powerful." She grins and turns to face me. "Now I need to explain to you why every single vampire that has ever been created, except you, is forever cursed."

She continues, "As I have said before you are the first of your kind. You are the true vampire; the vampire I was going to create before my blood was stolen from me and used to create the vampires you see today. They are the cursed ones. You were wanting to know why you don't react to certain things like the other vampires and this is the sole reason why. I call them the cursed ones not out of anger, but because their blood is actually cursed. The blood wasn't meant for their kind to begin with."

I just stand there speechless. This entire time I was being told that I'm a cursed abomination. She smiles at me and I know she heard what I was thinking. "No child, you are no abomination. They say these things out of fear. Fear of the unknown. They do not know why you don't feel the pain they do when they hunger, or why you don't feel sickened in the sunlight or how you can survive without a master. They fear what they don't understand. They also don't understand why it is you have no deficiencies because you are gay." She smiles as she continues. "The reason for all this is because of that very thing my child. My blood wasn't meant for them. Their kind isn't what it was created for. It was created for your kind."

She sits down on the floor and pats the floor next to her for me to do the same.

"Long ago when the world was still new, I lived with the humans as one of them. I was happy in my life watching the humans advance and learn. Back then people didn't care about homosexuals the way they do now. It was not frowned upon, to be honest some clans thought them to be enlightened, as did I. I lived this way for ages and eventually for the first time fell in love."

The light from her face faded and I felt my heart breaking.

"His name was Kain and he was beautiful. The most beautiful man I've ever seen in all my years. Of course, in time I would tell him what I was. It didn't matter to him in the least. We lived in bliss for years. In our town, we had servants who would tend to our every need and one of these servants happened to be gay. As I said before being gay wasn't frowned upon so I grew attached to her. Her name was Camilla."

"One night Camilla finished her cleaning and left us as she always did. Kain and I started a discussion that night about why homosexuals existed and what their purpose was. Seeing as though I didn't create this reality I could only come up with a conclusion from what I witnessed from all the years I've watched humanity. So, I told him that I noticed humans reproduce at an exponential rate, so maybe they are here to slow down that rate so they don't overpopulate and eventually destroy the planet. His face when I told him that made me feel small. He actually laughed at my conclusion. After that night, I decided to side with the people who thought you were enlightened. For some reason, I felt your kind weren't in the position you were meant to be in, so after a few days of contemplation I decided to alter your reality the only way I could. I felt that because your kind were never able to experience having children and because there were so very few of you that you should be granted a gift. The gift to watch over humanity and protect it from itself."

Lilith's face faded even more as she continued. "That night I told Kain about my plan. I've never seen him angry before. He didn't agree with me at all. For some reason, he thought he deserved the gift. It was then when I realized how power hungry he had become. He told me that very night that he should be the one who received the gift and that his plans were for us to rule over the earth forever together. After that he left me alone. I was so angry with him I went into action with my plan. I grabbed a goblet and went to my room. I then opened my wrist and filled it. I then used my gift to alter the blood into something else entirely. Gave it my immortal properties and then took it back into my body to complete the transformation."

After I finished the transformation Kain returned. He apologized to me and said he didn't mean any of it. That his jealousy got the best of him. He then said he would support any decision I made and that he loved me. I was so happy after that. He kissed me and I smiled and said I was almost finished with the ritual. He smiled at me and said he wanted to watch me complete it. So I did. I then opened my wrist again and filled the goblet one last time. He then walked over to kiss me. He told me that my first one should be Camilla and that he had brought her back with him to show his support."

I noticed her eyes water as she spoke. "He said she was in the living quarters waiting. I started to walk out and then turned around to thank him, that's when I noticed him drinking the last of my blood." She stands up and holds her hand out. "Brandon, that blood wasn't meant for him. It gave him great power but cursed him because it wasn't shaped for his kind. It also cursed me. The reaction that happened when he took my blood created an adverse effect on my own blood that banished me from that reality. As long as my blood is there I am not able to return." She walks over to the practice dummy with the stupid look on its face and stands with her back to me. I am devastated that she's so sad.

"Now you know the truth Brandon. Your blood is what mine was meant for. You are the first of your kind." I look at her "What do you want me to do now Lilith?" I say with fear in my voice. She then looks at me with a smile again. "Brandon do not worry, I'm not going to ask you to destroy the vampire population. They are innocent even though they are cursed. This is your gift, you do with it what you will."

I sigh with relief and then a question pops in my head. "Am I able to turn anyone I want?"

She puts her hand to my face. "I was wondering when you were going to ask me that. The answer is yes. You may turn anyone you want. But if you turn anyone that is not your kind they will be cursed as well. I'm not sure how, but the blood was meant for your kind and not theirs and it knows whose body it is in." That instantly brought a smile to my face. She walks over to me, places a kiss on my cheek and I start to tear up. "I've been watching you both, he loves you too. I agree he should be your first.

Now, I'm going to tell you what awaits your bloodborne. Your first three will be your most powerful. They will not have three gifts like you but will retain one of your three gifts as their own and with that they will manifest their own gift. So, your first three will have two gifts, one from you and one of their own. From then on, each bloodborne will have only one gift of the blood that sired them. I cannot say how they will manifest."

She seems excited explaining all this to me. 'This is your life now child. She says and then frowns. "I cannot go with you any further on your journey. After you leave me here, I do not know when we'll see each other again, but I have total faith in you. I've watched you grow from when you were born. I've seen you become a man. A wonderful beautiful kind man. Therefore, I believe with every ounce of my being you will become the perfect leader of your kind. Don't you ever forget that."

I turn around and look back to her. "So…so how do I go back?" She smiles and says, "It's your gift, you know how already." I look around and realize I do. I just have to will it to happen. The shadows open up and then release me from their reality and I'm back. I look around and I'm still the only one here.

I look down at my torn blood stained shirt and shake my head. I liked that shirt. Then three people rush inside the room in a panic. It's Daniel, my new master with those beautiful eyes, and a human I have never seen before. They stop and stare at me in shock. When the master finally remembers how to form words he speaks.

"How is this possible? You should be dead." I can't help but smile at him and it's at that time I realize I shouldn't tell them anything about Lilith and our conversation or my gifts. I don't know their kind well enough yet and I need to keep them in the dark for a while so I can get as much information as I can. I want to know everything about them and their intentions. I also want to find out what happened to Kain and the only way I can is to gain their trust.

I finally answer acting as confused as I can. "I…I think when he was taking his arm out I kinda stole some of his life energy and it healed me." I say looking at Daniel. His eyes opened wide." Holy shit! You can do that?" I realize when I said it even though it wasn't how I had healed that I could actually do that. I'm starting to understand my power now. This must be what she meant when she said I was now complete. I respond. "I think I can." I was going to play shocked and confused but it turns out I didn't have to act at all. I then look at my new master.

"Thank you for doing what you did to my wound. I think it gave me enough time to heal. If you didn't, I'm sure I would be dead now." He shakes his head and sighs. "I'm sorry that you had to go through this Brandon." He then walks up with an outstretched hand. "My name is Tristan, your new master. I wish we could have met under better circumstances."

I smile and shake his hand, "You and me both."

CHAPTER SIX

AFTER INTRODUCTIONS, TRISTAN asks to take a walk with me. He takes me to a part of the cave that I can only describe as completely amazing and impossible. It was a huge garden. A magnificent beautiful garden but inside a cave underground.

Looking around there is every kind of flower you can imagine and they all look so lush.

"How the hell can anyone grow anything down here" I say accidentally out loud to myself. That gets me a disappointed look from Tristan. "We are going to have to work on your language Brandon." I didn't mean to but I realized I gave him my are you actually telling me what to do face. "You also need to realize your position here Brandon." He says while sitting down on one of the many benches facing a small pond. I take a breath and try to say as politely as possible.

"I'm sorry, it's been kind of a stressful evening...well, a few weeks to be honest."

He nods and gestures to me to sit. "I do understand but I'm sorry to say there isn't as much time as I would like for you to have to feel at home here." He then gives me a pained look as he continues.

"Here's what you need to know. The twins are not members of this family. They are visiting with their master Kathrine at

62

the moment. They are both her bloodborne and off limits for elimination, as you are mine and off limits as well." I couldn't help but snort out a laugh. "Seems they didn't get the memo." He smiles and crosses his legs. "They know, trust me. There's something you need to know about the twins. The brother is overprotective of his sister as I'm sure you could tell, and a bit unstable." With a chuckle I respond. "You don't say."

His face turns serious as he looks at me. "That means nothing. You will come to find many of our kind are prone to violence. Vampires are not like humans, even though some humans are by their very nature violent. Vampires themselves are made for battle. We are stronger, faster and very hard to kill." I think back to when Lilith mentioned that her intention was to make us protectors of the humans. Is this what she meant? To make us stronger, faster, and better so we can fight for them? If this was true why? That would mean there had to be some kind of threat, right?

He continues "To be totally honest her visit was completely unexpected. Her family is investigating a cult that has been tracked to our location in Tuscaloosa and I'm saddened to say I think you might be caught up in the middle of it." Oh, come on! Can't I have five damn minutes before something new happens? I basically facepalm myself. "What now?" I say with a tired sigh. "It saddens me to no limit to say I have recently received information that possibly, my previous bloodborne was actually a member of this cult." I can feel the heat in my face when he mentions his first kid.

"You mean the guy that turned me? What kind of cult? I take it that it's not one that hugs trees and loves love kind of cult." With a frown he shakes his head. "No, not quite my child. They call themselves "The Hand of Kain and seek to resurrect the first vampire Kain." That revelation gets my total attention. "And why is this a bad thing? Not saying I would like it or anything, I am new here and would like to learn."

He loosens his tie a bit "Kain is our creator. He's the first of our kind. In the beginning when there were just a handful of us he was a fair and just ruler. He was strict but not unfair. He's the very one who created the blood order, the rule of law and power for the vampire kind. You will be informed of it soon.

Years later when the bloodline grew, the first gifted vampire was created. He was powerful and some say he had command of every element of nature. This made Kain angry as he was the first born and the King of vampires and should have been the most powerful of our kind. He called a meeting with the gifted one and flew into a rage.

He fed upon him like you would a human draining him dry. It should have killed them both, feeding on another vampire makes you extremely sick and can kill you if you take too much of them. Instead the gifted turned to ash and Kain gained his power. This is when Kain realized he actually had a gift the whole time, to absorb other gifts. He now had the gift of the one he fed upon. As time went by, other gifted vampires started to appear and he devoured every one of them to gain their powers. Eventually vampires began to fear their creator and you know what happens when someone fears something. They decided to kill him. The strongest of them confronted Kain and the battle of ages erupted. They tried taking his heart and then his head. Nothing seemed to work. He seemed indestructible, so finally the few remaining decided to bleed him. All of them at once sacrificed themselves by feeding on every drop of blood he had and bled him dry. Kain was defeated and the ones that drained him turned to ash and it's said the one remaining vampire took Kain's corpse and without telling anyone, hid it from the world.

The Hand of Kain is trying to bring back the one vampire who would devour us all. They believe they can rule by his side and worship him like a God, and that the gifted were his natural path to Godhood." He stands up straightening his jacket. "And that's your history lesson for the evening my child. Now we need as much information as you can give us about the man who turned you. We need to know everything Brandon."

I stand and stare at him." I don't know what I can tell you that you don't already know. I've given you everything I know. I wish I could help." I shrug "I met him in the parking lot, he bit me and it almost killed me and the last thing I know I watched him burst into flames while I was blacking out." He shakes his head "See Brandon, that's the part I don't believe. He couldn't have turned you by just feeding on you. And you say he was destroyed right after he bit you?"

Shit, well this isn't good. I've always sucked at lying.

"I don't know what to say. I don't even know how one turns another into a vamp. All I can say is I thought he was trying to kill me and I was pissed at the thought of being dead so of course I fought back some, not like it did any good." That grabbed his attention. "You fought back?"

I nod and just let it fly. The truth didn't explain much anyway. "Yeah, I figured if I'm gonna die then he's gonna remember me so I bit him back as hard as I could. I wanted to leave a scar." He seems shocked with my story. "You bit him back? Your saying you actually put up a fight?"

I shrug again "Well yeah. I'm not one to just let myself get killed without some kind of a fight."

He shakes his head then. "But Brandon, that isn't possible. When we bite a human, they are unable to move. We release a venom that incapacitates our prey so they can't move or even know what's happening while we feed. They also lose a few minutes of memory before the bite."

I blink at that and think back to the first-time I fed. The jogger seemed to move, he hugged me and seemed to enjoy it, even though he seemed to forget the whole thing and run off like nothing happened. "But I did. I mean it was hard to move at first but I did, also I felt the whole damn thing. It hurt like a bitch." He responds with a sigh and a shaky hand running through his hair. "I'm sorry Brandon but from what you are telling me we have to do a few more tests on you. We need to test your blood." Well shit, me and my big ass mouth. Well, it was fun while it lasted. Let's go get busted.

We leave the garden and walk down a few halls and come to a door. As he opens the door, I notice it's some sort of medical facility from what I can tell. There are people in white lab coats and others in scrubs walking around the facility. We walk through the main room past people looking into microscopes and doing various experiments and then down a hallway back to a private room where he tells me to wait. He then leaves the room and closes the door behind him. My mind is racing. After they find out what kind of vampire I am, what am I going to do? What will they do to me especially if they are scared of what I am? Should I do anything at all or just hope for the best? I decide it's probably in my best interest to try and plan something just in case the worst is realized.

I'm pretty sure even though I've never used my new amazing gift, I can jump back into the Shade and get away...at least I think I can. If it came right down to a fight for my survival I'm pretty sure I would be done for. That's of course only if they come back thinking I'm some sort of threat to their survival. I decide to play it cool and dumb. Tristan finally walks back into the room with someone who looks like a doctor. She is a pretty lady, maybe in her 40's, with light brown hair pulled up into a tight ponytail.

"Brandon this is Dr. Davis and she's going to be taking some of your blood. No worries though it's just for a simple test." I look her over and notice she's human. I smile. "It's a pleasure ma'am." She smiles back and pulls out a very large needle with a tube attached.

My eyes widen. "Um...how much blood are you going to take?" She grins. "Not much, you're new so you probably don't know how all this works yet. When the blood of a vampire gets too far from its host's body it turns to ash. It also does this simply when oxygen hits it. It doesn't burst into flames or anything rash like that, it just turns to ash. It's a defense mechanism for vampires to remain hidden from humans all these years." I nod and think how cool that is. "Ok Dr. Davis, go ahead and poke me." Needles have never been a big deal to me so I am not even nervous as she sticks the needle in my arm. Almost as soon as she inserts the needle, the blood runs from me through the attached tube and down to a microscope that she's looking through.

After a few minutes she raises her head from the microscope, that's when I notice my jaw is clenched so tightly my teeth hurt. She turns to Tristan and gives him the news. My foot is placed directly in her shadow and I think to myself that I'm ready, probably not truly ready, but what else am I going to do when Tristan learns of what I am and tries to literally take my head off.

"His blood is totally normal. One hundred percent vampiric blood." I let out a breath I didn't know I was holding and he looks in my direction. Shit. "Well, that doesn't explain much."

The doctor speaks up. "If I may, I think I have a theory." He looks in her direction. "You may."

She gives a slight bow. You're kidding, right? That's a thing, bowing and waiting on permission to speak? "With the information you gave me the only thing I can come up with is this. Him being gay, his DNA may have had a different effect on Jacob's body chemistry. I won't know for sure until I find out if he ever fed on a homosexual before.

Jacob's body chemistry might actually have had an adverse effect on the chemistry of homosexual DNA seeing as though vampire DNA does not agree with homosexual human DNA. His venom could have been ineffective on Brandon giving him free reign to defend himself."

I'm totally going to kiss this woman. She just saved my life, I hope.

Tristan looks at me with a smile. "That's a theory and I'll have to accept it as it's the only explanation that can be for now.

Thank you for your work and guidance doctor." She then bows again to Tristan. Come on, seriously. He holds his hand out for me to take. I look up not expecting a handshake and take it anyway. He just grabs my hand and pulls me up then takes my shoulder looking me dead in the eye. "My child I'm so sorry for how you have been treated, how you came to be, and all the tests you have to take. This is no way a vampire should come to be. I want you to know you are now, and always will be, my son. You are mine and what's mine is yours from now till the end of your existence." Holy freaking shit! I don't know how to react to any of what he just said, it didn't matter because the next thing he did was pull me in for a full-on hug.

After that I was allowed to walk back to my room. You know the one with just the bed. Anyway, the first thing I do is pull out my phone to call Sloan. He picks up the phone on the first ring. Shit, he's been sitting by the phone worrying his ass off. I can't stand making him worry.

"Hey baby, I just want you to know I'm fine and everything is ok here so please stop worrying." I hear him exhale like he's been holding his breath since I left.

"What's it like? Did you find out about turning me? They aren't all like the movies, are they? When can you come home? Can we still cook with garlic? Do they make king sized coffins for us? Are they letting you feed enough? Damn I miss your face baby. You don't have to live there forever do you?" I can't help but smile, he's just so freaking cute. I cut him off. "Ok, wait baby and let me answer the first question first please. And yes, I miss your ass too." He laughs a bit and I can tell he's feeling better about the whole situation now that we are able to talk.

We spend the next hour just talking. I only tell him about what I have learned here. I couldn't risk telling him anything else about Lilith or Kain or the Shade or any of that. I'm no moron. I'm pretty sure they are monitoring my calls. Hell, I would tell Sloan every little detail if I felt it was safe for both of us. Instead,

I tell him everything is going to be fine and I'll see him soon. We do our usual I love you g'night thing and hang up.

The next day I get a knock on the door and Daniel walks in. "Rise and shine pretty boy!" I sit up pissed. "Dude! Totally rude to just walk in someone's room! I'm naked here!" Yup, I sleep in the nude, no biggie. Me and the hubbs both do. The best night's sleep you will ever have trust me. He flinches "Woah man, I totally didn't mean to interrupt your private self love time." I growl a bit." Hey Mr. Rude Ass I sleep in the nude." He just chuckles "It's no big deal man. We got pretty much the same stuff." I roll my eyes at him." It kinda is a big deal man. Gay here, also married, sooo...Yeah." He smiles "So am I supposed to treat you like a lady or something?" I look at him and am not sure what to say. "No. I'm not a girl...But...I don't know. I guess it's complicated. Just freaking knock next time ok." He smiles like he's enjoying the shit out of this. I roll my eyes and groan. "Fine!" I fling back the blanket off of me and stand up to grab my clothes. As I get dressed he laughs.

"You are going to have to get over the shy thing. Especially with me. We are going to be together for a very long time and being naked in front of each other can't be a big thing. Just think of me as your big brother. Because that's what I am now." I finish pulling the shirt over my head and look back. "Brother? What do you mean by that?" He bows to me. Oh, freaking come on!!! Oh Hell no!

"I have been named your guard, I am your brother from now till the end of your existence." Well shit. This just keeps getting better. "Stop! Just frigging stop. I don't know what the hell this is all about but it needs to stop. You don't have to bow to me. Seriously how the hell is this a thing anyway? I get it, you're my guard but I'm still me and you are still you and you better not freaking change and get all formal and shit. I'm not used to all this formal shit and don't want it, you understand?"

He lifts his head and looks at me with a smile. "I do understand, and will gladly comply. But you also need to understand. I am your guard. You need to know what that means. I'm here to serve you, protect you, with my own life if necessary and aid you in anything you need. He then stands with a grin. "Now that you know the definition of what a guard is, get your pretty ass ready to go."

I can't help but grin at that. "Fine, where the hell are we going?" He turns around and as he walks out saying. "To learn all the rules of course. Can't have you pissing off the whole vampire community after all. You have enough vamps pissed at you already."

CHAPTER SEVEN

WHEN WE LEAVE my room, he takes me back through the garden chatting away trying his best to cram as much info into my brain as quickly as possible. "So, here's what you need to know right now. Tristan has already explained most things to you but I'm here to give you the basics. For instance, this place, headquarters. This isn't the norm for all vampires. This is the headquarters for guardsmen in Tuscaloosa.

We are a training facility for vampires to keep order in our community. We patrol the town, make sure feedings are kept private, investigate vampires who try to influence the human word and execute them accordingly." He said that like it's as normal as taking out the trash.

"Woah buddy, you execute vamps just like that? No trial or anything?" He grins "There is an investigation first. Every vampire knows the penalty for making our kind known to humans. There is a serious reason we stay hidden. Yes, we are superior to humans but there are very few of us comparatively. It would be easy for humans to wipe us off the face of the planet. Especially now with all the new toys they are creating."

I nod understandingly and let him continue "Anyway this almost never happens. The vampire usually ends up dead by human hands anyway. There are human vampire hunters out there too. They don't have tangible proof of our existence but they know we are real and they do their best to find us and kill as many of us as possible. We haven't heard or seen anything from them since our last encounter with them which was decades ago now.

The vampire hunters have either disbanded or have been in hiding for years now." He shakes his head. "Let's get back to what this place is and why it's important to our survival. Anyway, like I said we are the Guardsmen. We are the Vampire Law of Tuscaloosa. We enforce and keep order to keep everyone safe. We also have authority all over the world but only if our investigation calls for it or if we are needed." I smile at him "So we are basically the Vamp Police." He laughs. "More like the Vampire Secret Service. There is one in every larger town and city in the world. We are simply called the Guardsman. Now that you know what this place is, let me tell you how the vampire community is arranged. We of course are the law and order but there are houses that basically govern the vampire community as well. Those houses are concerned with the money and business that keeps us together and functioning.

See Brandon, this town's money for us comes from the club and bar scene. We have many clubs here that we own and operate to increase our cash flow and of course for feeding purposes. Now we don't influence the human population but we do have a few of our kind in power for very specific reasons. They are basically there to help us with the vampire community.

Then there's the Master of the State. It works like that here in the states, there is a master for every town then the master that rules the entire state. Just like a governor and mayor. That's about it for the community civics lesson, except for the Main House. It's basically the house that rules us all. It used to house the King named Kain until he was defeated, now it houses the three Elders. The Main House is located in London England now, but we literally have vampire houses all over the world."

I rub the back of my neck trying to take it all in. "Do the Elders ever make appearances?" He stops and turns to me "Rarely, but when they do you don't want to be around. It means something serious is happening and vampires usually start dying."

Well shit, why am I not surprised? "Sounds kind of cliché don't you think? I mean in just about every vampire movie ever made the elders are big meanies that like to kill for fun or because they are bored." He shakes his head "Dude, think about it. The Elders are probably thousands of years old. Boredom is their way of life now as they have done it all and seen it all, so I'm sure killing a vampire is as mundane as brushing their hair for them." I give him a nod. "Makes sense I guess." We continue with our walk through the garden and he continues with my quick education.

"So, as you know, every vampire is registered with headquarters and the reason for this is to keep track of them all. We need to know where they are when they feed just in case they run into trouble…." His face gets very serious now. "But there are a few who are off our radar. These are the vampires who have been turned by others that are also not registered, and are forced to live in hiding. They almost always don't agree with our way of life or our laws. They think that we should be the rulers of this world. They think our original maker, Kain, wanted it this way and are doing everything in their power to bring him back to life."

"They call themselves the Hand of Kain. This cult is the reason why the twin bitches and their master are here at Headquarters. Just so you know she's the Master of Texas and she outranks our Master, your dad, Tristan. This is the only reason that the little freak that tried to kill you isn't dead right now." Just thinking about him made my chest hurt. I rub it unintentionally and Daniel frowns. "I would totally kill him myself right now if I could Brandon. Just so you know, if he attacks you again you have every right to protect yourself, as do I. I'm your guard now and I will show him absolutely no mercy."

I smile at him and shake my head. "Thanks man, but hopefully we won't have to see him anymore." He frowns and I immediately get a bad feeling in my gut. "I'm sorry to say Brandon, but you will be seeing him again, sadly sooner rather than later. He's a part of this investigation and you are a big part of it as well." Now I'm getting pissed. "How many times do I have to tell everyone I don't know shit about shit?" He gives me a light pat on the back "As many times as you have to get them to listen to you Brandon."

"Now onto the feeding process, you now know you can feed at the bars and clubs in town. Also, you can feed here. There are feeding rooms available for us all at Headquarters, and also feeding rooms for the cursed." He says as he frowns. "Now I know you have already fed on a human and it went ok but that doesn't mean it will continue that way. Gay vampires always lose control eventually when feeding. When that happens, we have a special facility that helps with the feedings so you don't kill your prey."

I know that I'll never lose control from what Lilith told me, but I need to keep playing dumb so I nod and go with it. He finally asks, "When was the last time you have fed?" I realize it's been days, not since the jogger. "It's been a while I guess, how often do we need to feed anyway?" He stares at me in amazement. "You really don't feel the pain, do you?' I shrug.

"No, I've never felt pain like that. I just get hungry is all." He shrugs and his face is a mix of confusion and amazement. "Usually we feed every two days to make sure we don't have to experience the pain. But depending on how much you exert yourself it can be sooner." This revelation lets me know I should probably get a routine going so I don't draw attention to myself and fit in better among the other vampires.

"I guess I should feed then, it's been a while." He nods and I can swear his face is sad when he says, "Well that makes two of us." He takes us to the feeding area. It's a normal looking and palatial room that would not be out of place in any five star hotel in the world. There are flat screen televisions on the walls and huge comfy looking arm chairs scattered around. I see a few tables along the walls full of snacks and drinks. Not exactly what I had pictured in my head for a room where vampires feed on humans.

There are humans all over the room sitting in the arm chairs watching TV, reading books, playing games and chatting. I guess these are some of the humans who want to join club vamp. I see random vamps around the room feeding on the willing humans. I still can't get used to the blank stare the humans have on their faces as they are being fed on. I guess that venom we have is no joke and to be honest, it's spooky as hell. I turn to Daniel and ask the inevitable question.

"So, what do you do, just go up and ask someone if they can be my sippy cup?" He belts out a laugh "You can but I'm sure you might just piss them off. All you have to do is ask someone if they don't mind if you feed. That's after all what they are here for." I smile, "Well at least you're here to show me how it's done." That sad look returns to his eyes and all I want to do is make it go away any way I can.

"I'm sorry Brandon but I can't show you, I'm not able to feed here. My place to feed is in the room over there." With that he just walks off. The hell? I just stand there like a moron. Eventually a young lady in her early twenties walks up to me and asks me if I need assistance. She's your typical sorority girl, blonde hair, big smile and looks like she has had an easy life. She wouldn't look out of place at a beach resort bar ordering drinks poolside or driving her new convertible through Beverly Hills.

"Yeah, what's in that room over there?" She looks at me and responds with a nervous look. "That's where the cursed go to feed." Yep, my world just got turned upside down yet again. I swear the next thing that goes all wonky I'm gonna punch someone in the face. "You're freaking kidding me?" I say to myself but obviously loud enough for her to hear me. "No sir, I would never kid you about something like that." I totally forgot she was there. I look down to her.

"I'm sorry, I was talking to myself. This is kind of awkward, I'm kinda new here." She steps up with a smile. "I know sir. You are Brandon, aren't you? Well I'm here to serve. If there is anything you need to know, please just ask me and I will do my best to let you know. If you need a vein I'm here for you as well." Damn, this girl isn't shy at all, is she?

"How many cursed use that room?" I'm sick of being surprised and it's best to know who bats for my team here. "Only him sir." She says with a frown. I nod. "So, how does it work in there? What's so different?" She looks at me and frowns. "He's restrained with chains while he feeds. Others of your kind pull him away when he starts taking too much blood and heals the human as fast as possible."

I am about to tear up in front of her but I hold it back." Why can't he just get like a blood bag or something? "She smiles at that. "The blood for your kind has to be fresh from the vein or it is useless. As soon as it hits air its life force dies and is no good to you." I nod, I guess it makes sense.

"So...how do I do this?" This is so freaking weird. She grins and tilts her head. "Just go with it. It's why I'm here after all." Finally I lean into her neck and let my new fangs come out to play. As soon as they sink into her soft skin, she moans a bit, then she starts to hug me tight just like the jogger did. It's like she's enjoying every second of the feeding.

I look around while my mouth is on her neck and everyone is stopped and staring at me. I notice three vampires walk up and watch me feeding and they seem to be in shock. She's basically straddling me now and I feel full so I let up and lick her neck to heal the bite. It heals fully and instantly and I look at her to see her smiling at me. She finally blinks and says. "Well If you're not in the mood to feed right now it's ok I understand." She then looks around and notices everyone is looking at us

"Why is everyone staring at us?" I let her know the truth. "Because I've already fed on you. Apparently, me feeding is a bit different than everyone is used to around here." I'm kinda fed up with all the staring so I just leave the room and I head back to the garden to decompress. Wow, Daniel is gay. How the hell is this possible? Well I know how it's possible but damn. My gaydar is usually pretty freaking good. Why didn't he say anything? I'm totally going to kick his ass.

I'm sitting there when thinking of ways to kick Daniel in the face when a familiar voice interrupts. "So, I hear you've had your first feeding." I look up and see Kristin smiling at me.

"Word gets around fast I see." I can't help but sound all pouty. She sits down beside me, "I take it that it didn't go as planned?" Looking at the ground I shake my head. "You can say that."

"It couldn't be all that bad. I would have been informed if you went out of control so what's wrong?" I look up at her and try to form words.

"My feeding went fine, well sorta fine I guess. It seems humans don't react to my bite like they do to other vamps but I have full control so I guess it's ok. My feeding isn't what's got me upset." She nods and gives me a sad smile. "It's Daniel isn't it. You watched him go into the other feeding room." I can't help but get angry again. "I know everyone comes out to people in their own way but come on, why didn't he tell me? Me, of all people, I would understand the most." She chuckles and smiles. "Come out?" Shaking her head, she says. "Probably because he isn't gay."

I sit there with my head tilted like a confused puppy. "But the curse, doesn't it only affect gay people?" She nods "It's complicated but he should be the one to tell you. It's not really my place." I let out a long sigh. "So he loses control when he feeds but he isn't gay. No offence but how do you know?"

"Well for one as you know I'm pretty good at reading people and two because I'm his girlfriend." I sigh with an eye roll "Of course, you are. Why not, can't have anything simple in my life now can we?" She seems to be getting slightly pissed now." So how long is this pity party supposed to take?" Totally shocked the only response I had was. "Excuse me?"

"So, you find out Daniel can't control himself when he feeds. That he can actually kill someone if he does feed on his own and you get all sad because he didn't tell you right off? Get over yourself Brandon. I know this is all new to you but he hasn't known you that long and doesn't have to tell you anything and everything about his life." Shit, I'm a total ass. All I can do is look at her and feel guilty. "Wow, I had no idea I was being a total ass. I'm sorry." "Well look here, the pretty boy is apologizing. Looks like I got here just in time."

And there he is with that perfect smile. Just like Daniel to show up at the perfect moment. Kristin stands and gives him a quick kiss. "I'll leave you two to chat. And don't forget you're needed in operations in an hour." I guess they are dating. She walks off and he sits in her spot on the bench. "So, ask your questions Brandon." I just let it rip. "Are you gay and hiding because of the hate vamps have for us?"

He grins "Right to the point kind of guy I see. I'm not gay Brandon, I'm not one hundred percent straight either. I guess if you want to put a label on me I would be bi. I'm attracted to women mostly. I have only been attracted to a few guys but not like I'm attracted to girls."

And that explains it. "So, you're bi. I understand there are different levels of attraction and I guess the vamp curse doesn't give a shit about it. I'm sorry dude." He just smiles and gives me a pat on the back. "Why are you sorry? It's not like you did it. Anyway, we have been summoned so we should get going."

We walk for a while and I want to ask but just can't bring myself to. How bad is it when he loses control? Has he ever killed someone when he lost control? I decide he will tell me if he wants to, it's not my place. We get to the door marked Operations and walk inside. It's a giant office area with computers and big ass screens everywhere. There are only a few people here, I see Tristan talking to the Master of Texas and, yay me, my favorite psycho twins are here as well. I walk in and when they see me their eyes go wide. Is that fear coming off Ken doll? Is he on crutches? Tristan walks up to me and Daniel.

"You're late." Wow, not even a hello. Ken doll decides to speak up. "How the hell is he walking around?!" He didn't get an answer because his Master decided to speak up. "Well, it seems we have a replacement after all." Shit, she's looking right at me. "We absolutely do not!" Tristan seems pissed as he answers her. "This is your fault Tristan. We are down our most powerful soldier because you decided to cripple him right before the mission. We need a replacement and by the looks of it your new addition has a nifty ability to heal."

I can't help but speak up. "Don't all Vamps heal? Isn't that one of the perks?" Miss Texas walks up with a shit eating grin on her face. "Yes Dear, but not like you. From what my boy told me he did to your chest, you shouldn't even be alive yet walking this soon. For a normal vampire, they would be on some serious bed rest, at least for a few weeks." Well shit, looks like I'm going to have to keep playing stupid. She continues. "That's why you are going on your first mission."

Daniel interrupts. "He has no training! How is he going on a mission?" She cuts him off with a dismissive wave of her hand. "He's going because we have no other choice. We have a small window of opportunity for this mission and because your master just had to cripple our best soldier, he's going." Tristan looks enraged. "If your bloodborne didn't try and murder mine we wouldn't be in this situation! So why don't we try and put the blame where it belongs."

She rolls her eyes. Now I see where psycho bitch Barbie gets it. "What's done is done. He will be punished accordingly but right now we have a mission to complete. We got lucky receiving this information and it won't happen again. We have no choice, it doesn't matter if he is trained or not, we need three for this to be successful." Tristan sighs. "He has no training and that alone can make the mission a failure." "She holds her hand up, cutting him off like she did Daniel. "It doesn't matter, the decision is made. He is going, end of discussion." Oh goody. One minute I'm dying the next I'm going on a mission without any training. Good times had by all. All I can do is wonder how many times I'm going to die this week.

CHAPTER EIGHT

SO HERE I am, getting ready to go on my first mission. I'm kinda freaking out but I'm also super freaking excited. Daniel is trying to prepare me as much as possible. Basically, he's saying let him lead, stay close and when it comes to battle to let him handle it. You know, the usual, you have no training so stay out of the way and try not to die stuff. All I can think about is how I am going to use my new gifts on an actual mission. Should I use them? I really want to take them for a test drive.

"Brandon, are you paying attention?" It must seem like I'm daydreaming. "Yeah. I get it. Try not to die." He just grabs me by the arms and his gaze is so intense I feel like he can shoot lasers out of his eyes and fry my brain. "This isn't a joke Brandon. You have zero training and these vampires do. They will kill you as quickly as possible and probably enjoy doing it." I nod like a five year old who just got in trouble with dad. "I'm sorry, I'm listening." He nods and mumbles something under his breath that sounds like Texas and bitch.

It's dark out and the three of us are on a speed boat heading to some island down river on the Black Warrior. It's just Daniel, Janet, and little ole me screaming through the hot Alabama night on our water chariot to certain death. Janet can't keep from looking at me and I can't help but bait her. "I'm flattered hon but you're not exactly my type." She rolls her eyes like she always does and smiles at me.

Sarcastically she says, "I do hope you don't die out there, it would be a damn shame." Daniel quickly cuts her off. "This is a mission. We do not wish death on our team members in Alabama. I'm not sure how it's done in Texas, but here if one of us goes down not only can the mission fail but we could all die. So, put a sock in it Janet." He notices me smiling. "You too Brandon, quit acting like this is a game." He's right. I need to focus.

So apparently, we got good information that the Hand of Kain had a base of operations set up on this island. The island is a crescent shape that at one time was connected to the shore but over time has become an island to itself. There are hundreds of these along every major river in the south. Perfect hiding places where no one will bother you while you're planning a murder or the destruction of the world.

The intelligence tells us that the Hand of Kain is holding a certain item that could possibly have a part in the resurrection of Kain. We must infiltrate and retrieve this item at all costs. A full-blown assault would cause them to flee and we could lose the item forever, so it was decided that a team of three would be best. We are going all super stealthy and we have our basic supplies for defense. Apparently, we don't use guns, something to do with it just pissing off a vamp and not really killing them. So, we have two blades, something Daniel called a "Tanto". It's kinda like two long kick ass daggers that are about an arm's length. Well they got weapons I should say.

Apparently, I'm not allowed a weapon until I'm trained in its use. I guess I could accidentally cut my own head off…Or stab Janet in the leg. Ok so that thought made me smile just a bit.

We were supposed to split up and keep in contact through coms but because I'm a newb I was told to stick with Daniel. I'm still not sure why they had to have three of us for this mission. It seems to me I'm just dead weight. That's probably why Texas

made me go on this mission, so I can have the chance to be dead...
weight.

Janet will head to the left side of the building and we will take
the right. The building is some kind of old factory in the middle of
the woods. The building isn't all that big but it's still an imposing
structure with tall and thick brick walls. Daniel said that at one
time it was used to build and store munitions for the human war
effort but had largely been abandoned and the wild had pretty
much taken over. Trees are growing all over the compound and
bushes slowly taking over the structures. We are to use the trees
as cover, get a look good at the security, make our way inside the
compound, retrieve the item and get the hell out without getting
dead of course.

"So, what happens if we run into a cult member?" We've been
quiet going through the woods so I figured I would try and get as
much info as I could before we got to a point we couldn't speak. "I
kill them before they can inform any of the others." Wow, kinda
cold. "Just like that?" Truth is I've never killed anyone before. I
know I should feel some kind of bad about it happening, but I
don't really. Why don't I feel bad about it? Well I haven't done
it yet, maybe it's one of those things that doesn't affect you until
you actually do it. But why aren't I scared to take a life? Daniel
noticed me staring off into space while we walked.

"It's ok Brandon. You don't necessarily have to kill anyone.
Let me do all the dirty work, it's why I am here after all. You're
new and I don't expect you to even try the hard stuff." He thinks
I'm afraid to kill. Shit, I just realized that I'm supposed to be
scared.

"I'm ok Daniel. Let's just keep moving."

We eventually make our way through the forest and arrive
at the factory. It's as big as Daniel described and surrounded by
an imposing electric fence. We get as close as we can but not so
close that we could be spotted by the baddies. We climb one of
the tallest trees we can find and scout the area. Well I do anyway.

I use my vision to detect life inside and outside of the factory. Trying to get a good count. I spot three vamps patrolling the gate, five more vamps inside patrolling the building. I could swear there was another one in the middle of the building but for some reason its shape changed suddenly. It kind of like melted in on itself then came back to form. Hmm. Maybe I'm just tired and my eyes are playing tricks on me? Anyway, there is also a human in there that looks to be restrained. People just don't normally sit like that. I let Daniel know all the details of my reconnaissance. I'll be damned if I'm going to be useless during this critical mission. He gives me a serious look. "You sure you want to let her know what you can do?" I nod with a grin. "Go for it."

"We have a visual!" He tells Janet everything I said. "Well looky here, the mo is useful after all."

Wow, try and help a bitch and this is what I get. "And what have you done lately Barbie? Hope you didn't chip a nail." Truth is she doesn't really even piss me off anymore. "Well I almost did when I ripped the heart out of the last guard that came by but it's all good. Y'all need to catch up, you can make out later."

Ok that kinda pissed me off. "Enough Janet, where are you now?" Daniel didn't seem amused either. "She's making her way into the building on the other side." I know her little run when I see it. She speaks up with surprise in her voice. "Damn mo, your eyes are good. Now hurry up."

We come down from the trees and make our way to what looks to be like where they stored their old broken down vehicles. It's freaking amazing how agile I am now. I'm like a freaking ninja. We take cover behind a van and I decide to look through it to see when the cultist gets close enough to us for action. He's getting so close. My blood starts pumping through my veins like crazy and I've never been this excited before. I begin to realize that I'm smiling a big toothy grin from ear to ear and apparently so does Daniel. He's just crouched there looking at me like I'm completely nuts.

I nod to Daniel letting him know the bad vamp man is about to walk to our left around the van. He nods back and gets ready to pounce. Then it happens. The first thing I see is the cultist's foot come into view. The next is Daniel grabbing his arm and with his other hand the cultist's throat. He rips it completely out, damn. It is effective I suppose because he can't scream anymore, but damn. The next thing I know is Daniel pulling a blade out of nowhere and he takes off the throatless guy's head in one quick motion. And then just like that poof. Just a bunch of ash.

Daniel looks back at me like he was worried about me witnessing all that. I guess I should be in shock. I mean any normal person would be right? So why aren't I. All I'm thinking is how efficient he was at killing and trying to figure out why he went for the throat before cutting off his head. All I can do is look at him. What the hell, I'll just ask him.

"So why did you rip out his throat instead of just chopping off his head to begin with?" I ask like it was a simple math question. He walks up closer to me and looks me in the eye confused but answers me. "Because I didn't have a clean swing and I wasn't sure how tall he was because I couldn't see him yet and I had to make sure he couldn't call for backup. Are you ok Brandon?"

I give him a nod. "Yeah I'm fine. I'll try and find the next guard." He looks concerned but nods anyway.

The next two guards were easy, with my eyes and his blade we cut through them like a hot knife through butter. We finally make our way into the building and we take cover so we can observe. I can see Janet hiding in the broken-down machinery above us ready for action.

We see the human tied up in the middle of the factory floor and some crazy eyed vamp chick with a dagger standing over her. Then all of the sudden the air in the building gets electric, the wind picks up and that's when I notice some kind of hole opening up right next to the crazy eyed vamp and a guy with wavy long black hair pops out of it. The actual hell? Is that a real life portal?

His glow is silver so he has to be a traveler? They can do that? He says two simple words and then all hell breaks loose. "It's time."

As soon as he says those two words the crazy eyed vamp girl holds up the dagger and slashes the air above her, by the looks of it I think she slashed open a portal right above the terrified human girl. It looks like a hand coming out of the portal but the hand isn't solid like flesh. Holy shit I think it's made of ash. Vamp chick gives the dagger to the freaky ash hand then the next thing we see is that it looks like it's going to stab the human girl. All of a sudden it changes direction and goes to stab the Traveler instead.

The look of shock on the Traveler's face was the last thing I noticed before Daniel and Janet jumped out of the shadows and began the attack. They take to killing the vamps one by one. Slicing through them with ease, gliding over, under and off walls like some kind of kick ass video game. It's freaking spectacular.

Then I notice the Traveler. He's not in shock anymore, also for some reason not the same color as before. It seems his silver is turning blue. He pulls the dagger from his chest and smiles. The crazy eyed vamp grins at the battle that's ensuing and tells the Traveler that she can handle things here and he should go.

He makes for the door when Daniel tells Janet to go after him. She bolts out the door chasing him down. And that leaves just Daniel and crazy eyes to fight it out in the factory.

She just stares at Daniel grinning like a psycho one minute and the next thing you know is she melts into the friggin floor. Seriously just freaking melted. Shit! He can't see her. She's under him now but he can't see her.

"She's under you!" I screamed but it wasn't fast enough. She came up through the ground like an octopus wrapping her tentacle arms around his legs. The next thing I see is her taking form behind him with a blade in her hand. I jump down but by the time my feet hit the ground the blade is through his chest. He's going to die right in front of me!

I scream "You crazy ass bitch from Hell leave him alone!" That sure got her attention. She tosses Daniel to the side like a ragdoll across the room, and then comes at me. All of a sudden she's all over me and squeezing me hard. I can't take a breath and I hear cracking in places you shouldn't. I look over and see Daniel bleeding out on the floor and all I want to do is rip her crazy eyes out with my teeth. I've never been so pissed before or hated anyone as much as I do right now.

She looks at me and that crazy grin starts to fade as I just go for it and I bite her right in the eye. She screams and tries to let me go but I grab her and hold her with every ounce of strength I have. I feel her trying to go all liquid again, and that's when I decided she has too much power for her own good. I've never used it before at will but you gotta start somewhere right? Every tendril of my energy jumps to life and starts to latch on to her life force devouring it like a starved animal. She stops changing and starts to panic. That makes me very happy.

"I'm going to drain every ounce of life your crazy ass has until you don't exist anymore you evil bitch." Then I clamp down on her throat and start drinking her in. I can feel her blood and life filling me and I keep draining her. I want her dead like I've never wanted someone dead before. I realize that should scare me but it doesn't. I open my eyes and notice that now I see...everything. I see Janet chasing down the man with the dagger on the other side of the complex. I can see her leap and slash him in the back with her claws. I see him falling to the ground and the dagger rolling from his grip. I can see all the little ash piles she left behind after taking the hearts from the cult members on the other side of the building.

I can hear everything too. I hear the man scream as she claws his back. Her giggle as she does it, and him getting up and saying, "Your end will be the most painful!" as he summons a portal and jumps through to escape. For some reason I know, well I think I know, everything. I keep draining her until she's just a pile of ash.

Breathing heavily and with a smile I lick my lips clean. I've never felt so powerful. It's absolutely intoxicating. I look down at Daniel laying on the floor and frown. He looks so pale in a pool of his own blood. He will not end this way, I will not allow it. He's close to death now, but I'm not afraid. For some reason, I know how to fix him. I know how to make him better. I walk over and kneel beside him. The look he gives me breaks my heart. He tries to speak but just mouths "Run, live." Poor guy, I smile back and caress his cheek. "I'll make it all better don't worry." I look over to my left and notice some broken glass. I can see my reflection.

Holy shit! My eyes are glowing the deepest and darkest blue. My aura, liquid shadow, is flowing off me. There's so much! It's like the blackest of water is just flowing out, wrapping around, looking for something to devour. I take my eyes off my reflection and focus my attention back on Daniel. I kneel toward his head and bite down on his neck. He moans slightly but then stops. I take just enough to know his blood. I can feel his essence mixing with mine. I can feel his disease, his curse. I know how it happened and I know how to fix it. And that's exactly what I do. I simply fix it, it's not simple but to me it's the most simple and natural thing I've ever done.

Now I need power to get his new blood back to him and how about that, I've got an excessive amount right now thanks to crazy eyes. I grab his blade from his hand and cut my neck just over the vein to get the blood flowing and then lower myself to him so he can drink me in. I know he will lose control and try to kill me when feeding but it's ok, I need to fix him. This is all I can think about. It's all I care about right now. He starts to drink me in slowly, at first. I give him some of my life force to help him have the strength to feed. His eyes snap open and he grabs me tight. He's drinking much faster now. It's time. We must go now before he takes too much.

I pull my shadows over both of us and take us to my reality, the Shade. Here I have unlimited power and life force, I don't know how I know this, I just do. I use the shadows to carry us to where we had the boat tied up then I release us from the Shade. We are back in our own reality now. He stops drinking. I can feel him panic. "No no no! Brandon! Are you ok? Shit, no!" I look up and give him a weak smile. "You stopped. Good for you buddy." Then I see nothing but black.

CHAPTER NINE

I WAKE UP to a light being shined in my eyes. I feel like shit and my neck hurts. I put my hand to it and it seems I'm not healing like I used to. I did give him a lot of power and blood, I guess it's to be expected. "There is our fearless moron." Daniel walks up to me smiling. He looks to the nurse and asks her to go find me someone to eat. When she leaves, he leans in face to face with me. The look he's giving me is full of fear and panic.

"They will ask you what happened and you will tell them exactly this and nothing more. We were ambushed by a cult master and after I sent Janet to retrieve the dagger you tried to help me. She almost took your head right before I took hers. Do you understand me?" I blink. "But why?"

"Brandon, I wasn't unconscious when you did what you did. I watched you do... everything. I don't know how, or even if you know. But if people find out what you can do you will either be used or destroyed. A vampire as new as you, even if gifted, is not able to take out a master. I'm your guard, I'm sworn to protect you and that's what I'm doing. Just stick with the story right now ok. We will figure this out, I promise." I can't help but smile at him.

"Aww, you care." I try to make light of the situation because I'm starting to get scared as shit.

"This isn't a joke Brandon. This is probably the most serious thing in your world right now." I roll my eyes and sigh. "Well duh man, but do you want me freaking out or acting normal?" He nods in response. "Good point. Just stick with the plan and we will talk later."

"I will, and I'm glad you're ok." I try and sit up and it hurts like a bitch. He puts his arm behind my back helping me up then looks in my eyes with a kind smile.

"Thank you, Brandon. You saved my life." The nurse comes back with a red headed human man. He walks over to me with a smile. Yep, this is my midnight snack. I smile and tell him thank you before I sink my fangs in, he gasps and starts to moan. Soon, he's hugging me close like all the others do. I finish up and heal the bite, and as usual there's a smile on his face when I look up. I immediately raise my hand to the bandage on my neck. No pain. I start to take it off when Daniel speaks up.

"Nurse, could you take this gentleman to his room? He seems a bit dazed." The nurse looks confused. "Isn't he going to give him a suggestion?" The red headed man still smiling speaks up.

"Is he going to feed on me or should I go get someone else for him?" The nurse seems even more confused. "Let's go ahead and get you to your room." She leads him out of the room.

"Leave the bandage on." Daniel looks serious so I do what he says. "Is everything ok?" "You're going to have visitors and you need to keep up appearances." I pick up what he's putting down. "Gotcha, but could you check my neck for me?" I pull the bandage back just enough so he can see. "It's not fully healed yet. Are you ok? You seem to be healing fast but not like you normally do." I shrug "I'm fine, I just need time to get back to normal I think. Don't worry." I should be worried about myself but I'm not. For some reason, I can just tell what it's going to take to get my energy back up.

After a few hours, I'm called in for a meeting. I get dressed and head down with Daniel. As soon as we enter the conference room, I see the twins and their master speaking and Tristan seems pissed. "I'm impressed. I didn't expect a fag to survive as long as you have." There he is. Kevin and his smug ass smiling face. I really want to rip a hole in his chest. "Silence! You will show respect! If not for him your sister would be ash!" Tristan has had enough of his shit it seems.

"And how do you think his death would have anything to do with my sister?" Daniel speaks up. "If he didn't jump in and distract the Cult Master she would have taken my head, then taken Brandon's. After that, do you think she would have let Janet leave with the Dagger alive? Do you seriously think Janet can take out a Master one on one?" I look to Janet and she seems sad. She looks at her brother and walks away from him.

"He's right Kevin. Brandon saved all our lives." Then she does the weirdest thing. She gives me a smile and says..."Good Job Brandon." Umm....What, no snarky comment? "Um...thanks?" I look at her and grin. "You're secretly plotting my death aren't you." she just grins right back. "It wouldn't be a secret if I told you now would it." I don't know if she's playing or serious. Ava speaks up. "Enough, it's time we returned home. I'll take the Dagger and we will be on our way Tristan."

She gives a smug ass hair flip as she holds her hand out expecting it to be given to her right then and there. I look back to Tristan and notice he's smiling. "Yes Ava, you may return home, but the dagger stays with us here at Headquarters." Her eyes go wide "Excuse me?" Oh, the bitch of Texas seems pissed now.

"It seems the dagger was taken in my territory and the Master of Alabama has taken claim to it. It is under our protection now. Thanks for your assistance in the recovery of our artifact. We wish you a safe and comfortable trip home." His smile was so bright and perfect as he spoke. He enjoyed every word of it. She huffs like a spoiled child and says.

"We will see about that. I'll have a word with your Master. I shall return. But until I do I think I'll leave Janet with you to make sure you don't lose it again." Well hell. I look at Janet and she looks hurt. "But …" Ava gives her a stern look. "As you wish." She responds and bows in defeat. Ava leaves with Kevin and that's it. My first mission and I'm not dead. Yay me.

Everyone leaves except Tristan and Daniel. Tristan walks over to me with the brightest smile on his face and puts his hands on my shoulders. "You did well Brandon. I'm proud of you. Thank you for saving our agents lives and the mission." He then frowns. "I also want to apologize that you were forced to go to begin with. That should have never happened." I give him a smile and tell him the truth. "I'm glad you worry about me and am glad everything turned out ok. But you should know, I want to do it again. I want to train and become a Guardsman. Tuscaloosa is my town as well and I want to be able to protect it if the need arises."

The surprise in Tristan's eyes made me smile as I detect a rather noticeable facepalm coming from Daniel. Tristan finally speaks up. "You want to be a Guardsman? Ok, well I didn't expect that from you. You do have a gift that will benefit missions. I can't stop you if you want to train. You have my blessing." He shakes his head with a prideful smile. "I think you will be a fantastic Guardsman." He turns and walks to Daniel.

"His training will begin next week. He will need time to speak with his husband before he decides one way or another." Shit! I almost forgot. I guess blood and death will do that to a guy.

"One more thing Sir!" Tristan looks back with a slightly amused and shocked look on his face that I actually yelled. "Yes Brandon?" I guess this will be the deciding factor for me being here. If it's a yes, I'll stay, if it's a no then I will go and leave this all behind. So I just go for it.

"I want your permission to turn Sloan." I give him the most serious look I have. He walks up to me slowly. "Brandon. You do know if you try and turn him he will more than likely die. You are freshly born and even though you are gifted only a select few can turn a human."

I nod and have a plan to convince him. "Yes Sir I know this. But I have a plan. I think my gift can help me do it. I've been practicing and I'm sure I'm able to transfer power to him during the transformation. I think it will be enough to assist him in turning." My bullshit factor is off the charts right now.

"You're able to transfer your life-force? When did this happen?" Oops, gotta come up with a good one and quick. "When I almost died, and was taking Kevin's life force to heal myself, I just felt like I could. May I show you?" He flinches and then looks at me and nods. "You may. But please be careful my Son." I look to Daniel and he seems calm but I can see his Aura turning red. Yep he's pissed. I walk up to Tristan and smile nervously and look to Daniel.

"Daniel, I'm gonna need some juice." His Jaw drops. "Are you serious?" "Dude, I'm kinda drained here. Just a quick hit. I won't take much I promise." He walks over to me with a pissy look on his face and offers me his hand. "Ok, just be careful." I nod and take his hand. His aura is still red and I feed on it anyway. Wow, eating a life force while they are pissed is different. It's ... hotter. Like fire. But soooo good. I stop myself before I get too excited.

My hand automatically goes to my bandage and I take it off. Tristan's eyes go wide when he realizes I'm completely healed. I can't help but smile at him as he looks at me. "May I have your hand Sir?" He nods without saying a word and gives me his hand. I take it and focus my instincts on my own life-force. I notice his aura, a cool shade of blue. I stretch my life-force out to his and they fuse together. I feed his life-force with as much as I can without depleting myself and look into his eyes. They are wide with shock, sparkling and ... amazingly beautiful. He's enjoying this. He starts to breathe rapidly as his smile widens. I ease up and release him. He pants for a second or two and runs a shaking hand through his hair.

"Brandon, when you get back from speaking with your husband, we must sit down and speak of what you are able to do.

But until then, you will not speak of this with anyone else do you understand?" Shit, I've gone too far. "You have my permission to try and turn Sloan. But just know if you fail, he will die." I nod.

"Daniel, you will go with him. If he fails, you will make it look like an accident. And you will need to make sure Brandon returns to us alive." He looks at me in a strange way. Oh...he thinks I'll try and off myself. Shit. Now I'm sure that I'm able to turn Sloan but I've never thought what would happen if I did accidentally kill him. I don't know, I don't think I would be able to live with myself. I look to Tristan and give him a sad smile understanding what he meant by what he said. "Well Brandon, let's go get your man." Daniel says trying to hide how much he's mad at me.

CHAPTER TEN

I BARELY MAKE it through the front door before two old pups and a crazed husband just about knock me to the floor. So many kisses and puppy licks, my Jackabee {Jack Russel & Beagle mix} is screaming his head off and my Shorgi {Corgi & Shepherd mix} running through my legs like a cat.

After a good two minutes of lovin' Sloan realizes we are not alone.

"Oh, sorry Daniel. I didn't know you were with him." He seems totally embarrassed that he was showing me love and didn't realize that we weren't alone. We don't believe in PDA for a few reasons. One, we just don't need to. We know we love each other and don't feel the need to show everyone around us. Two, this is Alabama after all. Even though it's legal for us to be married it doesn't mean we still won't be assaulted for just holding hands in public. Daniel gives Sloan one of his bright smiles.

"It's ok. He's your husband and you have missed each other. I would expect nothing less."

Sloan smiles back. "Can I offer you something to drink?" He immediately gasps and puts his hand to his mouth like he can shove the words back in. Both Daniel and I burst into laughter. And I pull Sloan in for a kiss. "My perfect little host." We go to the living room and have a seat.

Daniel speaks up. "So, what do you have to drink in this place?" I blink with surprise. He looks at me and smiles. "You do know we can drink. Also, eat if we want. We just don't have to." My mouth opens but it takes a minute for words to happen. "Holy shit. Why didn't you tell me this?! I thought I would never be able to have a burger again. And bacon! That was just about enough to ash myself over!" He chuckles and I can tell Sloan is feeling out of place. I get up and go over to him and give him a peck on the cheek. "Is there still tequila?" He smiles and says "Oh, hell yes! There's always tequila. Would I ever be caught dead without Tequila?"

After a few shots, we start getting serious and inform Sloan of the whole turning him situation. I play along with Daniel. I know he knows I'm a bit more than what I seem but he doesn't know everything yet. I plan on keeping it that way for just a bit longer. I need more information before the big reveal.

"So, you do understand you could die from this. It would devastate Brandon if that happened." Sloan smiles at Daniel. "Yes, but you also need to understand that If we aren't together my life is already over." He looks at me and I smile back. "He's right." I look at Daniel.

"I know he told you to bring me back alive if I fail, but just know that even if you do I won't last long." Daniel gives a sad nod. "I understand." I smile back at him. Now I gotta get him to go.

"Ok, I know you want to help Daniel but I'm gonna need you to go now. This is kind of a private matter." Daniel seemed to blush when I told him that. "Of course, I'll go but just know I'm only a few houses over. If anything goes wrong, you call. If not, I will be back here in three hours." I blink. "Three? Why three?" He looks at me with a cold stare. "Because you will kill yourself if you kill him and I can't have that." He stands with a pained smile. "Good luck you two. I hope this works. I really do." He leaves.

As soon as he's gone I blow up with all the information I wasn't able to tell Sloan before. It took a good hour. Shit that leaves only two and I know he has a shit ton of questions.

"Holy freaking shit Brandon! You're telling me this just now?!" I should calm him down as fast as possible. "I was sure they were listening to our phone conversations baby. I couldn't risk it. We don't have much time and I wish I could answer all your questions but we only have an hour and a half now." He looks at the clock and gets his panicked face. "Shit, you need to hurry. Can you hurry? How long will it take?" I just nod and take him into my arms. "Hopefully not long at all." I sink my teeth into his neck. He gives me a big moan and pulls me in closer. I take just enough to taste him. I can feel his blood fusing with mine. I let go, lick the wound closed and see him smiling.

"Are you ok?" He blinks at me and smiles bigger. "I'm fine, are you going to bite me or not?" I can't help but smile. "No Sloan, you get to bite me. Well sorta, ok don't bite me but here." I take my wrist and use my teeth to open a vein. "Drink up. It will make you grow up big and strong." He gives me a grossed-out face but giggles anyway. "Ok, bottoms up." we giggle like school girls, then he drinks.

I'm not sure what I expected. But I didn't expect this. After he finishes drinking he gets dizzy and says he has to lie down. The next thing I know he passes out and then starts convulsing. His flesh is starting to stretch and his bones start to crack. All I can do is stare at him in horror.

His body is bloating right in front of me. It took under a minute and he was nothing but a giant cocoon.

A frigging cocoon. What the actual hell? My pups run upstairs scared shitless. I wanted to run upstairs with them and hide from what I've done. I calm myself down and try to focus. His life force is still there, I can see it clearly. He's alive at least, in there. His color is changing. It's slowly turning blue. I think it's working. I look at the clock. Shit, five minutes left before Daniel is back. I have no other choice. I pull my shadows to me and take us both to the Shade.

Once there I feel a bit safer. Not that I'm worried that Daniel will try and stop the whole process or anything, I just need time to think and plan. I look around at my world. It's so strange that it looks just like our townhouse. I look closer and can see the people that live in my complex. It's hard to explain but it's like their shadows have taken their form here. I look back to where my door is and can hear knocking. It seems that Daniel has made it to my door in the real world. I can see him knocking. Shit, I need more time. If he kicks in the door my neighbors will flip their shit. When he notices, we aren't there he will flip his shit. I start to freak out when he knocks a second time.

"Just frigging wait!" I scream like he can actually hear me. He starts to knock for a third time but before his fist hits the door it stops, he stops. I look around and notice my neighbors have all stopped. Holy shit. The world has stopped. Looking back at Sloan, he seems to have stopped as well. It didn't take long before he starts to move inside his cocoon. I can tell he's moving normally in there now. I look back expecting everything to be back to normal movement but everything is still frozen.

Then I hear a crack. He's hatching or something. Oh shit, he's actually hatching. I see his hand pop out first. This clear goop starts pouring out of the cocoon as he forces his way out. I look down and notice the shadows are eating it up. Gross. So, don't laugh, but I was half expecting Sloan to pop out with a pair of butterfly wings or something. Nope. it was just him, but hot damn. He was always built bigger than me but shit, he's massive. His body simply formed to the perfect version of itself. He's absolutely perfect, just perfect.

"I agree, you have done well." Lilith emerges out of the shadow like she is walking through water. I jump not expecting it and as Sloan emerges from his cocoon he starts to panic "Where are we Brandon? What happened? And who's this?" The poor guy is freaking out. "It's ok Sloan, you're safe. This is the Shade I was telling you about. We are safe here." I look to Lilith and she's smiling that beautiful smile of hers. "And this is Lilith.' She walks up to Sloan and lays a hand on his cheek. The smile on his face tells me he must feel it as well. It's like her touch makes everything perfect.

"You are beautiful and perfect. You have done well Brandon." She looks back to me "And it seems your power is growing." She waves a hand to my frozen neighbors. "Yeah, about that. How and what happened here?" She laughs and I'm instantly happy. "You wanted more time and that is what you got." She says it as it was as simple as that.

"You need to understand that in this place, "she looks at me seriously "Your place, your gifts are magnified greatly. This is because it is your world. You also need to understand that anything you can do here you can do on Earth. Maybe not as strong as what you see here but with time it will be." My jaw about drops right off my face.

"So, you're saying that I just friggin stopped time. And that it's one of my gifts?" she grins and sighs. "Haven't we had this discussion already? It's one of your three gifts of the Blood, your Tribus Sanguinem. I told you your power will increase with time." She looks back to Sloan and smiles. "And you my child, you will be powerful as well. Through the blood, you have received one of Brandon's gifts, but that's not all. Every one of our Bloodline receives their own special gift. Now let's play a game."

She looks back to me and then to Sloan and outstretches her arms. "Who here can tell me what gift Sloan received from the blood?" I blink and stare at Sloan with my mouth open like a moron. He looks back to me and then to her. We stand there trying to figure out what she wants from us when Sloan looks around. Sloan speaks up in excitement. "No way!" Lilith smiles at him with pride.

"You have guessed it, haven't you? You are impressive as well as beautiful." I just stand there staring at both of them like a dumbass. "What? What the hell is it?" I'm getting a bit annoyed as I'm the only one in the world that has no clue. "Look around Brandon. What do you see?" Sloan says with a smile. So, I do. I look back at my neighbors frozen in the middle of making dinner, back at Daniel frozen mid knock and then back to Sloan and Lilith.

"Wait, no way. He can freeze time too? Nice!' Lilith chuckles. "I knew you would get there eventually." Is she making fun of me? She's actually playful. "Hey, it's been a long day ok." I act like a toddler and cross my arms in a huff. Sloan speaks up in excitement. "What's my other gift?" Lilith shrugs "That's something your blood will tell you. It will come with instinct. You will just know." She steps away so she can look at both of us. "You will leave here soon but before you do you must know something. Something dangerous has escaped to your world, and I'm sorry to tell you that you are the only people that can send him back." I stare at her and I can see the fear in her eyes. She has the most pained expression on her face when she says. "Kain has returned to your world."

CHAPTER ELEVEN

AFTER SHE GIVES us that fun little tidbit of information about Kain being back she goes into detail about how he is back. It seems that the Dagger that Janet retrieved is just one of many magical artifacts created by someone called The Blacksmith. She was a traveler from way back when, whose talent was to create items and give them as gifts. The Dagger has the ability to transfer one's own soul to another by stabbing them in the heart with it. This is how Kain made his way back to our world. Back on the island, crazy eyes and that Traveler made it possible.

The Traveler opened a portal to the realm where Kain's soul was being held, the Cult Master offered the Dagger to Kain so he could stab the human that they had captured to transfer his soul to her and make him alive in our world again. Instead Kain stabbed the Traveler and took over his body. But he's not finished yet. He needs his own body to reclaim his immortality, so we still have time to stop him. There is one of the Blacksmith's tools he desperately needs to acquire before he can get his true body back. It's the only thing that can give his original body life again. We need to find it before Kain does and either destroy it or make sure he doesn't ever get his hands on it.

I'm sitting on the floor now running my hands through my hair. "Shit shit shit! He slipped right through my hands." Lilith shrugs. "No dear, you had bigger problems on your hands at that moment. You did what you had to do." Sloan sits down next to me. "We will get him baby, and we will do it together. Just think of all that you did all by yourself on that mission. And now you have me." I smile and nod. "You're right. He doesn't stand a chance against us." I realize looking at Sloan after his transformation just how fantastic he looks. I loved his body before but now, just damn. I also realize that we are not alone here.

"Aren't you cold, sweetheart? You've been naked this whole time, and in front of Lilith no less." He looks down and gasps, quickly covering up his naughty parts. "Holy shit. No, I haven't been cold. I've felt normal this whole time. I'm so sorry Lilith. I didn't realize I was naked."

She chuckles. "There is nothing to apologize for Sloan. People of your generation are such prudes. The human form is a beautiful thing and shouldn't be hidden. You should never be ashamed of your body no matter what. It is a gift, and an insult to the creator of that beautiful gift to be ashamed of it."

She then smiles at both of us." It is time for me to go now. Please be careful, my children. Kain may not have his body yet but that doesn't make him any less deadly. He will stop at nothing to reclaim his throne. Use every tool at your disposal to send him back." With that she fades into the shadows.

I look to Sloan "I'm afraid we might have to tell the others. I'm sorry, I was hoping to keep what we are a secret from them but we might need their help. We don't know shit about the vamp community." Sloan grabs my hand. "What if we can just guide them in the right direction. They are already after him, what if we can just give them a push in the right direction?"

I give him a nod. "It could work. But if it takes too long or if they can't get any leads we have to tell them what we know." Sloan smiles as he stands up. Holy shit, he is perfect. Lilith was right. I done did good. "We will, but let's try." He looks over to the frozen form of Daniel at the door. "So, what do you think we should do about this? Can you just make it go back to normal?" I look over and smile. "Yes, yes I can."

Seconds later I pull us out of the Shade and back to Earth. I made sure Sloan was upstairs and I was heading to the door with Daniel banging on it like a crazy person. I made sure I had my shirt off and my pants unbuttoned to complete the ruse. "Yes! Damn man! What?" The look on his face was classic. I wish I had a camera. Sloan timed it perfectly coming down the stairs in nothing but a towel. "Is everything ok?" Damn, he's gonna be good at this spy shit.

Daniel finally figured out how to speak again. "Shit, um sorry dude... It's been three hours and I was worried." I put on the best I'm so sorry face. "Shit, it has? I'm so sorry, we um, lost track of time." He grins and walks in the house. Rude, if we had actually been in the middle of something I would be pissed. "I can see it worked." he looks up at Sloan and smiles. "By the looks of it quite well." I notice the grin on his face. "Hey! That's my husband you're admiring there." He chuckles.

"Take it as a compliment!" He then plops down on the couch and grabs the bottle of tequila and tips it up like it was water.

"So, do me a favor and put some clothes on will ya. You guys have to explain how you two just appeared out of thin air like that." He gives a shit eating grin "I may not have your eyes Brandon but I know there wasn't anyone in this house while I was knocking at the door." I look at Daniel and have nothing to say. I go upstairs with Sloan to grab some clothes.

"Sloan, I think we have to tell him." He looks back at me and is visibly upset.

"Are you sure we can trust him? You've only known him a few weeks Brandon."

I just nod. "That's true, but yes I do trust him. I did save his life. Also, he's the one telling me I need to keep what I can do secret."

It seems he agrees with that. "Ok. But let's try and convince him to keep it a secret."

I put on an Alabama Football t-shirt and nod. "I'll try, but we can't force him to do anything. I don't think anyone can force that dude to do anything," We head back downstairs and I just look at him tipping up the bottle again. Man, can that guy drink.

"You're going to need to sit down for this." Daniel looks confused, "um... I'm already sitting." I sigh "Then maybe lay down then." I let the words fly. How we are from two different bloodlines, about Lilith, Kain. That I'm the Father of the Chosen. The whole thing. Without a word and with a calm face Daniel sits upright and slowly puts the bottle down on the coffee table. "Are you ok? Please be ok. This doesn't make us enemies, it just makes us different."

His face expresses no emotion as he stands up looking me directly in the eyes.

"You lied to me Brandon. You knew what you were the whole time and you lied to me." I can tell he's pissed, I'm not sure exactly, but he seems more hurt than pissed off. "I didn't know you Daniel. I didn't know what you would do, what the House would do. They made it clear they aren't against killing other vampires that don't fall into their perfect little roll. What the hell was I supposed to say when I found out? Hey, I know we just met a week ago, but I just wanted you to know that your entire bloodline is the one that is actually cursed and I'm the Father of the Chosen and am to birth a powerful new Bloodline. It's a pleasure meeting you, please don't kill me."

He takes a deep breath, I can tell he's starting to calm down. "Would you have ever told me?"

I shake my head with a shrug. "I don't know Daniel. It's not that I didn't want to. I was just scared of what that revelation would do to me and Sloan." "He wanted to tell all of you but I made him change his mind." Sloan says as he walks down the stairs with the pups. Daniel looks over to Sloan and then back to me. "Is this true?" I shrug "Yeah, I did. I was sick of lying to my friends and to be honest, we need help. We don't know where to begin with this whole tracking down magic items and killing Kain thing."

He sits back down and picks the bottle back up. "Well shit. I guess we are on the same side." He locks eyes with me. "Don't you ever lie to me again. I'm your freaking Guard Brandon..We don't lie to each other, ever." I sit down next to him and grab the bottle to take a swig, and about spit it all back up. "Holy shit, how do you do that? And you make it look so cool while you do it." He laughs as he takes the bottle from me. "Just because you're super powerful and shit doesn't make you as cool as me. Get over yourself." Sloan sits down next to me and takes my hand. "What are we going to do now?" Daniel Smiles at Sloan and then looks back to me. "We stick with the plan Stan. You have me in it now. You just lucked out big time." Realizing what he's going to have to do, I can't help but feel bad for him.

"Dude, you know that means you have to lie to Tristan. And there is another problem. Your girlfriend. You know, the walking lie detector. I'm pretty sure you won't be able to lie to her." He smiles from ear to ear. "Well it's a good thing she already knows." My heart skips a beat "What do you mean by that?" He chuckles. "How do you think I knew you weren't in your apartment? I can't see through walls." Shit, I look around through the walls of our house and around the complex trying to see if there was an army of vamps getting ready to take us out as we sit here.

"Calm down, she just didn't want me to wait for you guys alone. She is using her witchy ways to link to me right now and can hear and see everything. It's something we do sometimes, It's not weird at all. Trust me when I tell you it's a good thing she is because I was so pissed at you I was going to leave and let the cat out of the bag.

She's the one who told me to listen to you." I look closer and find her threads connected to him. I must say, that's a pretty cool trick. I trace them back and can see her walking to my door. I walk over and open it before she gets to it. She smiles. "You're getting really good at that" and walks right in, sits right next to Daniel and grabs the bottle from him then takes a swig. Shit, how do they do that? I notice Sloan standing up and I can feel the anger coming off him.

"Look, I didn't want to involve any of you. I don't know you and I've never even met your Master Tristan. From what Brandon has told me, your House just about got him killed, twice. The only reason I'm even allowing the thought of you people helping us is that Brandon trusts you and I trust him. But don't think for one minute that I trust any of you in the slightest. You seem to think that he's the only one calling the shots around here, but believe me you are mistaken. We are a team, always have been, and always will be. You may think of me as being just the weak little husband but you need to understand that Brandon might be the Father of the Chosen but I'm his first Bloodborn. That makes me the second most powerful vampire in this house. You will not walk into my home without being invited and you will show me the respect I deserve!"

Holy shit, his commanding presence has them both cowering, practically sinking in the sofa right now. It's totally hot and has me grinning like a schoolgirl. "I...I'm so sorry, I didn't realize we were being disrespectful. Please forgive us." Daniel says totally shaking in his boots. "Yes, I'm so sorry I wasn't thinking. Please forgive us." Kristin stands and gives a slight bow. Holy shit, he has her ass bowing to him. I can totally see why. His life force is magnificent. It's not blue but blood red mixed with blue and it's filling the entire room. Shit, I made that. Well my mother in law made that with my father in law but I remade that.

"Um... we will leave if you wish. But could you please pull back Sir? It's hard for me to breathe" Kristen says gripping her chest a bit. "What? What are you talking about?" Sloan has no idea what he's doing. "Baby, look at me." He looks back at me with a confused look on his face." Your power is showing and it's a bit too much for her to handle." I can't help but smile with pride while I tell him this. "What do you mean baby?" He seems to be calming down now, which is good for everyone involved. "You remember when I told you I can see people's life forces? Well she can too. And your life force is crazy big right now and it's kind of suffocating her. We just need you to calm down a bit is all." "Oh shit! I'm sorry." he tries to calm down. He takes a few deep breaths and his power slowly returns back to normal. I walk up to him, give him a hug and whisper in his ear. "That was friggin hot." He pulls back with a big smile and kisses me right in front of everyone.

After that we all calm down with a few shots of tequila and come up with a plan. We decide that it's just going to be the four of us, as we don't want to involve the other members unless absolutely necessary. Daniel and Kristin have enough knowledge of the vampire world and enough influence that they will be able to push the others in the right direction better than Sloan and I could by ourselves. With our help we are going to kick Kaine's ass so hard his momma's momma will feel it.

CHAPTER TWELVE

AFTER A FEW good hours and the rest of the bottle of Sloan's tequila, Daniel and Kristin decide to head out and inform Tristan of Sloan's transformation. Sloan and I have had an extremely long night and pass out as soon as the sun comes up. The next night we get a call from Daniel and are informed that we have been summoned to the House. Tristan wants to be introduced to our newest member, Sloan. After we get dressed, we hop in the car and nervously drive to HQ. We go through our usual entrance and I notice Sloan picking at his fingers nervously. I can tell he's also excited to see everything I've been describing to him firsthand.

As soon as the elevator doors open, his eyes light up like the Fourth of July. I don't blame him at all, It's a freaking amazing place after all. After a few minutes of Sloan stopping to look around in amazement, we eventually get to the front desk and it seems we have a new receptionist. She can't seem to take her eyes off of Sloan. Who can blame her? After introductions are made we head right up to see Tristan.

As soon as we walk into his office he stands to great Sloan with a smile. "I'm so glad you made it through the transformation in one piece. Welcome to the family Sloan." He walks up to him and shakes his hand. Sloan gives him a bright smile. "It's a pleasure to finally meet you Tristan, Brandon has told me so much about you." Tristan looks in my direction and chuckles.

"I'm sure he has. Please forgive me for him almost dying." Sloan quirks a brow and looks back at me. "He told me you did everything you could to prevent that, I don't blame you for it at all and want to thank you for making him as safe as you could. I also wanted to thank you for your part in saving his life after the attack." Tristan gives him a nod. "Of course, we are ashamed that it happened at all and I want to apologise to you as well for it happening." Tristan walks back to his desk and waves an arm to the chairs in front for us to sit down. "Please have a seat. We have much to discuss."

We take a seat and wait for him to start. "So, it seems you know much about us but unfortunately I don't know that much about you. To start, what do you plan on doing for the rest of eternity?" Sloan fidgets in his seat. "Well, to start with I plan on spending it with Brandon. If that means I need to join this House, then that's what I'm going to do." Tristin tilts his head with a smile. "And what makes you think you have to join our House to do that? You are more than welcome to live any life you choose, we will not prevent you from being together." That comment seemed to make Sloan relax quite a bit.

"Well I wasn't sure about your rules, if we actually had to join your House or not. I just wanted to make sure you knew that I was willing to do what it takes to be with him for eternity. To be honest I'm kind of interested in what you guys do here. Brandon makes it sound so exciting. You know, with all the dying and killing and all." Well there he goes. He's always been forward in that way. Right to the point with zero room for bullshit.

Tristan sits up in his chair with a smile. "Well, I can tell you like to get to the point Sloan so here's what you probably want to know. We're not all about killing and getting our agents killed. To be honest we do what we can to ensure that does not happen. We are a family here first and foremost and we protect each other. Our organization is here to enforce Vampire Law so yes, sometimes that involves bloodshed. Brandon just happened to come to us at a time of crisis."

Sloan relaxes a bit more in his seat and they start talking about everything. What is needed of Sloan and what he would be doing here at Headquarters if he joined the House. Sloan is the kind of guy that has to know everything about everything before he runs into something full force. In the end, Sloan surprised me. I didn't think he would join the House if he didn't have to but after all was said and done, he asked what he had to do to sign up.

After they were done chatting he sent Sloan to get all the registration stuff out of the way. Tristan asked me to stay behind with him in his office. "I'm glad you were successful with Sloan, but you need to know what you did is unheard of in the vampire world. The only vampires that can turn a human are Masters Brandon. So, you have a choice here. If word gets around that you did this, other vampires will become aware of your ability. They will come for you, either use temptation or fear to take advantage of you and your ability.

I have a solution but only if you wish it." I nod slightly spooked at what he just said. "Please, do tell." He leans back and continues. "I will say that I am the one who turned Sloan. Ultimately it's your decision, but for both yours and Sloan's safety I highly recommend we do this. We are the only people who know, and Daniel and I will keep it that way. This is your ability after all so the decision should be yours."

I didn't think of that. I had no idea turning humans was something so rare. No wonder they are so few in number. He does make a good point, I really don't need all this attention right now.

"I had no idea and I think that's a really good idea. I seriously don't want to be taken advantage of like that. Thank you, Tristan. I'll let Sloan know as soon as I see him." Tristan seems pleased with my answer.

"Good, you are my Bloodborne Brandon and I'm here to protect you. I would have been ok with whatever decision you made. This one makes it much easier on all of us so I thank you. I do hope you will grow to trust me more in the future." I can't help but feel a bit guilty, he holds up a finger shaking it side to side. "No no. Don't try and cover. I know you don't trust me yet. Why should you? It's ok. You are still new and we barely know each other. Now that the crisis is over, we will have more time to get to know each other. As for your training to be an agent, you can start today if you wish. You do still want to, don't you?" I smile with excitement but also feel crushed inside because he doesn't know that the real crisis has just begun.

After our chat, I find that Sloan has finished registering and he is ready to go. I was told he could come with me to start training so he can see what he would be getting into. With my surprise I find our situation being very convenient. We find out the two training us are our very own Kristin and Daniel. They greet us with smiles and then lead us to an unexplored area for me and we hop onto an elevator and head up.

The doors open and much to my surprise our floor leads directly to the outdoors. It's an open area full of rocks, trees, and boulders fashioned around an obstacle course. Looks like a great place for target practice with all of the combat dummies. This place is obviously used for mission training. Perfect place to train a super-secret army of vamps. We walk out and Daniel smacks his hands together and rubs them together with excitement then looks at Kristin.

"Brandon is all yours, I get the newbie." He grabs Sloan and smacks me on the ass when he passes. I can't help but chuckle and feel bad for Sloan. He has no idea what he's in for. Kristin just stands there and smiles at me. When they are out of earshot she starts walking to an open area. "He hasn't been this happy in a very long time Brandon. I want to thank you for that." I can't help but look shocked.

"What do you mean? I've been nothing but a pain to him." She shakes her head. "That's not true. He's right about you though. You really are kinda dense. You need to open your eyes. Besides the human's, Tristan and I, have you ever seen another vamp pay any attention to him? Or even say hello for that matter." I think back and the answer is no. Why haven't I noticed that? "Wow, I guess I've been pretty self-absorbed. Why doesn't anyone talk to him?"

She seems sad when she says. "Because they think he's gay Brandon. They think he uses me as cover to try and prove that he isn't."

I can't help but want to kick every vamp's ass in the House. "Some family. I guess they don't like me either. Why does it feel like there are more homophobes in this House than the entire state of Alabama?" Kristin nods. "It seems that way, and I'm sorry." I shake my head. "I don't care, I'm used to it, but Daniel doesn't deserve it." When we get to the spot she wants to train in she tells me to sit.

"So, Brandon. We know about your gifts, but the one everyone knows about is your sight. It will make the entire vampire community shit bricks if they found out you had more than one gift, but the one they know about is still shocking to everyone. The reason for this is that the gift you have is one that vampires can't have. It's a gift of the Traveler. Vampire gifts tend to stick with the physical aspects. You kinda lucked out by having Tristan as your Master. There are very few vampires that have gifts related to energy manipulation. His is a very powerful gift." I nod. "You're telling me, I saw it up close and personal. Freezing people solid is kinda cool." I chuckle at the pun. She does not.

"He doesn't exactly just freeze them Brandon. He saps the heat energy from them and he can use that heat energy as well. I've seen him freeze an object solid and with the heat energy he created an explosion inside it and watched it shatter into dust. He's an extremely powerful Master. That's why he's the Master of this House."

I'm not sure if my mouth is on the floor or not but I'm finally able to speak up. "Holy shit. He can do that?" She smiles, "Yes he can. And I'm not sure but I think you can too." At that moment, I'm totally shocked that I'm still conscious. "Um.... ok....um, please explain."

She takes a breath to gather her thoughts.

"Ok here's the best way I can put it. We have seen you leech power from people, and watched you also give it back. We also know you can see the life force of others and feel that life force. I've seen you use your power on me even. I think you have yet to tap into your potential. That's why you are training with me to start. So, here's what I want you to do. First I want you to close your eyes and take a deep breath." I do so, and she continues. "Good. Now tell me what you see Brandon."

I know what she's asking so I look around with my mind and can see Sloan and Daniel talking over next to the obstacle course and I can see Kristin's aura doing that web thingy again. "Are you going to trance me again?" She giggles "No Brandon. I just wanted to know if you can see me. I figured you could. The things you see with your eyes aren't actually seen with your eyes. All the life forces you see is actually in your mind. Now do me a favor, you see the rock in front of you?"

I look with my mind, and see nothing. "No, it's not a living thing so I don't think I can." She speaks up. "Concentrate Brandon. Look closer" I sigh and do what she says. I try harder. I sit there for what seems like hours and then I see something different. It's like a pulse coming off the ground, more like vibrating water. Suddenly something snaps in my mind and I get dizzy, my head hurts for a second.

"Brandon, are you ok?" I take a breath. "Yeah, I'm ok. Let me try again. I think I noticed something happening." She looks worried but nods. I close my eyes again, take a few deep breaths and there it is again. But the vibration is everywhere now. I can see everything. It's on everything. I try to touch it with my mind and notice it's heavy. I focus on the rock in front of Me and I use my mind to feel it, its shape, its density. It's smooth, both the rock and the energy. That's it, it's energy. A heavy energy...no, that's not it. I can't eat it. It's more like a force. It can't be can it? I must try. I use my mind and touch the force that's around the rock. I use all my willpower to force it to obey.

I want to make it go in a different direction. It starts to fluctuate and eventually changes direction. It starts to go up And I can see the force around the rock rise in front of me. It's so cool. It's just floating there in front of me. I hear a gasp. "Oh, my God! Brandon. Open your eyes!" I thought she was just freaking out about me manipulating a blob of force, but when I opened my eyes, the only thing I saw was a rock hovering in midair.

"Holy frigging shit..." I'm shaking and I don't know what to do. "Don't panic Brandon. This is amazing. Let's see what you can do with this. Move the rock Brandon." I do. It was shaky at first, but then I understood it. I wasn't controlling the rock. I was manipulating the force that was keeping it on the ground. I was manipulating frickin gravity!

"Holy shit!!! No freaking way! I release the rock and stand up. "Brandon, are you ok?" I smile and hold my hand up to her. "Oh, hell yes I am, you stay right there, I want to try something."

She seems scared. "If you are going to do what I think you are please be careful." I laugh "I promise." I close my eyes and put all my focus on my own body. I focus on the force around me that's keeping me tethered to the Earth. The vibrating force around me, just like it was around the rock, and I do the same thing that I did with the rock. I make it do what I want. I feel it instantly. I'm freaking floating. I open my eyes and Kristin is standing there in shock. I go all out and make myself go higher.

"Holy shit! Brandon!!" Sloan is screaming from across the training area at me as he runs up to me so fast he's almost a blur, or I should say under me. "Sloan! Baby, I can frickin fly!"

Daniel and Sloan start to panic. "Brandon come down please! You are too high!"

Kristin is a bit calmer. "They are right Brandon. You are too high. This is new and you need to be very careful!" I can't help myself, I'm frigging flying for God's sake. Flying! It's so perfect. I can see everything.

The excitement is making me feel light headed. Looking down things are getting blurry so I lower myself toward the ground. I guess getting too high up can make a dude dizzy. Getting lower doesn't seem to help. My head hurts. That pain is back. Oh shit, I'm falling. I guess the excitement wasn't what was making me dizzy.

"Brandon!" Sloan is screaming. I can't move, can't speak. Can't even open my eyes. Can barely breathe. Someone catches me. I think it's Daniel. "Lay him down gently" Kristin seems to be taking charge. "Brandon, can you hear me?" I wish I could answer her. "His energy is practically nonexistent. He's used up just about everything." Damn Kristin, wish you would have told me that earlier. "What are we going to do? Does he need blood?" Daniel asks. "No, that's not what he needs. He needs life. I've been trying to give him mine but he's not responding."

Well shit, I didn't even feel it.

"What the hell is that!" Why is Daniel screaming like a fourteen-year-old girl? "Holy shit! Get him away from that!" Kristin is just as girly, well she is a girl so. "No! Don't move him. It's here for him. Let it touch him." Sloan? That better not be a snake you're letting touch me.

The next thing I know my mind snaps. I feel a familiar energy but see a world I've never seen before. But it's familiar. I know what it is. It's the Shade. It's before it was destroyed. It's amazing. Like nothing I've ever seen. There is no way to explain it. There are living beings, like water but not. It's full of life, but not physical life. Everything is made of energy. Dark energy. They feed on light and seem very intelligent. So beautiful, so peaceful. Then a blast of light explodes out of nowhere. A horrible creature with no face emerges from the light and is burning everything. Why? Why is it killing everything? It burns everything and everyone to nothing. This is what happened. This beautiful world was destroyed by a faceless demon. My world, that's what destroyed my world.

Those poor creatures.

"Is it eating his hand?!" Daniel is still shrieking like a little girl.

"No, it's feeding him." Sloan, he must be talking about the shadow holding my hand.

"He's right, his energy level is much better now." Kristin could be such a good doctor. I can finally open my eyes.

"Well shit. That kinda sucked." Oh hell, they look pissed.

"You ass hole! You almost died, again!" I'm pretty sure one of these days Daniel is actually going to kill me for almost dying so much. "I'm sorry man." Sloan looks calm. That's not a good thing. He's at his most evil when he's calm. "The next time you almost die I will kill you myself. What the hell were you thinking Brandon?" I do really need to stop doing that.

"I'm sorry, I was thinking I can fly. And I did!" Kristin moves up closer to the shadow on my hand while speaking. "Yea, so you can fly. Good for you. But you need energy for that dumbass. What the hell is this thing feeding you?" I look down at my hand and smile. This is mine. My little version of reality. I can show you if you want. You two will be the first non-chosen to see." Daniel and Kristin seem a bit afraid.

Sloan speaks up. "You are spooking them Brandon. You got that devious face on again. They aren't used to it. It scares the normals." I chuckle. "My bad. I don't realize I do it sometimes. But I'm serious. I would love to show you. While I was out I had a vision of the world, what it used to be. It's so sad what happened, I want everyone to know what happened." Kristen stands up with a serious look. "Brandon, are you telling me that is from another world?" I shake my head. "No, not another world but another reality" The look of panic on her face scares me. "This isn't possible, it's just not possible. Brandon, only Travelers can do this. No human, vampire or any other creature can do this. Only a Traveler."

I shrug and stand up. "Until now I guess. Would you like to see?" They all still seem a bit standoffish. Sloan sighs. "It's totally safe, he's not gonna drop it until you agree to go see his Shade." Daniel steps up. "Fine, show us. But I swear if anything goes wrong I will end you." He takes Kristin's hand and closes his eyes and they stand there like I'm about to shoot them or something. I shake my head with a smile and pull their shadows over them to take us to the Shade.

Once there I just watch their jaws drop. They walk around fascinated. As I've said before, everything is still the same but with light and dark switching rolls. They walk around touching everything. Kristin stands in amazement. Sloan just holds my hand as my world recharges me. Kristin walks up to me with a look of fear on her face. "What are you?" I don't know why but that kinda hurt. "What do you mean? I've told you. I'm what a vampire was supposed to be before Kain stole the gift."

She shakes her head "No Brandon, that isn't possible. Vampires are not Travelers. They don't have this gift. They are the opposite of us. There is a balance to things. Your very existence is throwing everything off balance." I stand there speechless. Sloan squeezes my hand. "And what exactly makes you an expert in vampires and Travelers my dear?" And there it is.

That voice. That beautiful voice. Kristin jumps and you can actually see the chills on her skin. Daniel stares wide eyed in amazement at her. Sloan is smiling like she's a long lost loved one he hasn't seen in years. I just smile and walk up to her. "Lilith, it's great to see you." She takes her hand and caresses my face and it's as beautiful as usual. "I see you have been making friends." She turns to them and they seem to be in shock. "Do they speak?"

I chuckle a bit. "Lilith, this is Daniel and Kristin. Guys, this is Lilith. The Mother of all vampires." She smiles and walks up to Kristin face to face. Kristin takes shaky breath and says.

"Yeah, she's also the Mother of all Travelers." Then she bursts into tears right in front of us.

CHAPTER THIRTEEN

LILITH STANDS THERE with that beautiful smile. "Yes dear, I am, among other things as well." She puts a hand on Kristen's arm and her crying stops instantly. Kristin looks up at her with an amazing smile. I know exactly what she was feeling. "Tell me, why do you cry my child?" Kristin smiles. "Because I've offended you. I'm so sorry." Lilith smiles and tilts her head. "You haven't offended me dear. Even if you did it is no reason to cry. I know what your people teach you about me. I must say they have many things wrong and just a few things right. If I could, I would go to your world and correct your records." Kristin runs a nervous hand through her own head of silver hair. "Why don't you? Why haven't you ever come back? We thought you abandoned us." Lilith smiles and walks towards Daniel. His eyes grow bigger the closer she gets. "Because child. Because of his kind."

I can't help but get defensive of Daniel. "He's not like them Lilith!" She gets right up to him face to face like she's inspecting him. Her smile lights up. "You are correct, my child. He is not like them at all now, is he?" She looks back to me with the happiest of smiles. "What have you done, my love?" I have no idea what she's talking about. She walks up to me and hugs me tightly like a mother does her child. I'm in total shock and have no idea why

I start to tear up. She takes a step back smiling at me. "You silly boy. You could have died. You should have died."

Well shit. Again? "What are you talking about?" She starts pacing back and forth looking to Daniel then to me. "That must be it. It's because my blood was so fresh in you. Yes, that and this place. I remember you bringing him here. That makes sense." She finally stops and with the most serious expression I've seen on her as she says. "You must never ever try this again. You will fail if you do. It will kill you and the one you are trying to turn. Never try it again, promise me."

I start to panic even more. "What are you talking about?" She chuckles. "Why, turning Daniel my child."

We all just stand there like a bunch of morons. I finally decide to speak up. "What do you mean? I didn't. He's already a vampire." She turns to him and flips her hair back and walks in his direction again. "But you did. You did the impossible. You turned a full-blooded Vampire." She turns back to face me again. "And you must never attempt to do it again. It will be the end of you." I look to her and to Daniel. "I don't understand." Then I think back to when he almost died. I took his blood and fused it with mine then had him drink from me, used just about every drop of life force I had to make him better. I did the same thing to Sloan. Holy shit. I didn't know. I look at Daniel in horror.

"Daniel, I'm so sorry. I didn't know. I swear I didn't know." His breathing starts to get heavy.

"What the hell are you talking about?" Kristin looks at him in confusion trying to make sense of what we are saying then speaks up. "Daniel, when was the last time you fed?" He gives her a look like the question wasn't that important. "I dunno? About a week, I guess. I guess I am kinda hungry......"

His face goes white as a ghost. Kristin takes a deep breath. "You are hungry?" He seems like he's about to pass out. "Kristin, there is no pain!" He starts to tear up and I feel horrible. Kristin walks over and wraps her arms around him. Dear god what have

I done? "Daniel, I'm so sorry." I start to tear up. Daniel raises his head and looks me dead in the eyes. He says nothing and starts walking in my direction. I'm just going to stand here and let him do it. If he wants to beat the shit out of me, I'll let him. This is my fault. He gets face to face with me and I can see the tears in his eyes. The next thing I know his arms are around me. His hug is so tight I almost can't breathe. I can hear his sobbing in my ear.

"Thank you! Thank you so damn much!" The only thing I could do is hug him back.

Lilith's face is smiling with pride when she speaks up. "Why is this so confusing to you Brandon? You seem to think he should be angry with you? You have given him a gift that should you never have been able to give. You changed his fate."

Daniel pulls back from me and looks to Lilith. "Does this mean, when I feed? Will I have control?" Her face is full of pity when she responds. She knows how much pain that has put him through. "That nightmare is over my child." She walks up to him and kisses him lightly on the cheek. "You are my child now." He just drops to the floor and bursts into tears. Kristin walks over and pulls him in for an embrace and they both sit there crying in each other's arms.

Sloan turns to me with a bright smile. "You seriously need to stop trying to get yourself killed." Then he kisses me. My head is spinning from all the shock. "This is just too much. Too damn much" Lilith walks over to me. "You will be fine, just stop trying to die and you will be just fine." She giggles and I feel better. Did she just make a joke? She looks back at me.

"My time here is growing short. You need to ask your questions. It might be the last time we speak for a while." I look to her and have so many questions but I can't come up with a good one.

"So, does this mean Daniel is my second? She looks at him. "Yes, yes he is. He is the third most powerful Vampire of the Chosen." She smiles brightly "And he will be powerful." He looks at me and then back to her. "What do you mean? What kind of power?" She lets out a quiet laugh. "You have to come into your own power my dear. I can't ruin all the surprises." With that she takes a few steps back. "It's time for me to go my children. Please be careful, when Kain finds out you exist he will stop at nothing to destroy you." With that she fades into nothing.

When she leaves all we can do is stand there staring at each other for a few minutes. Finally, Sloan speaks up. "So, I guess we are all related now." Daniel bursts out laughing, breaking the tension. "Well that's kinda gross. I mean if that's true I'm dating my sister and you are married to your brother. I mean, this is Alabama but I'm pretty sure you shouldn't do that."

I can't help but laugh. "Dude, you just had to go all hillbilly on me, didn't you?"

Kristin smiles. "Hey Brandon, I do appreciate you letting us see your fancy world here but it kinda gives me the chills. Mind if we head back?" I smile. "What do you mean? This place is awesome!" I shrug. "Guess it's not for everyone." I then bring us back to Earth. For some reason, everyone takes a deep breath like they haven't had fresh air in ages. Daniel walks up to me with a pained look on his face.

"Brandon, we have to tell Tristin." My eyes go wide. "What the hell man? Are you kidding?" He shakes his head. "No, I'm serious. This is too much to keep from him. We will never be able to hide all this without his help." I'm not convinced. "Daniel, I don't trust him. I like the guy but I barely know him. What if he tries to have us killed?" He puts a hand on my shoulder.

"You trust me, don't you?" I give a slight nod. "Good, he's been my Master for one hundred and thirty years. He took me in when every other vampire rejected me. He's the only vampire in all these years that has treated me like an actual person and not a freak. It's been killing me keeping these secrets from him. Please trust me with this."

I look him in the eyes and I believe that he believes every word of what he just said. I have no choice but to trust him. He's got a point. This is too much to hide. We need help. I look back to Sloan.

"What do you think?" He looks at me and shrugs.

"I'm not sure Brandon. He makes a good point. We need all the help we can get. I'll support any decision you make." I nod and look back to Daniel. "Ok, I trust you. We will tell Tristan." And with that we head back to the House to tell our Master that he's not really our Master.

CHAPTER FOURTEEN

WE TAKE THE elevator back down from the training area and on the way my mind is racing. What the hell do I say to the guy? What if he goes all crazy and tries to kill us? I don't want to have to take the guy out. He's a good guy. If he tries to kill me will Daniel protect him from me? Shit? I didn't have time to think this through. Daniel is staring at me but not saying anything.

"Dammit man, why did I let you talk me into this? There are so many things that could go wrong. What if he tries to kill me?" Daniel shakes his head. "He won't. He's not like that. Not like... us. He stays calm no matter what." I can't help but doubt him. "Daniel, there are so many things that can go wrong. I know you trust the guy but this is big. This information is game changing. Literally game changing. Just tell me one thing. If he tries to kill me, you know I will have to defend myself. Who will you be protecting when that happens?"

His eyes go wide. "That will not happen. I won't let that happen." I sigh and shrug. "You can't predict what will happen or stop it from happening. Think about it. You will have to protect one of us if it happens." Shit, I'm not sure if he will be on my side if it happens. I can't rely on his protection. I feel a tight squeeze on my hand. Sloan is standing there smiling at me.

"If anyone tries to kill you they will die, it's as simple as that. I will make sure of it." He looks to Daniel and Kristin. "I will make sure of that, and you can be sure of it as well." I can feel the fear radiating off of the two of them. You go hubby. Smack the fear on em.

We end up walking to his office in complete silence. We go in after knocking and see that he's sitting there at his desk doing paperwork. He looks up and smiles. "Well hello, I take it training went well? Did you learn anything new?" I belted out a nervous laugh. I just couldn't help myself. "I take that as a yes then. Please tell me all the details." He rolls his chair back from his desk and crosses his legs.

Well...here goes nothing. I just let her rip. "Tristan. We have something important to tell you and I have no idea how to do it without sounding like I've been betraying you." I sigh and shake my head. Haven't we been doing just that? Just by not saying anything? He doesn't flinch and waits for me to continue.

"First off I need you to know that Daniel has just now found out this information himself and is the one who convinced me to come to you." His face hasn't changed at all. Shit, Daniel wasn't kidding. "So here it is. I'm not your Bloodborne. I'm not even your kind. I am what is called ``Chosen." Still, his face hasn't changed. "Um...yea? So, I've known this from the beginning and I'm so sorry but I've been using you and this House for information. I didn't know anything about vampires and needed help in finding Kain and defeating him." Man, his aura isn't even changing.

"I'm new to all this and still trying to find out what I actually am and in doing so I accidentally turned Daniel." His brow twitched ever so slightly and his aura flickered the slightest bit. I hear Kristin whisper behind me. "Oh shit."

The room is getting much cooler now. "Tristan, it was an accident. He was dying and I had to do something and I just reacted." He stands up. "You just reacted? You do that a lot, don't you? You don't know anything about vampires so you react and lie to use us. You find a teammate bleeding out so you react and turn him." He takes a few steps closer. "A vampire starts feeding on you in a parking deck and you react and kill him." I stop breathing. Shit, he knows? How does he know? "You killed my Bloodborne Brandon. Because you reacted. You never think. You just act."

I take a breath. "It was an accident. He was killing me." He waves a hand and frost comes off it. "Silence! You will not interrupt! He wasn't trying to kill you, he was just feeding!" I don't care who this guy is, I'm not going to keep quiet. "With all due respect, Tristin. You don't know shit. You weren't there. I bit him yes, but that's all I did. I don't know what happened. All I remember is that he started puking everywhere and then started to burn. I didn't kill him!"

Wow, that's right. I didn't. All this guilt I've been feeling about killing him is finally gone because I didn't kill him. It was an accident. He didn't know what my blood was. I look back to Daniel and his face shows me just how much pain he's in.

"I swear I didn't kill him. He didn't know what my blood was. It must be poison to vampires. Just like when you feed off one of your own it will make you sick. Mine will kill you. I didn't know this, he didn't either." I turn back to Tristan. "It was an accident and I'm sorry. But that doesn't explain how you knew."

The air keeps getting colder. Then a circle of power starts to form next to him. I take up a defensive stance and am ready for whatever he throws at me. I glance back and Sloan has his eyes on Daniel and Kristin waiting for them to make their decision when Kristin says. "Wait Brandon. He's not attacking!"

That's when I notice the spot grow and a figure emerging from it. "Tristan, would you mind calming down? It's a bit too cold in here for my taste." An extremely gorgeous woman emerges from the portal. Her hair is long and wavy and almost as black as Lilith 's. Her eyes are as green as a rainforest. The black dress she wears is painted on her beautiful curvy porcelain skinned body.

She's about as tall as Tristan but only because of the four inch heels she is sporting.

"Everyone is so tense." She says with a beautiful smile. "Tristan. Is this because of you? You told them already haven't you?" She sighs and pouts and I notice she has a slight Russian accent. "You were supposed to wait for me."

She looks to me "He knew about your involvement in his Bloodborne's death because I told him." I can't help but to stand there and stare, completely speechless. She chuckles in response to my silence. "Well I guess I'll introduce myself seeing as though Tristan isn't going to do so. My name is Vanessa. I'm Tristan's Bride." Well shit, no kidding?

"I didn't know you were married Tristan." Vanessa chuckles as Kristin speaks up.

"No Brandon, they aren't married. She's his Bride. She's connected to him by blood and he's connected to her by power. They are joined. It makes her immortal and increases his power." I run my hand through my hair and let out a breath. "Well that's new." Vanessa gives me a hair flip. "Actually, it's not. Brides have been around for ages."

I don't care anymore. I'm sick of all the damn surprises. And to be honest they don't surprise me anymore. "Just tell me how you knew. The cameras were out and there weren't any witnesses." She sighs and sits on the edge of his desk. "It was a simple spell my darling. All I had to do was go back to the place where the attack happened and replay the night like a movie."

Figures, why not. Why not magic. "So, you knew the truth all this time and just let me lie to you like that? Tristan finally speaks up. "We have known for a few weeks now. We wanted to see how long you could last, also wanted to see how good you are at lying. I have to say you have impressed me." Yea, I'm so good at lying I've impressed a Master. Go me.

"You know why. I didn't do it because I wanted to hurt anyone…." he cuts me off.

"I don't care, Brandon, we have known for a while now. It doesn't change the fact that you changed Daniel." Yep, that was the breaking point for him. I kinda figured that it was. Daniel finally speaks up. "I would have died if he didn't intervene, Tristan." Tristan gives him a sideways glance. "I know that Daniel. I have no idea how he did it and don't care. It doesn't change the fact that you are no longer mine. I no longer have a single Bloodborne. He's taken both of you from me!"

Vanessa giggles at him. "You silly man. Is that what's got you all pissy today? Well then let me kiss it and make it all better." She stands up and walks to him. "They are all your Bloodborne you silly man." He blinks and glances at us. "Explain Vanessa. This makes no sense to me."

She gives him an eye roll and looks at Kristin. "Men, am I right?" She sighs and they exchange a giggle.

"Fine, just try to follow along, ok. When Brandon was turned, the blood that he took in was of your Bloodline. Just because it mixed with the blood of the Chosen doesn't make it not so. Actually, it means that your Bloodline is the flame that ignited the Chosen. You are in fact Brandon's Sire, and with him, Sloan's and Daniel's and any other they turn. Your children are breeding like bunnies Tristan."

She giggles and turns to us. "Now just so you know I'm not just jumping to conclusions about this. You should know I can see this in the blood. His blood is connected to me and with my power fused with his I can see his children. That's how I knew you weren't your typical vampire when you came to us." Well damn, she's known about me from the beginning? "So, where do we go from here? What do you plan on doing with me Tristan?"

He seems to have calmed down, but looks at Daniel. "What has he done to you Daniel?" Daniel walks up and puts a hand on Tristan's shoulder. "He's fixed me. The pain is gone. I won't kill by accident anymore Tristan. He fixed what was broken." I can see the tears in his eyes as he speaks. Looking at Tristan I can see his eyes on the brink as well.

He looks back at me. "Is this true? You are able to do this?" I shake my head. "Actually, not anymore. It almost killed me turning him. If I attempt to do it again, it will kill the one I'm trying to turn and me along with them. It was a one-time deal I guess."

He walks up to me and holds out a hand. "If it's true you have fixed what was broken in him and I owe you my thanks. You have no idea the pain it has caused him. The amount of pain it caused me to see him go through it." I look down to his hand. "You're not gonna freeze me if I shake it are you?" He just chuckles. "Won't know till you try, right?" I shrug and shake his hand.

CHAPTER FIFTEEN

WE SPEAK FOR hours and I let him know about everything. About my powers, about Lilith and Kain. It feels amazing not holding anything back anymore. Like a massive weight has been lifted and can finally breathe again. He lets me know he doesn't trust her and that's not because he trusts Kain either, it's just that from his experience with beings of that much power there is always some kind of power play and they love to use people as their tools. I can tell he's being truthful. To be honest as much as I like Lilith I don't think I've ever completely trusted her either, I just can't help but love her when I'm in her presence.

I let him know this. "I'm glad Brandon. This tells me you're smarter than I expected. In my circle, there are very few people I trust completely. You have met three of them, they are all in this room." I look around and can tell it's Daniel Vanessa and Kristin. "I hope one day we can trust each other like you trust them." He gives me a sad smile. "You coming to me and telling me in person is a start." I nod and then bring up the bad news.

"So, it seems Kain has been released and is trying to get his body back. Do you know anything about this? Like where the body is, or what magic item the Blacksmith created that he's after?" Tristan starts to pace the floor thinking as Vanessa speaks up. "I can tell you what the item is darling, well what I think it could be anyway. It's the Blacksmiths Bracelets. Two bracelets crafted for the one purpose, to transfer blood from one person to another without it dying in the process. They were created for one of the cursed vampires to help them with feeding. It makes it so the vampire doesn't have to use his fangs."

I look up from the floor and ask. "Why would he need this?" She smiles. "Think about it Brandon. His body has been dead for centuries. There is no way he will be able to feed to regain his body's strength." I smile at her. "Huh... that makes sense. So, where are these bracelets?"

She shrugs. "Why would I know this thing?" I give her a little head tilt. "Well you are an all-powerful Traveler, why wouldn't you want to know these things? I sure as hell would."

She giggles "I'm glad you're not just pretty, you will live longer because of that. I don't know where they are but I do know where we can find out. And if we get lucky we might just find out where Kain's body is." I get excited. "Sweet! Where?"

She stands looking excited. "Get ready boys... And Kristen. We are going to a ball!" Tristan facepalms and sighs. "Dammit, please no." I can't help but laugh at his reaction. "Well I guess it sounds kinda fun but why a ball?" She walks up to me in that flirty way she does. "Because Brandon, this is where everyone who is anyone in the vampire community is going to be. The most powerful vampires and Travelers are going to be there. One of them is bound to know something." Tristin stands and shakes his head. "You're forgetting one thing Vanessa; the Elders will also be there."

Daniel looks nervous. "They could challenge us. What if they challenge us?" I'm totally confused now. "What do you mean challenge us? Like to a duel or something?" I chuckle a bit when I say it. Tristen speaks up. "Exactly that Brandon. They could kill one of us. Sometimes they spare the life of the one they are dueling and sometimes they rip them apart slowly just to hear the screams."

I stand there blank faced and breathlessly mouth. "Holy shit." Sloan shakes his head. "You have gotta be kidding me. They are that bat shit crazy? You're telling us the most powerful vampires are sadists?" Kristen takes Daniel's hand in hers when she says. "Yes Sloan, that's exactly what we are telling you." Sloan looks pissed. "When is this ball?"

Vanessa smiles "In two weeks." Sloan gives an exaggerated sigh. "Then we need to start training immediately." I look at him and smile. "That's a fantastic idea. But I think tonight we need to just rest up." Tristin grins slightly. "Yes, tonight rest up but be back here in the morning to start your training. Vanessa, you do your thing and get us into this ball and bring me a list of the guests. I want all the info we can get."

We head back to our townhouse and we are greeted by two fur babies at the door. Our pups are so damn cute. The grey on their faces shows the fourteen happy years we have had them, both rescues. Sloan is on the floor rolling around with them in the puppy pile. I can't help but smile because it's the cutest thing ever. My baby Sheba runs lightly into the wall every now and then because she has become blind in one eye. Poor girl.

"I'm going to get a shower. You mind feeding them while I do?" Sloan looks up with a smile. "Sure Baby." I smile back at him and head upstairs. As the hot water hits my face I can't stop my mind from racing. How are we going to get this information we need? When we find Kain's body how are we going to destroy it? From what I know it can't be destroyed. Shit, just a few weeks back all I was worried about was paying rent. I smile a bit when I realize that I can fly now so there's that. I towel off and head back downstairs to get some play time with the fur babies myself when I see Sloan sitting there next to them both.

It looks like they are sleeping but Sloan has the strangest look on his face, also blood on his lips. Shit. "Sloan?" My heart starts racing. I get in front of him and his eyes are white. No pupils, no nothing. Just white. "What the hell! Sloan! Are you ok?" I look around in a panic and notice the pups have a bit of blood on them too. Around their mouths. I check them to make sure they are ok. They are breathing but not waking up.

"Sloan! Shit! Sloan wake up!" I check his aura and it's his usual mix of blue and red and check the pups thinking I can give them some of my life force to make them better. Their auras are the usual gold but it's going dim. I start to panic a bit more and start petting them about to try and give them some of my energy when I realize that their auras are getting brighter again. I start to breath better until I notice a shade of blue joining their gold.

What the friggin hell? I look at Sloan "What have you done?" His eyes start going back to normal. The pups start shaking like they are having a seizure. I start crying just petting them, then they just stop. Sloan comes to his senses. "Sloan what have you done?" He looks at me confused. "What do you mean?" I point to the pups. "What did you do to them?"

He smiles at me. "Made them better baby. I made them better." I look at him with a shocked look when I feel a warm tongue licking my arm. I look down and start crying harder. My babies are awake and the grey is gone from their cute little faces. I look at Sheba and her foggy eye is crystal clear. I look back to Sloan and he's smiling at me. "I think I've found my gift Brandon."

I can't stop hugging the pups. "You scared the shit out of me Sloan!" He looks sad when he says. "I'm sorry Brandon. But I didn't mean to do it to begin with. It just happened. One minute I was petting them, the next I just knew how to make them better. I don't know how I just knew what to do. It broke my heart when I bit them to taste their blood because it hurt them but I knew it would be over soon.

After I tasted them I let them taste mine. But soon after that the most amazing thing happened. My body spoke to me. Every cell in my body spoke to me. I now know what every cell in my body does and what it can do. After that, the pup's blood spoke to me. Brandon, the pups are part of me now." I stare at him dumbfounded. "What do you mean Sloan?" He smiles and stands. "Let me show you."

As he stands he holds out his arms. I try to stay as calm as possible but inside I'm absolutely flipping my shit. Fur starts to grow on his hands and arms, his nails start to form claws. When I look up into his eyes I notice they are pure red. He looks feral when he speaks. "They are part of me now. Brandon, I think I can become anything I feed on." My jaw drops." Holy shit!" Sloan laughs, I laughed, the pups barked and started to do what we used to call greyhounding, running in circles around the coffee table chasing each other. They haven't been able to do that in years. Yes, today is definitely what you would call a good day.

CHAPTER SIXTEEN

MY MIND IS racing as I pace back and forth in front of Sloan and the newly changed pups. Every now and then I cast them a glance. Sloan is looking at his clawed hands petting his fur and smiling and the pups are just sitting there next to him staring at me with a curious look on their adorable faces. They look... smarter somehow.

"So, you are telling me you have total control over your DNA and every cell in your body?" I say with a smile on my seventh lap of pacing back and forth in front of him. "That's exactly what I'm telling you Brandon." He says with a smile on his wolfy face. I can't help but laugh like a madman. "Do you have any idea how many possibilities you have? So many damn beautiful amazing possibilities?" He quirks a bushy brow at me and grins. "Yes, yes I do."

I stop and look at him. "Ok, that's not what I was thinking but let's put a pin in it. No, I meant if you can take in the DNA of any creature you feed from....." I look to the back door and grin. "Let's go outside Sloan." He jumps up "Are you sure?" I nod to him and smile. "But you should change back for now, It isn't Halloween and people will probably freak out."

He chuckles. "Good point." He closes his eyes and I turn mine on.

I want to see how he does it. I watch how his aura works as he changes. It's amazing. His colors change so quickly from red gold to red blue as his fur just retreats into his body. I can see waves of energy like water rippling off his skin. It's like gravity but different. What is that? I want to touch it but not without his permission. I'll ask later. When he's back to being his beautiful buff perfect self, we head to the back door. I look down and notice the pups are with us.

"You wanna grab their harnesses? We can take them for a walk." Sloan smiles at me. "They don't need them anymore" I blink. "What do you mean by that?" He gives me a shit eating grin.

"Ask them to do something simple Brandon." I stand there blank faced for a second and then look down to them. "Um…. guys, go jump on the sofa." They give a quiet bark and jump up on the sofa and look at me panting all excited and I smile from ear to ear. "Ok, now go to the kitchen." They again give me a bark and do just that. I look back to Sloan and see him smiling at me.

"Holy shit Sloan! They can understand us?" He nods with that bright smile on his face. "Yes they can! When they took in my blood it increased their intelligence. Not to a full human level but basically it evolved them enough so they can understand us." I look back to the kitchen and they are standing there wagging their tails in excitement. "Guys come here so I can hug the shit out of you!" They bolt out of the kitchen and I drop to the floor and take in all the face kisses.

I look back up to Sloan. "As amazing as this is we still should have their harnesses on in public. It is the law and we don't want to draw attention." He looks down at me with a grin. "Good point." He goes and grabs the harnesses and we head outside. There are woods behind our complex and I lead them there.

"Lots of yummy DNA out here." He looks back to me with a grimace. "Please tell me you're not suggesting what I think you're suggesting." I stop between some trees and look back to him. "I'm pretty sure you don't know what I'm about to suggest, but go ahead and tell me what you think I'm going to ask you to do." He sighs and runs his hand through his hair nervously. "Shit Brandon. So, what do you want me to hunt? There isn't much out here except bunnies, deer, and snakes...Shit you want me to eat a snake?!"

I can't help but laugh out loud. "I'm sorry, your face was so damn cute. No Sloan not a snake, but that's not a bad idea. That can be next. No, we aren't hunting mammals or reptiles. We are hunting insects." He gives the biggest gay gasp I've ever seen him do. It was impressive. "Oh, hell no! That's just so damn wrong!"

I smile at his adorable panic. "Listen Sloan. Insects are amazing. The abilities they possess are of the most useful there are. Just think about it." He calms himself down, somewhat. "Fine Brandon. But I don't have to like it. I'll give it a shot." I smile and grab his hand and we go hunting for some creepy crawlies." The first one was perfect. A nice bloodsucker cousin of sorts. A mosquito. The possibilities of this one for feeding is perfect. I grab it alive and show it to Sloan and he looks at me with horror on his face.

"Brandon, come on. Really?" I smile and nod.

"Yes really. Just do it and see what you can do with it. You might like it, who knows." He growls at me and I can tell it's the pup in him growling. "Ok, that's cool as shit but still, you gotta eat it." He rolls his eyes and sighs with an open mouth. He swallows and his eyes open and turn cloudy again. It's freaky as hell when he does it. It's like a trance from some spooky movie. I open up my mind to see what he's doing. His aura is nonexistent.

What the actual hell? He's alive but his power isn't there. I look closer and notice that it actually is there. It's inside him, completely inside his body. Then boom! His power comes erupting out and becomes normal again. His eyes go back to normal as he's staring at me. I look at him with a smile. "Well? Are you able to use insects?" He looks at me with a blank shocked face, nods and holds out a hand. I look at it and tiny drops of blood start to come up from his palm. They start to take shape. They grow tiny wings and a cloud of mosquitoes erupt from his palm and swarm around his head.

"Holy freaking shit!" I take a step back and he smiles at me. He then gives me a wink and the cloud launches itself in my direction. I panic and make time slow down then move out of the way while watching the cloud slowly move towards the area I was just in and look back to Sloan. He's smiling and moving slowly but then his eyes speed up and look directly at me. He laughs and the cloud speeds up as well.

Oh shit. I slow time even more and notice a rock that I kicked up practically stop in midair. It's moving so slow it almost looks like it's not moving at all. I look back to Sloan and he's just standing there grinning at me.

"You forget I can do this too." My jaw drops. And I stand up straight.

"Why are you attacking me? Are you ok?" He chuckles at me and the cloud of bloodsuckers move back in his direction. I walk up to him past the floating rock and he starts to laugh. When he stops, he holds his hands out and absorbs them all back into himself.

Ok that's totally creepy as hell. "I was just playing with you. I wanted to creep you out as much as you did me by making me eat a damn bug." I roll my eyes. "Yea ok, point taken but shit man! Look what you just did!" His smile was so bright "I know right! That's not all. I can control them because they are a part of me but I can also see through each of their eyes. It's so frickin amazing." I run up and give him the biggest kiss. "Let's keep hunting!"

By the end of the night we hunted like seven more bugs including ants, flies, spiders...yeah, I know it's technically not an insect but whatever. Wasps, bees, dragonflies and we even found a scorpion. He also found a cat, a bat, and a bird. And how he got those things was just plain creative and amazing. He used his mosquitoes to drain their blood and bring it back to him. In the end, he got a snake and I think he loved it.

Walking back to the house through the woods the pups were playing off their harnesses and loving every second of it. We discussed the uses of his new-found gift and how it will benefit us greatly at the ball. He smiled and chuckled as he turned to me. "I can't wait to bug the place. I'll find out all their dirty little secrets." Yep, that's my devious little hubby.

He stops at the edge of the woods and I turn and look to see his serious face. "Brandon, what's your plan?" I look back to him confused. "What do you mean?" He shakes his head and waves his hands out to nothing. "Your plan Brandon. Yeah I know we need to find and destroy Kain and all, but after that, what's your plan?" I scratch my head. I've never really thought about it. "I'm not sure. I like what I'm doing so far. I like our team, and Tristan. I think he's a good guy. But to be honest I've never thought that far ahead. I suppose eventually our family will grow, I mean we do have a third that's supposed to join my Bloodline. I have no idea who, but I guess we will have to cross that bridge when we get to it. What do you want to do Sloan?"

He looks at me and gives a small smile. "You know I'm with you no matter what. But I'm worried about the future. We have such a long one…. Well if we don't get killed first. Eventually our Bloodline will grow larger than the Cursed. You do know there is a large possibility we will have to go to war with them." I frown at him. "It has been in the back of my mind, yes. I'm going to do everything I can to make sure that doesn't happen. But for right now Sloan, I think all we can do is just keep moving forward and learn as much about ourselves and the Cursed. Right now, I'm pretty sure we don't know shit about what's out there. Let's just keep our heads down as much as possible and learn everything we can." He smiles then walks up to me to pull me in for a hug. "I think that's a good plan. I love you."

I hug him back. "I love you too."

CHAPTER SEVENTEEN

THE NEXT DAY we head back and meet up with Daniel and Kristen to get some training in. When we get to the training field I see Daniel and Kristin smiling at each other, holding their hands out in front of themselves. I walk up and Daniel turns to me and beams with excitement.

"Brandon! I can see you!" I tilt my head a bit confused. "Did you go blind last night or something?" He runs up and holds his hand out to me. "No Brandon. I can see you now.

"I look down to his hand and see his aura flickering and taking shape. It stretches out to me like Kristin's does when she turns it into webs. My eyes go wide and I take a step back. "Holy shit dude. That's amazing, but don't surprise me like that again ok? You can see my aura now?" He looks like a toddler at Christmas time when he nods. "Yeah! You're all blue and black and shit. It's pretty damn cool." I look at him and smile. I take a closer look and realize his blue aura is mixed with white. That's interesting.

"Did you find out what you can do with it yet?" Kristin walks up and smiles. "That's what we were doing when you guys showed up. He woke up this afternoon and kinda freaked out thinking things were on fire. His control of it is pretty damn impressive. Kind of like you."

I can't help but to be proud and give a big smile back. "It's his gift of the Bloodline. It's second nature for him. I'm excited to see what he's able to do with it." I look back to Sloan. "Looks like you're not the only one coming into your power." He gives Daniel a smile. "Congratulations. Daniel." Training is definitely going to be fun today.

Daniel puts a hold on his new power for the time being. He and Kristin want to focus on us for now because we are the ones with the least amount of training. I walk over to Sloan. "So why don't you go ahead and show them what you have learned baby." He smiles pointing at me. "Don't freak out like Brandon did last night." I look back to him and roll my eyes. "Hey, I had no warning at all. How was I supposed to react?" He chuckles and takes a stance with his hands out to his side slightly slouching like he's about to pounce on something. The next thing you know I see black fur growing on his skin. His face cracks and grows and starts to take a feline shape. His eyes are fantastic. I've never seen a cat's eyes that big before. His hands have turned into claws and look like they can shred anything to tiny little pieces. I notice that strange energy over his body again that looks like water and decide to ask him later about it today. Looking back at Daniel and Kristin I couldn't help but laugh. Their jaws are just about on the ground in amazement.

"So, what do you guys think?" Daniel looks back to me and stutters a bit.

"He's...he's like some kind of werecat? Holy shit." I giggle and look back to Sloan "They think you are a werecat. Don't you think you should correct them?" He growls a chuckle and things start to change again. This time he takes off his shirt and the fur goes away. Replacing it with a finer brown fur. His face changes just slightly and this part amazed the shit out of me. Out of his back sprouted two big ass wings. They were massive and beautiful, shaped like a bat. He flaps them a couple of times but then spreads them out showing them and himself in all his fantastic glory.

The three of us stand there for about a full minute just staring at him in amazement.

Kristin finally speaks up. "How? when...how? What?" I turn to look at her and my face is actually hurting from all the smiling. "He found his own gift last night. Isn't it amazing?"

Daniel doesn't take his eyes off him. "Can he fly?" I look to Sloan. "I don't know. I've never seen him in this form before. Hey Sloan! Can you use those wings?"

He looks directly at me and I think he's actually trying to speak but stops after he makes some growly squeaky sounds then nods and starts to flap his wings hard. After a second of being blasted from wind and dust we look up and see him hovering above us.

"Yes! Holy shit yes! That's my baby!" I run up underneath him and take control of my energy and reverse gravity on myself again. This time I'm prepared. I've realized that the ground wasn't the only thing that holds shadows. All I need is a small shadow to connect me to my power. I use the shadows that my clothing leave on my skin to connect. That way I won't pass out again. I launch myself into the air to join him. There we are, both hovering in midair and I can't help but feel excited and powerful. We fly for a few minutes diving and spinning and just getting the hang of it. I can tell Sloan is getting a bit tired so we land and he changes back to my husband's normal form.

We walk back toward them and he puts his shirt back on panting like a tired pup. Daniel and Kristin are speechless. Sloan gives a bright smile and looks right at us. "That made me hungry as hell." Kristen's face keeps it's shocked look when she says. "We... we can go back to feed if you want." Sloan looks at me and gives an evil grin. "That won't be necessary hun." He then holds his hands out to his sides and swarms of mosquitoes erupt from his palms and take off in all directions.

"I'll be fine shortly." I guess Daniel couldn't contain himself anymore. "What the hell?! You can't just do all this amazing shit and not explain!" Sloan gives a big laugh. "Ok, sorry for showing off but I couldn't help myself. I'm now in full control of my own body's DNA. I can change it to whatever I want whenever I want." Daniel runs a hand through his hair and brushes it from his face. "That's the coolest shit I've ever seen!"

After showing off we decided to get serious. As we walk off I ask Sloan if I can try something when he changes the next time. I want to kinda taste the energy he gives off while he does it. He looks kind of confused but agrees. I tell him he doesn't need to fully change. Just his hand will be fine. He holds out a hand and starts to change it into a claw. As he does I use my own energy to touch the strange water like energy he is giving off. When I connect, I not only feel reality crack, but can actually hear it. It was like glass breaking. I look up and everything has stopped completely.

Time itself has stopped. I've always been able to slow time to a crawl, so slow it seemed like it stopped, but here, after touching his energy, it stopped completely. Looking around everything seems fuzzy, like sort of in a fog but vibrating. I move my feet to back away a bit but the strangest thing happens. My foot slips into the ground. The ground has no substance.

No that's not right, it's not the ground that doesn't have substance looking at myself I can actually see through myself. I have no substance. I try and kick a rock but my foot goes right through it. Oh shit, I'm floating here frozen in time. My mind is racing trying to figure things out. I need to get control of my movement first. Seeing as though I can't actually walk because I pass through the ground I try and take control of my gravity again. Thank you baby Jesus, it actually works. I can move around at least. I float back a bit and try not to panic. I have the ability to control this. I take a breath and think, I notice Sloan's hand starts to change extremely slowly and barely noticeable but it's changing.

His hand is the only thing that is moving here. Well shit. That makes total sense to me finally. There is no way that matter of any kind can alter its own makeup and change as fast as Sloan was changing. His aura was actually time speeding up the process. That's friggin amazing. I wonder if he knows he's actually doing that. Well I can't ask if I'm stuck here. I breathe in deep and try to make time speed up. I open my eyes and nothing is happening. Shit, I start to panic again. I look at his hand and notice its furry now and claws are starting to form. I get an idea. I stretch my power to his hand again and touch it. I hear the loud crack of glass sound again. Things are still fuzzy but are starting to clear up. That's gotta be it. His power threw mine out of whack.

I try to wait it out till his hand finishes changing. It should throw me back to normal, I hope. All I can do is hope for the best. It turns out I was right. After his change was complete, time cracks again and everything goes back to normal. I'm back to reality, but about five feet back from where I started, and floating. Everyone loses their shit. I guess to them It seemed like I just teleported. "Well that was certainly interesting." I look at everyone and grin a bit. "I'll explain later but don't let me do that again Sloan." He nods with a confused look but doesn't ask questions.

After escaping from being lost in time and space, I have to say I am a bit shaky. Eventually we all end up splitting into two teams. Daniel takes Sloan again and Kristin takes me. They go off on their own and Kristin and I take a seat on the ground again. "What happened Brandon?" I let out a sigh and can help but feel stupid. "I was reckless again. Apparently, the aura that surrounds Sloan when he changes is time itself. I was frozen in time. Completely stuck." I look up at her and I have no idea why but I was starting to tear up. "I've never been that scared before."

She responds to my almost display of waterworks by smiling at me. "Good. Fear is a good tool for learning." As much as I want to be pissed at her response I can't, she's not wrong. "The reason why you are so reckless Brandon is because you think nothing can touch you. You need to understand that just because you are powerful doesn't mean you can't be defeated. Let me show you. I'm going to use my power on you and want you to try and stop me."

I look at her and can't help but be afraid for her. "I don't think that's a good idea. What if I hurt you?" She sighs "Shut up Brandon. That's the kind of thinking that will get you killed. Now, get ready." I have no idea what she's planning and no time to figure it out because her webbing launches itself at me so fast I have no time to react at all. Perfect, My head is fuzzy now, and where the hell am I? I have to figure out what's going on, and I need to know where I am. Why is there a Christmas tree here? I hear laughing around me. Oh, it's my baby brothers and sister. Oh yeah, It's time to open the presents! I smile and look down and I have one in my hands as well. I hope it's what I asked for. Everyone else has a Nintendo and I've played Mario on my friend's system, but I've been asking all year for one of my own.

I start to rip the paper and my little brothers look at me and are just as excited as I am. I shredded that paper and there it is! Nintendo! I scream, my brothers scream, my baby sis has no idea why we are screaming, but screams along with us. The next thing I know I'm in the middle of a training area with a blade to my throat.

"This is what I'm talking about Brandon. If I was your enemy your head would be rolling on the ground right now." Holy freaking shit. "What the hell was that?" I say with panic in my voice. She lowers her blade and sits back down. She looks at me and smiles. "That is proof that you can be killed, and quite easily I might add." Well damn.

"Ok, point taken. I need to be careful." She nods

"What's the most powerful thing you have?" I answer right away. "It's the Shade. My own reality of course." She shakes her head disappointed. "No Brandon, that's just power. Your true gift is your mind. Power is nothing without a mind to use it. But because we are talking about it we should explore this place you call the Shade. You say it's your own reality?"

I nod smiling. "Yeah, it has actually shown me what it was before it chose me. I changed it into my own world, connected it to this one actually." She stands up. "Then let's go. I want you to show it to me." I look up. "But you have already been there." She shrugs. "Yes, but you have never shown me. You just took me there." I stand up and take her hand. "Ok, why not?" I command the shadows to open and there we are.

I expect Lilith to be here. She's usually here to greet me when I change realities so I look around. I notice a form standing next to that large wall in the obstacle course that people are supposed to climb over. I walk over to say hello expecting it to be her but realize halfway to it it's not Lilith. I stop dead in my tracks with Kristin behind me. I notice it's in the shape of a man but its form is totally black. Its flesh is like liquid shadow. It starts to move closer.

"Brandon. Don't be frightened." I should be scared shitless but for some reason the figure feels familiar. "Don't come any closer. Who are you?" It stops as soon as I speak." I'm your creation Brandon. I stand there confused. "My creation? What are you talking about?" It responds. You created me, You gave me life here. I absorbed your essence the first time you brought Sloan here. When he became what he is now, he left behind what we needed to take physical form."

Gross, I remember the shadows eating all the goop that cocoon leaked out when Sloan hatched. "You have got to be kidding? But why?" He doesn't move at all but speaks somehow without an actual face. "So, you can complete your connection with your reality Brandon. You are not complete. We have given you our power but your physical body isn't in tune with this reality. You are not complete."

I can't help but freak out about what he's suggesting, "Why do you keep saying we?" Again he doesn't move but responds. "We are your creation formed from you and fused with this reality. We are the memories, the abandoned reality of this place you call the Shade. You need to complete your connection to understand what we are."

"Um... I'm not sure if I want to. What would that do to me actually? Will I look like you? No offence but I kind of like the way I look right now." He shakes his formless head. "No Brandon. You will be the same person you are now. You will not change, but you will finally be in tune with us. You will have a full understanding of what we are."

I look back to Kristin. "What do you think? I have no idea what to do here." She looks to the creature and then back to me." I'm not sure but by the looks of his power, it's like a mirror to yours. I don't feel any malice from him at all. To be honest there is no emotion there at all. This is your world Brandon, I'm not sure my opinion here would be of any use anyway."

I look back to the creature. "Your opinion is always useful Kristin, thanks." I take a few steps forward. "Ok, so how are we going to do this?"

It nods. "You gain power the way you always do. You feed from me. Leave nothing behind." I can't help but be shocked. "You want me to kill you?!" It looks at me with its formless face.

"We are dead already Brandon. The only reason we are here able to talk to you is because of you. We are you. You just need to take us in to be complete." This is confusing as shit but I can't help but trust him. For some reason I know he's telling the truth.

"Ok, I guess. Will it hurt you?" He tilts his head to expose his throat. "We only feel what you do Brandon. You must complete yourself." I walk the rest of the way up to him. Hold out a hand to touch him. He is flesh. Warm to the touch. The energy coming off him feels exactly like mine. He's not lying. I can tell. I lean in and sink my teeth into his neck and wrap my arms around his body. I drink him in, blood and power fill me. As I'm doing so I can see everything here. Oh, my God. It's not just here. This world is connected to Earth but not just Earth. Everything in that reality. The moon, the sun everything. The universe. It's so breathtaking.

I'm starting to understand the shadows now. How they work. I can see through them. Every shadow on Earth is like a window for me. I am connected to all of them. Holy shit. I can give them form. Physical form. Because of Sloan they can take physical form.

The creature was right, he wasn't alive at all, he is just information. My complete connection to my reality. I open my eyes and notice his body melting into the shadows and look back to Kristin and notice she seems frightened.

"Are you ok? I'm sorry if I spooked you but he wasn't lying. He wasn't alive really. He was just a shitload of information like downloading a file from a supercomputer." She shakes her head. "That's not what's freaking me out. It's your aura, it's pure black now and the size of a freaking mountain."

I look at it myself and notice she isn't kidding. "Holy shit! Ok, this could be a problem." Kristin takes a few breaths and regains her control. "Don't panic. That's your energy Brandon. You control it. Bring it back in." I nod because she's right. I take a deep breath and concentrate, I take it all back inside myself. Kristin lets out a breath. "How is it so damn easy for you?"

I give a shrug. "I don't know, it just is. So do you want the grand tour?" She shakes her head no.

"I think I've had enough for now. I need some air...some actual air from my own world."

I give her a smile and take us back through the shadows to Earth.

CHAPTER EIGHTEEN

WHEN WE RETURN back to Earth, I notice that Daniel and Sloan are still sparring. It's very entertaining. Sloan is landing blow after blow on Daniel, but every time he does he gets overconfident and Daniel takes him down. It seems that it's easy to manipulate time to land a blow but if they get a hold of you it's not as easy to get out of it. This is when I realize if we had never met these two we wouldn't have lasted long at all. Kristin is right. We may be powerful but our arrogance would have gotten us killed quickly. If they weren't in our lives I don't think I would have realized this. I turn to Kristin, give a big smile and pull her in for a hug. She jumps in response.

"Um…...Brandon? Are you ok?" I squeeze her. "Just realized how grateful I am that you two are with us. Thank you." She lightly hugs me back and pulls away. "You are welcome. I take it you understand now?" I give her a nod. "Fully and I'm sorry for being such a child."

She chuckles at that. "It's understandable. Those gifts of yours can be intoxicating." I turn back to see Daniel putting Sloan in a headlock for the third time. "Extremely."

After training we are all spent and pretty friggin hungry so we decide to go back to feed. As we get to the elevator a swarm of insects return to be absorbed by Sloan. Kristin and Daniel stand there in amazement as his eyes go white. Sloan is frozen for about a minute as he takes in the DNA of God only knows how many new creatures.

Kristin finally speaks up but in a whisper. "Brandon, is this normal?" I look back at her understanding why she's concerned. "For him, yes. It's freaky as all hell isn't it? It scared the shit out of me the first time I witnessed it." She shakes her head and doesn't say anything. Daniel walks up to him and waves his hand in front of his face and turns to me.

"Don't let him do this out in the open again Brandon. He is extremely vulnerable right now. I could have killed him like seven times already." I jump at the realization of how stupid I've been. He's totally right. "Shit, I didn't think of that. Thanks Daniel." He nods and Sloan wakes up. He blinks at us and gives us a shit eating grin.

"Are you guys still hungry?" I smile back and realize the blood that he's been taking in isn't all human. "Sloan, do you need to feed?" He gives me a grin. "Nope, I'm fine." Well that's interesting. I look back to Daniel. "Can vampires feed off animals?" He shakes his head. "They can, but it's gross and doesn't give us much. We need human blood to keep our bodies alive."

I look back to Sloan. "You can feed off animals, can't you?" He nods excitedly "I was wondering when you would figure it out!" Kristin speaks up. "Wait! Those bugs you released and just absorbed just fed you?!" I turn to her and smile. "They did more than that for him. But yes."

Daniel looks to Kristin. "Remember, everything he feeds on he can become now. He probably just took in hundreds of new strands of DNA." I shake my head and walk up to Sloan. "That's freaking amazing. But you shouldn't do that out in the open anymore. Daniel brought to my attention you could have been killed easily while you were in your trance."

His smile fades. "Shit, I didn't think of that." I give him a nod. "Neither did I."

Sloan turns to Daniel "Thanks. I had no idea." Daniel shrugs and smiles. "Can't have you guys dying on me that fast. It would be embarrassing at the annual Guardians conference." I chuckle. "Yeah, that would suck for you." We then head back down the elevator for a bite to eat.

After we feed and review what we learned in training with each other, we get summoned to Tristan's office. We walk in and he's at his desk chatting with Vanessa. She turns and smiles when she notices us. Tristan waves us in. "How was training?"

Daniel speaks up. "Extremely enlightening. I think they learned quite a bit. As well as us."

Tristan nods. "I'm excited to hear all about it. But for now, we need to go over our plans. It seems Vanessa has gotten us all invitations to the ball." I give an excited smile. "That's great!"

The look on her face makes me nervous. "Not really darling, it was too easy. This leads me to believe they have heard about you already. The Elders probably want you to introduce yourself to them." Kristin sighs. "Shit, I bet that damn twin Kevin and his Master started talking."

I take a deep breath. "So, what now? We should go, there is no choice. What do you think they will do?"

Tristan responds calmly as usual. "They will test you. Power interests them. They will want to know everything about you." I rub the back of my neck. "So, we need to hold back as much as we can so they don't suspect?" Vanessa speaks up. "No Brandon. Not just hold back. You must not let them know you have more than one gift. It is possible for a vampire to have an extremely powerful gift, but to have more than one isn't possible in their eyes. They will either kill you if they think you will become a threat to their power or claim you as their own to add to it if they find out."

I stand there trying to imagine what they would do with me if they claimed me as their own. It wouldn't end well. I'm sure one of us or perhaps all of us would die. "Well shit. Ok, so the only gift they know about me is my energy manipulation. So, there's that.

But Sloan has two. What one should he use?" Tristan walks closer to him. "I'm not sure, but I think it should be on the lines of your energy manipulation. The way gifts usually work in the vampire community is that the Bloodborne's gift is taken and transferred from the Master and then manipulated into their own version. The Bloodline usually stays with the same type of power but in different variations."

Sloan gives a nod. "Makes sense. So, I guess I'm going to be using my speed then. Got it. I'm getting the hang of it anyway." I look at Vanessa. "Ok so we know what gift we are using so what's the plan? I've got some suggestions if you all don't mind." Tristan's smile grows into a large and toothy grin as he looks at me. "Suggestions you say. Do tell." I stand and give him my most confident face.

"As we told you when we came in we learned a few things recently. A few of those things I think will benefit us greatly." I look back to Sloan and see the smile on his face, he knows what I'm getting at. "Show them what you can do baby." He steps forward and holds his hand out. "Let me show you how a pro bugs an office." With that a single drop of blood leaks from the tip of his finger and takes the form of a fly. "I'm literally the fly on the wall." Vanessa walks closer and takes his palm getting a closer look at the fly.

"Now that is an extremely nifty gift you have there Sloan." Sloan's smile is so bright I'm expecting shit to burst into flames. Tristan's normal stoney look of confidence shatters with shock. "That is impressive indeed Sloan" After he regains his composure he looks back to me. "Now I'm really looking forward to seeing what you can do Brandon. What exactly have we learned today?

I smile. "Quite a bit, but let's start with this. I'm going to need some assistance. If you don't mind Vanessa, would you leave the room and say something quietly in the next room? Also, write something on a piece of paper in that room please."

She shrugs. "Ok sure." She walks out of the room and closes the door. I find a seat next to a plant that's casting a shadow on the wall close to where my head would be, and take a seat. The shadow is in the perfect spot, covering my left eye. I then take control of the Shade and manipulate it to show me every window in the area I'm in. She's in the training area standing there with her arms crossed tapping the pen on her elbow. I look at Tristan.

"Go ahead and text her if you don't mind and tell her I'm ready when she is." He pulls his phone out and gives it a quick text. I can see her pull her phone out and roll her eyes. "You know this is kind of annoying, it had better be good child." She pulls out the paper and holds it to the wall so she can write on it. She scribbles "I have no Idea what I should wear to this damn ball. Any suggestions?"

With that she folds the paper and makes her way back. As she's walking she passes the shadow I was spying on her with and stops. She folds her arms and gives me a smile. "You naughty naughty boy." She makes her way back to the room and hands Tristan the note. "So, go ahead Brandon." I look to him then to Vanessa and feel kind of disappointed.

"Well, it seems she already knows. I'm not sure how but she does. Anyway, she has no idea what to wear to the ball and thinks this demonstration is annoying. She also thinks I'm a child."

Tristan gives the note a glance and smiles then looks to Vanessa. "He seems to think you know what he's done already. Mind enlightening the rest of us my dear?" Her face glows with pride when she walks up to me.

"First off, what you did is extremely impressive. But there is one problem with it on this particular mission. If it were just vampires, humans and regular Travelers at this ball, it would be perfect but it's not. I'm one of the oldest and most powerful Travelers in existence. That's the only reason I noticed what you were doing, and even I almost missed it. But I'm not the only powerful Traveler and there will be more at the ball. It's risky to use so I don't think it's a good idea."

I frown a bit. Tristan takes a few steps forward. "And what exactly are we speaking of?" Vanessa smiles and waves a hand to me. "Why don't you go ahead and explain." I feel like my party was ruined so I decided to show off a bit. I take hold of the shadows and make them slightly take physical form. They outstretch from the plant to touch my own shadow and then take the form of a shadowy human figure on the wall. I make it wave at them. Vanessa is standing there shocked. She looks to the shadow and back to me and then back to the shadow.

"You must explain how you are doing this." Tristan walks closer to the shadow and decides to touch it. It surprised the hell out of me that he did that. He would have to trust that it wouldn't hurt him. Is he starting to trust me? "Yes, you must Brandon." I look at Tristan.

"Would you mind telling me what it feels like Tristan?" He looks back at me.

"It's kind of soft and cold. Kind of like cold smoke."

I nod. "I control shadows. I can see through them seeing what they see and can give them physical form through my own reality. It seems it chose me for some reason. It's called the Shade." Vanessa looks back to me and for some reason she's crying. "Is this true?" I nod.

"Yeah." She walks up to me and puts a hand on my cheek. "It's not destroyed? They still live?" I look her in her eyes as tears roll down her cheek. "You know, don't you Venesssa?" She smiles and pulls me in for a hug.

"Yes child, it was the biggest mistake one of my kind has ever made. To find out they weren't completely destroyed is the best news I've received in centuries." She pulls back and seems genuinely happy. I think we both need to have a drink or seven, together to learn more about each other. Tristan walks up and puts a hand on her shoulder.

"That is an impressive gift Brandon. You must show us more later but for now we know it's too risky to use at the ball. It was a good effort and a very good idea. You should not be disappointed." I release the shadows back to normal and stand next to Sloan. "Thank you, Tristan." He nods and for the rest of the night we go over the ins and outs of vampire society.

CHAPTER NINETEEN

AFTER HOURS OF grueling vampire politics, Vanessa takes us to a part of the cave we have never been. To be honest, I'm sure there are so many parts of this place that we will not get to see all of them in a hundred lifetimes. I know I shouldn't be surprised anymore with all that has happened, but I can't help but be when we walk into the room.

It's an actual tailor's shop. The room is full of rolls for the most beautiful fabrics, patterns hanging everywhere and tailors and seamstresses working on some very rich looking clothing items. Of course they would have everything here at Headquarters considering it's basically a small underground city for the vampire world in Tuscaloosa.

After niceties and introductions, we are measured and asked what kind of style of suit we prefer. Sloan seems perfectly at home here as he is very into fashion trends and watches all the fashion shows on TV. He prides himself on always being impeccably dressed and always in style. It's one of the things that attracted me to him when we met.

I'm not stylish at all, The Ying to his Yang I guess you can say. To be honest, all those stereotypes that people think gay people have, I have zero. All my friends are straight. I'm not uncomfortable around other gay people at all because, duh. I just like to hang out with those who I click with. I hate musicals, Reality TV makes me barf and I can't stand shopping unless it's for video games online.

Of course I do have friends that are gay but for some reason I can't seem to find anyone gay with the same interests as me. The only thing gay about me is my attraction to dudes. In truth this should be the only thing expected of me. This is what I hate about stereotypes. They put you in a group and for some reason people expect you to only like those things. It's stupid as shit to me and I don't understand it at all. You like what you like and that's it. It's that simple.

After we get measured for our tuxes, we head home to get some rest before the big shindig and meet back at HQ the next day. We get home to the pups and get as much fuzzy time in as possible before we rest up.

The next day we head back to HQ and as soon as we walk in we are directed to the shop to try on our new suits. Mine is amazing and fits me like a glove. It's black with a deep blue shirt underneath. It kinda doesn't have a collar. It goes around the back of my neck and curves down to the buttons. I ask what it's called and all the shop owner says is that it's a Brioni. Like I'm supposed to know what that is. I really don't care, I look hot as hell.

Sloan walks in and as soon as I notice him I want to rip off my new suit and jump him. His form fitting suit has a deep purple shirt and it's made perfectly. He walks strutting his stuff knowing he looks good. "So, you ready to go make everyone at the ball jealous?" I chuckle.

"Damn skippy." We meet up with the others in Tristan's office. They look freaking amazing as well. I'm wondering how much money was thrown at these outfits we will probably never wear again. Vanessa grins. "Are we all set? We know what we are going for, correct?" I look to the others and give a nod. She then waves her hand in the air and a glowy ball of light forms. I look at her in astonishment.

"I was expecting a stretch limo." She grins. "That wouldn't get us there in time dear." Tristan walks through the ball of light followed by Kristin and Daniel. I take Sloan's hand and we walk through as well.

As soon as we step through the light I can't help but look confused. We are in a small stone room with absolutely no doors or windows. The only thing here is a stone door frame in the middle of the room with strange markings on it. There are two people on each side of it. They bow as soon as we arrive. "We are ready to take you to your destination ma'am." Vanessa smiles at them "Go ahead and get it ready." Kristin looks at me noticing my confusion. "It's a portal we have created to take us to any part of the world we wish." I cough out a laugh. "Well that's just damn nifty." Sloan takes my hand and pulls me to the side.

"I'm kind of freaking out a bit here." I squeeze his hand. "It's ok, I'm kinda nervous too. But you know what makes me feel better? It's you. With you by my side we will own this bitch. Think about it. We are the two most powerful vampires in existence. I've seen what you can do, you have seen what I can do. Those people we are about to meet have no idea what's waking into their little fancy party. They are assuming that we should be scared shitless just because they are the Elders, but we know that we can take them out with a flick of our wrists. I know we shouldn't be arrogant about our power because that's exactly what they are doing, but we know the truth. And don't forget, we have the element of surprise on our side."

He gives me an evil grin. "Oh, I'm not worried about me, Brandon." He takes my hand and puts it underneath his stomach. I feel a heartbeat. I immediately put my hand to where his heart should be. It's beating up there as well. I figured it out. Hot damn he's a genius.

"You didn't!" He nods grinning. "I did. They can take my heart as many times as they want. It won't do shit." I grin and give him a kiss. "That's my smart hubby." He smiles back. "Again, I'm not worried about me. I'm worried about you." I hug him close. "You don't have to be. You forget, anyone who tries to kill me will die. It's as simple as that."

He pulls back and still looks worried. "Stop worrying, remember when I told you that I'm totally connected to the shade? Well I am, I have an unlimited source of power to heal. Also, an unlimited source of power to take them out. We own these bitches, so hold your head up high like the badass that you are."

He smiles, kisses me and we walk back to the group like we own the place even though I know all they have to do is take my head off and I'm dust. Tristan looks back at us. "I do enjoy the confidence you two are showing, but don't forget why we are here. We are here for information only. No showing off, no starting fights. They must not find out what you actually are." We all agree and the two Travelers put a hand on each side of the door frame. The markings around the frame start to glow a deep red, then a second later a glowing pool of gold forms where the door should be. Tristan takes Vanessa's arm and walks in. Daniel takes Kristen's arm and follows and I hold my arm out and take Sloan's. We look each other in the eye and he says.

"We own this bitch." With that we walk in.

On the other side of the glowing door is a massive ballroom like something in a castle. There are massive carved stone columns along the wall. In between the columns are the most elaborate stained glass windows I've ever seen. There are tapestries hanging from the balconies along the sides and the chandeliers look as if they are centuries old. It looks like something out of a movie. A royal ball. The decor is full of deep reds and crystal.

At the other side of the ballroom are three tall elaborate gold thrones. Seated are two men, one on the left and one on the right and a woman in the middle. The men look gorgeous of course. The one on the left has perfect raven black hair, a close shaven goatee, silver eyes and a slender build. Pale and beautiful. The one on the right's hair is a deep cherry red. His beard is thicker but frames his face perfectly. His deep blue eyes seem to glow because of the color of his hair. His complexion is soft and powder white like a redhead that hasn't been in the sun for a very long time.

I've always had a soft spot for redheads and this one is knocking my socks off right now. The woman in the middle looks to be of Asian descent, beautiful shiny black hair and perfect features. Petite, but with a strong build with a commanding presence. As we enter we are introduced.

"Master Tristan and his bride Vanessa!" They walk in towards the Elders. "His Bloodborne and bride to be, Daniel and Kristin!" Bride to be? The hell man? Oh is he gonna hear it from me later about this shit.

"And introducing, Master Tristan's newly formed Bloodborne children, Brandon and his husband Sloan!" He actually made a face when he said husband. We both make our way to the Elders when I see a single fly pass by my face. That's my baby. He made sure I knew he has already set his plan in motion. I can't help but smile. We walk up to the Elders with our heads held high. This is our party after all.

We walk past all the whispering vamps and their Travelers, also some humans. There must be snacks at the ball after all. We can't help but notice that most of the vamps are snickering and giving us grossed out faces as we walk arm in arm past them. I can't help but smile brightly at them. These morons have no idea what they are dealing with. It's true, ignorance breeds hate. They will be enlightened soon enough.

We eventually arrive at the thrones. I am in the middle of our pretty group with Tristan to my left and Daniel to Sloan's right. The ladies are on the outside. They bow to the Elders and we do the same. We look up and I give them a friendly smile. The redhead grins back at me.

"This one seems pleased to see us." The black haired male chuckles. "Usually they about piss their pants." The redhead says with a grin. The female beauty rolls her eyes."Are we doing this again? Can't you two come up with anything else?" Tristan speaks up. "It's an honor my gracious Elders. We thank you for inviting us. It's as beautiful as ever." They look to him with bored eyes.

The redhead grins again and looks back to me. And suddenly I hear something like glass cracking, I can feel it shatter in my mind. The next thing I know I'm bleeding from my arm. I look around and nobody seems to be surprised. Sloan is about to jump into battle, I grab his hand and squeeze. I do this because I notice Mr. Redhead grinning at me with a drop of my blood on his face.

He looks down at me and his smile grows. I had no idea how tall he was. The cracking of glass happens again and I'm bleeding from my stomach. I look up and he's not there, but I can feel him at my back. I turn quickly and see him standing behind me with a shit eating grin on his face.

"I've been rude. Please excuse me. My name is Connor. It's a pleasure to meet you Brandon."

I've realized I know what that cracking glass feeling is. I've experienced it before. I didn't mean to, but I cracked a smile. He notices and I feel glass crack again. This time I'm prepared. I slow time as slow as I possibly can and don't move a muscle. I was right. I see him coming towards me with a knife in his hand. I must think quickly.

How am I going to stop him without outing myself? They know I can manipulate energy but not time. I have an idea. I start to produce an intensely strong field of energy around my body, I'm going to have it drain the life of anyone who enters it. I let him cut me. He is smiling as he gets right up to me and thrusts the blade deep in my stomach. Not a killing blow for a vamp but shit it hurt.

As soon as the knife goes in, the field grasps his arm. It starts to suck the life out of him instantly. I go back into real time and notice he's starting to do the same. He starts out as a blur but takes form right in front of me. I've sucked his energy so much he can't hold his speed. He jumps back holding his hand. I look down to the knife that is still in my stomach. I pull It out and the wound heals instantly. I hold the knife out and drop it on the floor and say nothing. He smiles at me and then pulls another knife out of his jacket, then looks at Sloan.

Shit, this isn't good. His power is exactly the same as what Sloan was going to show to the world. I don't know why but I just know it's the right thing to do. I hold my hand over my mouth like I was panicking. The shadow gives me the ability to speak into it. I connect the shadow to the one in Sloan's ear and whisper.

"Don't use time." As soon as I say it I feel glass cracking again. The redhead is gone and the next thing I know he's in front of Sloan with a knife in his chest. Sloan looks down to the knife and back up to Connor. The knife missed the heart by inches, not that it mattered. Sloan looks up to Connor's face and gives him a pissed off smile. Then a low growl comes from his throat. He grabs the knife that's still in Connor's hands and pulls it out. As soon as he does, the wound heals up without bleeding a drop. Connor looks down and smiles and then looks up to a pair of cat eyes staring back at him. Just the eyes. His beautiful face with big bright cat eyes. Damn, I'm glad that he actually heard me.

"Enough!" The Female Elder stands and makes her way down to us. Connor is standing there staring into Sloan's eyes smiling at him. Miss Queen speaks up. "These are impressive gifts you have given your children Tristan." Tristan smiles and bows. "Thank you." She makes her way to me.

"So, the rumors are true. You are a life drinker." I blink. "Aren't we all?" She gives me a small smile. "Yes, but you know exactly what that means. She grabs my hand and for some reason it burns. Not like fire but like how a really hot jalapeno burns your mouth. I want to pull away but I don't.

"My name is Sayo. It's a pleasure to finally meet you."

I smile and give a bow. She makes her way to Sloan. She holds her hand out to him and he takes it. He didn't even flinch at the pain. "Sloan. It's a pleasure. Your eyes are quite beautiful. I would love to see what you can do." Sloan looks to me and then to Tristan. He looks back up to her and his hands start to form claws while her hand is still in his. She doesn't flinch but seems fascinated. She looks down at his claws and releases it.

"Now that's impressive indeed. I've only seen one bloodline able to do this and it's not the bloodline you are in. She looks back to me and smiles. His gift is impressive indeed. She walks back up to her throne and turns to all of us before she sits. "They have been tested and have my approval! All shall welcome the newest members of our family, Brandon and Sloan of house Tristan!" The palace erupts in clapping and she turns and sits in her golden throne.

After that, the celebration continues. We mingle and Tristan and Vanessa put the word out discreetly about the artifacts. Their plan was to start rumors throughout the party and get people talking to each other about it. Sloan's bugs would spy on all conversations and with any luck we would get a lead. Well that's not the only thing we are relying on, Tristan and Vanessa have some old friends they plan to speak with as well. I take this opportunity to use my eyes. I'm going to play the arrogant newb that went on his first mission and kicked ass. Every now and then a vamp would come up to me and ask how it went and I would let it slip about a special object we were to retrieve. I watched their auras closely to see their reaction when I mentioned it.

Most of the female vampires, for some reason, were only interested in Tristan. I figured it was because he was the Head of the Guardians and of course he's super hot. The guys barely even spoke to me. One or two would say hello to be polite. I use that opportunity to strike up a conversation whether they like it or not. Talking about the mission grabbed their attention easily. Vanessa walks up to me after my last conversation ends. She puts a hand on my cheek and smiles with a glass of bubbly in her other hand and gives it to me.

"You are doing well Brandon." She leans in closer still smiling. "Any luck?" I take a sip of champagne and smile. "Nope, nothing. Seems most of the girls here only want to bone Tristan and the guys only like to talk when they want to know what going on a mission is like." She puts her arm in mine and walks with me. "No worries dear, the word is out and in this vampire community word travels fast. I do have a question. Why did you tell Sloan to change his tactics?"

I panic a bit but don't let it show. "I don't know, for some reason I felt that Sloan showing the world that he has the same gift that Connor possesses, was a really bad idea." She stops in her tracks and turns to me with that smile still on her face. "What are you talking about Brandon? That is not possible." I look back at her. "Why do you think that?"

She sighs. "Brandon, Connor's gift is phasing in and out of reality itself. It's a form of teleportation." I grin and realize she doesn't know and she seems frustrated at me. "What do you know that I don't?" I take another sip of the bubbly. "He's not phasing in and out of reality. Is that what he's telling everyone?" She grabs a glass of champagne from a tray walking by. "No, vampires with gifts never tell their secrets. It makes it easier for others to find a weakness. It's a conclusion we came up with."

I start to get a bit pissed off and force a smile at her. "If vampires with gifts never reveal them to others why the hell are you having us reveal ours to you?" She giggles and puts a hand on my shoulder brushing off fake dust. "You're so adorable. Yours is a special situation. It's because your gift came in full. Gifted vampires come into their power slowly. If you were a normal vampire, your gift would probably start out as sight and would progress gradually for years before what it is with you now. That is, if you survived that long. If you were a normal vampire the

Elders would have probably killed you here tonight. Life drinkers are considered too powerful."

I jump slightly at that. "There are other vamps with my gift?" She takes a sip and smiles again." Very few. Most can't control it and must be put down. The fact that you have control and haven't drained the life out of everyone in the room saved your life tonight." I nod to her with a grin. "I'm guessing that the cursed blood of Kain taints the gift so much they can't stop when they start. Kind of like when Daniel used to do when feeding on blood. It does feel amazing to drain the life force of another."

She gives a sigh and starts walking. "That's a possibility. Now, tell me why you think I am wrong about Connor's gift." I smile and nod to the passersby. "Because I have the same ability. I've seen it in action." I look at her and her aura is flickering a lot. She's starting to freak out. I smile and pull her close to give her a kiss on the cheek. "Your emotions are showing. I think you need to breathe."

She pulls back and giggles like I've just told a joke, then takes a deep breath and lets it out. "What power are we talking about Brandon?" I take her arm in mine and start walking again. "Speed, love. The gift of time. He moves so fast it seems like he's teleporting. He's just manipulating time" She chuckles. "Well that was our other conclusion, we tested it numerous times with cameras but found nothing. Are you sure about this?" I give a nod.

"Yes, I've seen him in motion." We start walking towards Tristan. "Well, in that case you made the right decision. If Connor found out Sloan has the same gift as he then he would have taken his head right then and there. He can't have another with the same gift that's just as strong as his." I chuckle. "Sloan's is stronger." She waves to Tristan. "What do you mean by that?" I give Tristan a nod. "Well I guess you guys know pretty much everything about us anyway and will find out eventually. Connor can speed himself up enough it makes time crawl and seem like it's stopped. Sloan can actually stop time completely." She jumps slightly as we get to Tristan.

"That is definitely something we need to look into soon. But for now, you did well. Let's focus on the mission at hand."

After a while, Sloan walks up with Daniel and Kristin. They look like they are having a good time. Sloan comes in for a kiss and I return it. I look around and people are staring and shaking their heads. "I think I've got a live one." Sloan says as he pulls back. Tristan grins. "Do tell."

"There is a woman on the other side of the room next to the exit speaking with two others. They are talking about pushing up the timeframe. They say they found out where the artifact is located and are afraid they might be running out of time. The guys are talking about the boss getting impatient and are afraid he won't last much longer." Daniel chuckles. "Betcha a dollar that the boss man Is Kain!"

Vanessa nods. "I'm sure you are right. It seems what we learned was true. The transfer of life force from one person to another through the dagger isn't permanent. The body will die soon and send him right back." Kristin looks to Sloan. "Can you put a bug on her? I think I have a way we can use it like a tracker. They will lead us right to it." Vanessa gives her a big smile. "Impressive thinking, daughter." Daughter? Son of a bitch. Why don't these people tell me anything?

"Seriously guys, as much as we tell you, you don't tell us much at all." They all look at me and shrug with a smile. Daniel pats me on the back. "Gotta keep it interesting for you buddy. Can't have you getting bored with us. You won't want to hang out with us anymore."

Sloan was successful in bugging the cult member, not just her, he bugged them all. It's kinda gross but he made a few of his flies fly into their hair and change into an insect nobody wants. It took all my willpower not to shoot champagne out of my nose when he told me he just gave them crabs. It was perfect. We chatted and partied for a few more hours and then left to head back to HQ to form a plan to track them down. Time for mission number three. I'm starting to dig this secret agent shit. I think Sloan is a natural. My own little secret agent vamp.

CHAPTER TWENTY

WE GET BACK to HQ and head into Operations. We get as much info on the three suspected cult members as we can utilizing all the intelligence contacts we have and of course the good ol internet. The woman in the group is named Jessica Danbridge and the two others are her brothers Phillip and Jason. I guess culty things are kept in the family. They are big money in Tuscaloosa and own most of the properties here. Big donors to the University as well. I've noticed that most of the vamp community is big money.

Kristin and Vanessa are speaking to Sloan and apparently have some kind of spell to make the connection to his bugs much stronger so he can pinpoint a location just like GPS. I can't help but be a small bit jealous of that nifty gift of his. He's really kicking ass with it. Daniel walks up to me and gives me a pat on the back.

"You ready for the big-time buddy?" I can't help but be excited as shit. "Hell yeah man! It's about time we get rid of these crazy ass people." I look him in the eyes. "Why would anyone want to bring back a tyrant that kills anyone with a gift just so he can have it anyway?"

He lets out a big sigh. "They think he's a God. They think those born with a gift are just vessels for his power to complete him in this world." I rub my hands over my face in frustration.

"This world is never gonna be free of stupidity, is it?" Daniel laughs while shaking his head.

"Probably not."

Tristan walks up with a look of concern on his face. "The plan is now made. We will track down and secure the artifact as quickly as possible. All cult members are to be destroyed without question. The artifact is our main objective and as soon as it's retrieved, it's to be returned here immediately. Vanessa will open a portal when it's obtained so that she is able to steal it away faster and get it back here to safety. There are likely masters there and the possibility that Kain is there as well. I would like to say that nobody is to engage Kain in combat, especially our newest members, but I can't."

I can see the sadness building in his beautiful eyes. "I want to say that you two are not ready for this mission and should stay behind where it's safe. I want to say this but I can't. I'm not sure if I believe your Lilith, or that you two are this Chosen breed you told me about. You believe this and I'm not going to stop you from doing what you believe you were made to do. I just ask one thing. If you think at any point that you can't defeat him, you get the hell out there and not try to be heros. You certainly can't defeat him if you are a pile of ash. I won't have you killing yourselves out of pride, do you understand?"

I can't help but smile looking at Sloan and back to Tristan. "We understand Sir. Trust me when I say we don't want to die either." He gives off a sad smile as he nods. "Good, let's get to it then." His eyes turn to Vanessa. "Have you two come up with a spell for Sloan yet my bride?"

Vanessa chuckles "Of course we have." She then turns to Sloan. "Are you ready dear?" Sloan gives her a nod. "Yes, let's do this!" All our years together I never thought he would enjoy this stuff more than me, or at all, but here he is all excited about going to war with a cult. Well I shouldn't say more excited, because I'm looking forward to it as well. I want to test my limits and see how powerful I actually am. I want to show the vampire world they have been wrong this whole time about our kind and they can suck it.

We end up being taken to yet another room that I've never been to. It's a large space that is pretty much empty with the exception of strange markings that are carved onto the stone floor. I'm guessing this is the room where the Travelers practice their spells. Sloan is taken to a carved circle that is in the exact middle of the room and is told to just stand there and try to relax. Vanessa and Kristin walk to the outside of the circle on opposite sides and stand with their arms spread out stretched. They both let out a deep breath and close their eyes and start whispering to themselves in some odd language I've never heard before.

After about a minute I notice that the air in the room starts to feel like it's actually vibrating. I can see the energy coming from both of them and then notice the outline of the circle around Sloan starts to glow a brilliant silver. The inside of the circle seems to be filling up with energy like a pool of water but it isn't spilling outside the circle itself. Eventually it fills up over Sloan's head and I can't help but think he can't breathe in there. I only panic for a second before I tell myself that it's energy and not actual water surrounding him.

The next thing I know, the girls smack their hands together in front of themselves and a shockwave emits from the clap and all that energy starts to be absorbed into Sloan's body. He looks like he's in pain and enjoying it at the same time. After it's all absorbed I hear a loud pop and the circle stops glowing and the room suddenly goes back to normal. I look at Sloan to make sure he's ok and still my Sloan in there. I can't help but blurt out in excitement,

"That was freaking amazing." Sloan looks down at his hands and then back up at me.

"You're telling me." Kristin speaks up. "Your connection to your blood should be strong enough to find them now." Tristan smiles at Vanessa. "It's the Blood Bond spell. Impressive use of it." I just have to ask because you know...magic. "Blood Bond spell?" Vanessa nods.

"Yes, it was created to locate a missing vampire long ago. More like a traitor. The Master of that traitor was infused with this power and could see his location. The traitor was found using this spell and was ultimately destroyed. We still use it from time to time for the same reasons, or if one of us goes missing." I nod. "Nifty."

Kristin has Sloan sit down. "Now close your eyes and feel for that connection to your blood. As soon as you get it you should be able to give us an exact location." He nods and takes a deep breath and relaxes and after a moment he speaks up. "Ok, I can feel them but I can't tell how far they are from me. I know what direction they are in and can see their surroundings, but I can't tell you where they are."

Vanessa sighs. "I was afraid of this. His bugs are just too small and have no intelligence to actually know where they are." Daniel speaks up. "We can use him like a tracking device."

Kristin shakes her head. "They could be on the other side of the world for all we know. By the time we get to them it could possibly be too late."

I take a step forward. "Not necessarily." They look back at me. "I think I have an idea." I walk up to Sloan. "I have a way to get to them instantly." Tristan smiles at me. "The Shade?"

I nod. "The Shade." Tristan walks up to me and puts his hands on my shoulders looking me in the eye. "I wish I could go with you but for the sake of this organization I cannot. The Leader of the House has to stay behind." I nod. "Makes total sense and I completely understand. I'll kick some extra ass for you." I say with an evil smile.

He gives a small laugh. "I'm sure you will. Just be careful and make sure you all come back alive." He walks up to Daniel. "Protect them and yourself, understand?" Daniel gives a serious look. "I do." With that, our team gets battle ready and meets back up in the middle of the room. Daniel gives me a smile.

"As soon as we get back I'm teaching you how to use a blade. It sucks we haven't had the time to do that yet. I know you want one." I smile so big my face starts to hurt. "Damn right! They are cool as shit and I'm ready to learn how to slice and dice!" With that, I take us to my world. Daniel shakes his head. "I'll never get used to this place. It's so freaking creepy." I chuckle. "It's not for everyone I guess but I like it." Sloan lets out a chuckle.

"You would." I can't help but smile back.

"So, I'm going to try something new." He nods. "And what would that be?" I walk up to him and take his hands. "I'm going to try and connect you with this place. That way you can pull us to your bugs." Vanessa walks up to me. "You really think you can do that?" I nod. "Yeah, I've kind of done it before. It's like transferring energy. Everyone move in close to each other because as soon as he's connected I'm taking us directly there." They all get as close as they can and I start to fuse my energy with Sloan's. It feels nice, kind of like home and it's easy to connect with. I guess this is because he's my Bloodborne. I don't think about it much though. There are much more important things to do right now. I use the part of my power that's connected to this world and infuse it into him. We are both connected now. His eyes open wide and he starts to breathe rapidly.

"Wow..." He says breathlessly. I smile. "I know right." He looks at me with a look of amazement. "You see all of this? Holy shit Brandon, you see everything." I grin. "I know it's a bit overwhelming and amazing baby, but right now we need to focus on finding your little bugs." He takes a deep breath and nods. "Right. Let me focus." He closes his eyes and I can actually see what he's seeing. He's looking through every window here feeling the energy coming from it. Both of our eyes pop open and we say at the same time. "Found them!" I look back to everyone. "Get ready because it's time to kick some cult ass!"

CHAPTER TWENTY-ONE

I START TO take us directly there to them but then I realize they are in a cave. There are so many shadows there, why not use that to our advantage? I look back to the team. "I have an idea." Daniel chuckles. "You seem to be full of those today." I grin. "I'm usually totally against doing this but we are going to split the party and flank them."

Kristin smiles. "And how do you suppose we are going to do that?" I point to the window down to Earth. "Can you see there?" Her eyes widen as a window appears in front of her. "Wow, I can now. Can they see us?" Apparently, they weren't able to see through the shadows until I wanted them to. That's interesting. I shake my head getting back to the task at hand.

"No, they can't see us." Daniel steps a bit closer to get a better look. "Ok, I see Jessica and her two brothers, no Kain. Guess he doesn't like to do the heavy lifting. Wait." I look through the shadows to see what he's trying to see. Another woman enters the cave with the cult members. A brunette with a familiar build and a man at her arm. I can't see her face so I use another shadow on the other side of the cave to get a better look at the situation.

"Holy shit! Guys! That's the Master of Texas, Ava!" Vanessa leans in. "Are you sure?" I nod and Vanessa's eyes go wide "Shit. this isn't good. She's a Master. If she's a cult member this could complicate things." I shake my head. "If she's a cult member then she has to be taken down, we have our orders." Vanessa grabs my arm. "Did you not hear me? She's a Master. Masters are extremely powerful." I look her dead in the eyes.

"I know, not my first one." She blinks with a shocked look on her face. "You killed the last Master at the factory on the island, didn't you?" All I do is nod. "Shit. I guess then we have no choice in the matter." I shrug. "Nope. and I think I've found what they are looking for." I pull a shadow into view so everyone can see what I have been looking at in the cave. There, on an altar behind some broken stones are a pair of bracelets resting on two stone arms sticking out of the altar. I notice the cult members are getting closer to our relic.

"Vanessa, I'm going to send you there now. You get the bracelets and port your way back to HQ, that is your only objective. We will distract the cult members while you get the bracelets."

She shakes her head. "Brandon, there is a Master there and three other talented vampires..." I cut her off.

"I know that Vanessa. We know our mission. Tristan said our main objective is to secure the bracelets and terminate anyone who gets in the way." I give her a toothy grin. "Trust your team, beautiful." She sighs and grins. "Flattery will get you everything darling. But one thing before we go. If my daughter doesn't return to me your pain will last very long, and when I finally do kill you, you will welcome death's embrace."

Holy shit, I've got to use that one. Also, I believe her. "Um... ok. Damn lady, you scare me more than Kain." She grins and heads to the shadow. I send her in. I look at Kristin and Daniel.

"Ok, you two will be the frontal attack. Sloan will take their left and I'll attack from behind." Daniel is smiling from ear to ear. "One question kid, when did you become leader?" I jump at that. "Um... sorry? It just seemed like a good plan." He smiles.

"No, it's a damn good plan. I just didn't expect you to be that good at this. When we get back to HQ we have to have a chat about where you learned this shit." Sloan chuckles. "His nerd nights playing Dragons and magic or someshit." I give him a punch in the arm.

"That's not what's it called and you know it, nerds rule so stop being jealous." Sloan laughs and shakes his head. "You do baby. Now let's finish this." I nod and pull the shadows into place and take us to our positions. When we pop out, the first two they see are Daniel and Kristin.

They actually jump. Ava has a pissed off look, probably because she's been busted conspiring with the enemy. Ava asks in a very demanding tone, "How did you all get here?" Kristin smiles. "You've been a busy little traitor, haven't you?" I guess Ava and the other traitors weren't much for talking because the only response Kristin got was. "Kill them all!"

Jason goes directly for Daniel with a quickness. He launches himself at Daniel's face with a blade that comes out of nowhere. Jessica goes directly after Kristin. Not running, but pulling out daggers with an evil grin on her face. The next thing I know she's throwing them directly at Kristin.

Ava finally notices Sloan and heads in his direction. Shit, that bitch touches him I'll shred her face. I start to make my way towards her but Phillip notices me and runs full speed in my direction. I need to work on my sneaky skills I guess. I am totally ready for his ass though.

When he gets to me swinging his blade, I dodge it easily, looks like my training is paying off. I punch that S.O.B. right in the stomach as hard as I possibly can. Much to my surprise my hand goes straight through him and at the same time I feel a foot at the back of my head. He's behind me? The image I punched has turned to mist and disappears. What the shit was that? Kristen smiles as the daggers that were launched at her stop in midair and reverse direction and head straight back to Jessica's face.

Kristin runs up to Jessica while the blades fly towards her. Jessica spins and dodges one of them and catches the other in her left hand. When Kristen gets to her, Jessica makes a slash with her blade at Kristen's stomach. Kristin drops to her knees sliding and maneuvering under the attack kicking Jessica directly in her kneecap as she slides by. Jessica screams in pain as she jumps back a step, tossing a dagger at Kristin. Kristin deflects the dagger and it hits the wall. I get a glimpse of Kristin at this point and see her webs all over the damn place. Nifty.

I realize I need to pay attention to my own vamp when a face appears out of nowhere in front of me and a fist hits me square in the jaw. This punch was not as hard as the brother who is on Daniel though. Daniel is dodging every blow that Jason makes. When he throws a punch, Daniel dodges and Jason's fist goes through the cave wall ... not kidding, through the damn wall. Fragments of rubble and dirt fly everywhere. It gets stuck in the hole it has just made and Daniel takes advantage of the situation and takes his hit.

He swings his blade and lands a direct hit to Jason's throat ... and the blade freaking shatter as Jason chuckles. Daniel punches him in the face and I hear a horrible crack. Daniel's hand is broken. "I take it you have never heard of me." He says in a scottish accent. Jason pulls his hand from the wall and kicks Daniel across the cave.

I get back up off the ground after taking a hit from Mister Poofs A-lot and try to figure out how the bastard is doing this. I breathe and slow time, thinking that he's just damn fast. I throw a rock at his face and it goes right through it. With time slowed I look behind me and he pops out of nowhere. Shit, he's actually teleporting. I dodge his punch and grab his arm, I taste his energy before he disappears again. It tastes strange, but apparently I got enough that I'm able to tell where he's gonna pop up next. That's new. It's something I can work with though. I'll keep draining his ass till he can't attack anymore.

Ava is swinging some freaky ass looking claws at Sloan. I notice they are leaking something and it's not his blood. Sloan dodges them easily, smiling. She's pretty pissed off now because of his dodgyness. "You arrogant child, you shouldn't pick a fight with a Master. You may be fast but I will make you wish for death." Her body starts changing right in front of him. Sloan stands there in shock as she grows twice her size, scales covering every inch of her flesh, her fangs extend and her face molds into a reptilian form.

Sloan chuckles. "Cute trick, but let me show you how it's done bitch." With that, his hands form long and pointy black claws. His face becomes a mix of a rat and a cat, his legs extend as he grows at least two extra feet. Out of his back sprouts what I can only explain to be two spider legs and they are dripping some kind of nasty acid out from the tips. He growls a chuckle at Ava.

Holy shit, my baby is the stuff nightmares are made of. Ava takes a step back but then launches herself at Sloan. He easily dodges the first few blows from her. He grabs her arm with his massive claws and then slings her hard across the expanse of the cave and into the wall. She gets back up blood dripping from her mouth smiling.

"Finally, someone who can actually last more than ten seconds against me without dying. Now let's see how fast you can die, you little stain." With that she hisses and her body starts growing yet again. She grows two times larger than before. Her legs start fusing together and a massive snake tail takes their place. Her arms stay and grow longer and the claws are sharper, I can tell that there is some kind of poison dripping from them.

She's become some kind of giant snake human hybrid and is fast as shit. Sloan blinked and she is on him slashing with all she has. He takes a direct hit from one of her claws. Blood goes flying and the claw marks on his chest start foaming. Her tail swings and smacks him across the cave into the wall. He gets back up stunned and she's already in front of him. She wraps herself around him in a vice grip like a python choking its prey and squeezing hard.

I hear bones cracking and hear him struggle to breathe. I start to run in his direction in a panic.

It was the perfect distraction for Phillip. He appears right in front of me and sinks his blade into my stomach pushing up trying to get at my heart. It hurts like a bitch too! I grab his hand and start eating his power. His eyes go wide and he disappears again appearing two steps back. I'm too angry and worried to deal with him anymore. I grab the blade in my chest and pull it out making sure he sees my wound healing right in front of him using all the power I leached from him. I decide he's just gotta go now.

I extend my power absolutely surrounding him, switching gravity to use it to lift him into the air. He levitates in midair flailing his feet and arms freaking the hell out and I decide to try something new. I pinpoint a small area in his chest and make that the center of gravity for him and I increase the force around it.

His arms and legs curl into a ball and he floats mid air in a fetal position.

I've never felt so powerful seeing him like that. It's intoxicating as hell. I walk up to him and touch his face. "Time to go. You're in my way." I open up my power and pull every last drop of energy he has in his body into myself and all that's left is a small floating pile of ash. I release it and it floats slowly to the ground, I then make my way to Sloan.

Before I get there, he's stabbing at her furiously with his spider legs while still in her grip. They can't penetrate her scales though. I get about ten feet from her and watch her claw as it enters his chest and rips his heart from his body. I freeze. Oh God no.

She grins holding his heart in front of his face. "You lasted longer than most. You should be proud." Sloan looks up to his heart then to her face. He gives a feral grin and growls a low and menacing chuckle. The look of shock on her face is beautiful and delicious. It gets even more beautiful as the heart in her hand starts to form a gigantic swarm of insects that fly directly into her mouth. With a look of pain, fear and panic on her face she starts choking and coughing up insects as she drops Sloan to the ground.

Her claws scratch around her neck then suddenly she grabs her chest like she is having a heart attack. I realize exactly what he is doing. I sense it. His insects are devouring her heart while still inside her body, literally eating her alive. She looks back at him and tries to scream but all she can do is turn to ash. And all I can do is stand there in amazement. Sloan looks at me exhausted with a shit eating grin and says. "Don't you just hate it when you swallow a bug?"

Kristin is dodging and deflecting daggers left and right. At one point, Kristin punched Jessica in the throat and I notice that she leaves webs attached. Kristin takes four steps back looking at Jessica's furious reaction. After a second or two choking she finally was able to belt out a scream. "You're going to regret that bitch!" Kristin laughs. "Don't think so." Kristin snaps her fingers and all the blades that she attached to her webs are suddenly pulled onto Jessica's throat. The next thing I know there are six blades forming a collar around Jessica's neck. Kristin spins her finger and the blades do the same taking Jessica's head clean off her body creating another pile of ash.

All I can do is stand here speechless. That was the most amazing thing I've seen since I watched a bunch of bugs eat a heart from inside a living body. I notice Daniel having problems with Mr. Punchy so I head over after making sure Sloan is ok.

Daniel is getting his head bashed into the wall and he doesn't look good at all. Jason is attempting to crush Daniels skull through a wall. I hear a horrible cracking sound and I think that I'm too late. Suddenly Daniel's head goes directly through the wall. For a moment it seems like I'm actually too late, until I look a bit closer realizing that his head didn't smash but it actually goes right into the wall. Daniel's body seems to be fusing into the wall itself. He is now absorbed into the wall completely and Jason starts to step back confused and just staring at the blank wall. Suddenly, Daniel is on the floor under Jason taking form with his arms wrapped around Jason's body. I get a closer look and realize that Daniel is made of freaking stone! Getting a good look at his stoney face I can tell he's pissed the hell off.

"I guess you haven't heard of me either, jackass." Daniel then takes his hand and fuses right through Jason's chest, crushing his heart and turning him to dust. I look at Daniel. "The hell man?! When did you learn how to do that?!" He looks back to me panting. "Just now I guess."

I laugh. "Guess it's as good a time as any to find your own gift. Lucky bastard! That looked like it hurt." He stands up, cracks his arm back into place and the stones fall from his body unveiling his usual badass self. "Yeah, it kinda did." With that, we had taken out every damn cult member here. Shit... I guess we could have tried to take one alive. Oh well.

CHAPTER TWENTY-TWO

AFTER WE REGROUP in the cave and check to see that there are no vamps hiding anywhere, we make sure the bracelets are gone with Vanessa. We head back into the shadows using them to get back to HQ. When we get back we notice everyone running around in a panic. Daniel pulls the first person that is running by and stops them.

"What's going on?" The poor girl is crying and freaking out. "A bomb just exploded in Operations!" We didn't say anything. We just run there as fast as possible. The smoke is just starting to fade when we arrive. The emergency system that we have in place had doused the flames so there is no fire danger anymore. The destruction however, is pretty bad. People are being dragged out on stretchers, bloody and some are missing body parts. I use my eyes to see if there is anyone else that might have been missed by the rescuers. I noticed three bodies under some of the rubble that was once our mainframe. Their life forces are very weak and I run to them as quickly as I can. Without thinking I levitate the rubble off them as carefully as possible.

The emergency crew stops and stares at me in amazement. "Hurry! They don't have much time left!" They run in and get the victims out as quickly as they can. I notice two of the wounded are females. One with blond hair and the other with black. As soon as they are clear, I drop everything and make my way to them. Sadly I realize that my worst fears just came true, it is Vanessa and Janet. I have a bad feeling about what happened but there is no time. Their life force is extremely weak. I follow the emergency crews to the medical unit.

Doctor Davis is running around giving orders and patching up as many victims as she can. She sees us coming in and stops what she is doing then gives orders to one of her nurses to take over for her. "Shit, Is that Vanessa?" I nod. "She's fading fast." Dr. Davis gives her a hurried examination.

"She has internal bleeding. I'll need to operate fast." I can't do anything except watch as they take her to another room for the operation. Daniel walks up and puts his hand on my shoulder. I look up to him with anger in my voice as I say. "This was planned." He looks me in the eye.

"I agree. We have to find Tristan." I nod as I try and sense where Tristin is in the building. I've been around him enough that I've got a feel for his energy signature. "He's upstairs." Daniel nods and we make our way upstairs with Kristin and Sloan.

We get to his office but there are guards blocking our way. "Let us in, we need to see him now." They look at us and speak into their wrists then nod to us as they open the door. We walk in and notice Tristan is fairly bloody and banged up pretty bad.

"Shit! You ok?" He looks up to me with a pissed and pained face and growls.

"It was freaking Kevin." Daniel shakes his head. "Of course it was. Ava was a cult leader." Tristan looks shocked. "What do you mean, was?" Daniel smiles. "Sloan took care of her for us." Tristan blinks in amazement and looks to Sloan. "She was a Master..." He shakes his head. "That's for a later discussion. We have to get the bracelets back." I realize something that I didn't pick up in the middle of the commotion.

"Janet was one of the victims under the rubble that I freed! I need to get to her before she gets away!" I don't ask for permission,

I just stop time completely this time. I'm there floating in the air with my feet dangling through the floor. It should be easy to get there now that I can fly. I glide down through the walls to get to where Janet's being worked on. I then bring time back to normal and hear a screech behind me. The poor nurse is spooked but recognizes my face and calms down slightly.

"I'm sorry, it's ok. Here to help, I promise." I say with the friendliest smile I can put on my face." I turn back and notice Janet laying there in tears. I walk up to her to look her in the eye and keep my face as calm as I can. "Janet, tell me what happened." She looks up at me and I can see the pain in her eyes.

"Kevin… he, he went crazy. He took the bracelets. I tried to stop him. I swear I tried, but he wouldn't listen and when the others realized what he was doing he…" She started sobbing. "He had a bomb Brandon. He used it, he used it on me." By the time she finished talking the others burst into the room with guards. Daniel speaks up. "Take her into custody."

I walk up to Daniel and I don't try to stop them. He looks over to me and I realize he's very pissed off at me. "You really need to stop acting like you are in charge. It was fine on our mission because your plan was sound but here, I'm in charge understand?" I feel like shit and am totally embarrassed. "I'm Sorry Daniel. I'm just freaking out. It won't happen again." He seems to calm down.

"I understand Brandon, but you have made a mistake and I'm not sure if we can cover it up." I then realize everyone walking by is staring at me. Shit. I've just outed myself. "Shit." I look up to Daniel. "I had no choice. Vanessa, Janet and the other person under the rubble would have died if I didn't."

His smile is sad. "I know Brandon. You wouldn't be you if you didn't." He pats me on the back and we walk back up to Tristan's office. I notice he's all patched up now as he looks up from his desk. "If you are finished running around this entire facility panicking we can actually formulate a plan." Oh crap, he's pissed off at me as well.

"I'm sorry Sir." He cuts me off.

"Later. Right now, we need to figure out what to do." I nod. Daniel speaks up. "Janet is in custody." I take a step forward. "She said that she tried to stop Kevin and that he tried to kill her with everyone else with that bomb." Tristan shakes his head. "I didn't know they were traitors. When Vanessa returned, she gave me the bracelets and went over to the computer to look up something. Kevin walked in before she noticed him, and said that Ava was requesting him to guard the bracelets until she arrived. I didn't think twice about it because she talked to me earlier that day about the need to guard the bracelets if we recovered them. Before I realized it, Kevin swiped them from the case we had them in. Janet noticed and yes, she tried to stop him.

As soon as we noticed them arguing, Kevin pulled the bomb from his jacket and thrust it in the middle of the room and shoved Janet to the floor. He fled the room and the bomb went off."

That crazy assed cold hearted piece of shit,. When I get my hands on him he will suffer. "So, Janet was telling me the truth?" Tristan nods. "I think so, but just to make absolutely sure of that. Kristin would you mind asking her some questions?"

She nods. "Of course." She leaves the office and we go over what happened on the mission with Tristan. Sloan speaks up. "How did they know we even had the bracelets?" Tristan looks at him. "That's a good question. Kevin must have been their plan B." Daniel scratches his head. "Yeah, but we had just taken them out. There was no way for them to know what was happening. even if one of them escaped word could have gotten back to them for them to deploy Kevin." I try my best to come up with an answer to explain what all could have happened.

"There is no way that anyone would have even had any kind of cell service down here. The only reasonable answer I can think of is that someone had to have teleported out of the cave, but I checked for signs of life before and when we got there. There were only four of them, and I killed the only one who could teleport."

Tristan gives me a confused look. "You said there were only vampires there, right? You didn't mention there was a Traveler with them."

I look confused. "There wasn't. He was a vamp." Tristan shakes his head. "That's how they knew. The one that you killed had a Bride." I'm really confused now. "How do you know?"

Daniel speaks up. "Because, vamps don't have that kind of power. Teleporting uses massive amounts of energy. The only way he could do it is if he was connected to a powerful Traveler."

Damn, I'm pretty sure someone told me that already. Bad Brandon. "So, what happens to the Bride when the vamp dies?" Tristan looks up with a sad face. "The Bride dies as well." I get a bad feeling in my gut. "And the reverse?" He nods. "Exactly the same." I know he notices the sadness and panic on my face. "Shit." I look back to Sloan and he's standing there with a sad look in his eyes as well. I turn and look at Tristin. "I might be able to help Vanessa. I've done it before with vamps but I might be able to help her too."

He realizes what I'm saying. "I don't know Brandon. It could make things worse."

I nod. "I'll only do it if the doctor says it's ok." He gives a sad nod. "There is nothing else we can do here now. Only with the doctor's permission." I give him a quick nod and head out with Sloan behind me.

I get halfway down the hall when Sloan yells. "Brandon, Stop!" I stop and look back to him.

"What? We don't have much time Sloan." He grabs my arm and looks me in the eye.

"You know what you're going to try to do won't work Brandon. It only works on vamps because of their regenerative ability. She's not a Vampire. She's mortal."

I pull back. "I've never tried it. You don't know for sure, it might work."

He steps closer. "Brandon, yes I do. It's what I'm good at, remember? I know every cell in the human body completely. I'm sorry, but you can't fix everything." I start to get frustrated because I did know that already. He pulls me in and hugs me. "You did your best and probably gave her a fighting chance because you got her out of there.

All we can do is wait now." I hug him tighter. "If she dies then he dies and then what will happen. They are the only two in power that are protecting us." I pull back and look at him.

"I don't want to have to go to war with them Sloan, I really don't." He gives me a sad smile.

"One thing at a time Brandon. Let's go see how she's doing first before you decide to take on the whole vampire race."

When we get there she's still in surgery. I ask one of the nurses if she has any info, but all I get is we won't know until she's done. I walk over to a chair and sit with my head in my hands. Sloan sits beside me and rubs my back. "Don't panic Brandon." I sit up. "I'm trying Sloan, I really am." He smiles at me.

"I know, you always plan for the worst possible outcome. There isn't anything we can do right now but wait, so stop thinking about going to war. You don't know their reaction to us yet." I lean my head against the wall so I can see him. I'm so tired.

"Are you sure about that Sloan? You noticed their reaction to us at the ball as well. You see how they treat our kind. Now add being powerful vampires to being gay and how do you think they will react to us? Vanessa told me something at the ball that makes me sure Sloan. She said there were only a few vampires created that could drain power like me and they killed them baby. They killed them because they were too powerful."

He shakes his head. "If it comes down to it, we will do what we have to do for us, my love. Just try not to get ahead of yourself." I nod because I know he's right and lean my head back and close my eyes. I'm not sure but I think I'm asleep. I hear a raspy disembodied voice whisper to me. "Brandon." I open my eyes a bit and look around. Sloan is sleeping in the chair next to me and the hallway is totally quiet. It's just me and Sloan here in the hallway. I hear it again. "Brandon."

I look next to me and my shadow is much darker than normal. A dark shadowy hand comes out and holds out a finger suggesting I come forward. I stand up and walk into my own shadow. When I emerge into the Shade, he's standing in front of me. It's my shadow self again. He's the same liquid shadow faceless figure of a man he was last time I saw him in the Shade. I can't help but be confused when I speak.

"I thought I killed you. How are you here?" He doesn't move.

"I've always been here. I am here. I'm the part of you that is connected to this place. I'm the other you." I sigh. "I'm way too tired for this, shadow me." His faceless head tilts.

"I'll try and explain it better, in a way that you can understand." He steps forward and offers his throat. I take a step back.

"Are you serious?" He doesn't move but says.

"Very serious. You are tired because you have depleted your power in battle. You are confused because I am not able to explain myself to you correctly. This way you will learn what I'm trying to explain to you and feed to replenish your power."

I remember back to the last time I fed from him. I learned so much and my power increased dramatically. I decide to give it a try. I lean in and let my fangs sink into his shadow skin. It's strange how his blood is different from any other blood I've tasted. It's full of power and amazingly full of knowledge. As I drink him in, I understand what he's saying now. He is my other half. The me that is part of this world. The me that was born in this reality. We are the same person. He is this reality, and holds every drop of knowledge about this place. I pull back not draining him completely this time and he stands up straight.

"You understand now?" I nod feeling the power flow through my veins. He holds his dark hand out. "Then come, I have a secret to share." I take his hand and we walk directly through the wall that looks like the waiting room I was in. The other side is amazing. The world is totally alien to me. It isn't really a planet, but patches of land just floating around with strange plant life growing everywhere. Some floating boulders of land that look to be populated with what looks like castles and some small towns.

"Is this what your world is supposed to look like?" He nods. "Yes, the world that you created is a mirror of your own. This is the true reality And I'm rebuilding it for us." I smile. "So, your kind wasn't completely destroyed then?" He shakes his head. "Unfortunately, it was. The only reason I'm able to do this, is because of you. I wanted to show you what you have made possible. This place holds many secrets. I believe it might hold something that may be useful to you right now."

I look at him as he takes my hand. We soar over to another floating mountain of land. There I see what looks like to be ruins of some sort. He points. "In there you will find what was left behind of the being that destroyed this world." I can't help but look shocked.

"It left something behind?" He nods. "Yes. come and I'll show you." I follow and we go through a set of gigantic wooden doors and we emerge into a huge room with gigantic stone walls. The floors look to be made of the blackest marble I've ever seen. The place is beautiful. In the middle of the massive room is a single table with an object glowing very brightly. It's the only thing in this entire world that emits light. We walk up to it and my shadow self stops half way there.

"I'm sorry but the light hurts me." I nod and proceed. When I get there, I can see a single glowing stone. The stone itself wasn't glowing, but there was a liquid inside that was creating all this light. I look back. "What is this?" My shadow self explains. "The being that was summoned to destroy this place did not do it of its own free will. It was controlled. After he was finished with the destruction, sadness overtook him when he realized that he destroyed all life in this reality. What you hold in your hand are his tears." I stand there staring at the glowing liquid.

"What kind of creature can be so powerful to destroy an entire reality but be controlled? Shit, what kind of creature can control something with enough power to destroy an entire reality?"

All he says is, "I believe the closest description those in your reality have is, Angels." I look back at him shocked. "Holy shit, Angels are real?"

He looks back at me. "Yes, but not exactly the creatures that your reality portrays them to be. They have their own reality. An extremely advanced realty." My head is spinning. "So, there are other realities?" He nods. "Many. Some that are good, some that are bad. Some that are extremely advanced, and some primitive." I have to ask but before I get a chance to, he answers. "Primitive, your reality is considered to be very primitive, comparatively I mean."

I should say I'm not surprised. "Ok, so this is all amazing and I have so many questions, but how is this supposed to help me?" He looks at the glowing liquid. "The tears of an Angel can heal any wound, no matter how deep. The tears can revive a being from death itself as long as that being died recently."

The smile on my face grows. "This can save them?" He nods. "Yes Brandon." I look back at him. "So why didn't he use it to bring any of you back?" His head hangs low. "There was nothing left to bring back. It was total destruction." Damn. As much as I would love to encounter one of them, I really don't think I do. I put the stone in my pocket and the glow fades. I walk back to him. "How do I use it?" He shrugs. "Just hold it over the person you want to heal. The stone was created to hold the tears until they are needed. It will release what is needed." I can only stare at him in amazement. "Did you create the stone?" He nods. "Holy shit man. That's amazing."

He shrugs. "I suppose. I think you should get back to your reality as soon as possible." He's right. He takes me back to my mirror Shade reality and I use the shadow to get back to Earth. Sloan is still sleeping in the chair. With excitement I run and shake him awake.

"Brandon, oh my god what's wrong? Is she ok?" I shake my head with a smile.

"I don't know but I can make her ok." Sloan holds his hands out and grabs mine.

"Brandon, we talked about this. It won't work."

I give him a smile. "I'll explain later, now I need to get to her." I realize I can't just barge in and use the stone in front of everyone, so I need to come up with another plan. At that time, Dr. Davis walks out looking extremely spent. She looks in our direction with a sad face, making me feel like I'm too late.

"Is she?" She shakes her head. "Vanessa's resting and still in critical condition. I've done all I can do but I'm going to be honest, it doesn't look good. All we can do is wait and hope for the best." I nod. "Can we see her?" She looks slightly confused but says. "You can but she needs as much rest as she can get. She's sleeping and won't be able to say anything." I nod. "It's ok, we just want to see her." She shakes her tired head. "But just the two of you, and you only have five minutes."

I smile and take Sloan's hand in mine and we go inside her room. Vanessa's laying there with tubes coming out of just about every part of her and she's hooked up to all kinds of machines. That beautiful, powerful, confident, and loving being I've known for only a few short weeks looks so frail and fragile now. I walk up to her and look at Sloan.

"Make sure nobody barges in here ok baby?" He gets a panicked look on his face. "Brandon, no. It could make things much worse for her and also for us my love." I look back at him with a smile. "I'm not doing that. I have something better in mind." With that, I pull the stone from my pocket. Sloan's eyes go wide with confusion. "What the hell is that? Some hippie crystal crap?" I chuckle at his question and hold the stone over Vanessa's forehead and simply say.

"It's life Sloan." A single drop of light forms at the tip of the stone and falls. We watch as it slowly releases from the stone and lands gently on her forehead. The fluid itself is deep blue in color and thick like mercury. After it lands, it seems to move on its own as if it's internally guided to her closed eyes. Once at her eyes, it pools on her eyelids like the most perfect eyeshadow and then is completely absorbed. The color instantly starts coming back to her ashen face. The black and blue marks from the rubble bruising her skin fade and all of her open wounds heal instantly.

We hear the sound of bones cracking and they appear to be fusing themselves back together. It's pretty damn cool in a disturbing kind of way. Finally she opens her eyes, and is blinking slowly. I can tell she is trying to focus her vision on us. I put the healing stone back in my pocket before she is able to see it in my hand and ask questions about it that I may not want to answer just yet. Sloan stands there staring at me in complete astonishment and is uncharastically unable to speak.

Vanessa pulls out the ventilator tubes from her throat and chokes a bit. She coughs out "Kevin!!" I smile and take her hand. "We know. We are trying to find him even as we speak." She looks down at herself in surprise. "What happened?" I can't hold back a giddie chuckle.

"Well, you kind of blew up. Now I need a favor."

The look of confusion on her face makes me want to explain everything but unfortunately we don't have the time. "So, I kind of outed myself to the house when I was getting you out from under a bunch of rocks. And now that I sorta brought you back from the brink of death, I'm afraid that people will start to talk and ask some questions that none of us want to answer. Would you mind acting like you're still hurt just for a little while longer?"

It takes a minute for her gaping mouth to form words. "How did you save me Brandon?" I shrug. "Would you believe Angel tears?" She bolted up. "Are you serious?!" I give a nervous laugh. "I take it you know about them then?" She nods and seems panicked. "Yes, of course I do. They are extremely dangerous! Please tell me you didn't summon an Angel to get their tears. Dear God please say you didn't!" I can see she was scared shitless.

"I didn't, it's ok. I'll explain later. There are no Angels here and we are totally safe at the moment so just relax. But I do need for you to pretend like you aren't safe and healed, so that nobody finds out what was used, ok?" She nods slowly. "It's best if I do. If word got out you had Angel Tears, people would stop at nothing to get to you." We had to make sure it was believable so Sloan had to do something he didn't want to do. He had to make her injuries real again. He used his blood to cut off her sense of pain to do it at least. He then broke the bones that the tears healed and damaged her just enough to show signs of the injuries that she had before. Just enough to make her live and be conscious but look as though she was still very injured.

She looks like total shit now but at least she will live. That's all that matters. She grabs my hand. "If you have any more Angel Tears you need to hide them now. Nobody can know you even know of them. Understand?"

I nod. "I'll make sure of it. Don't worry. I'll explain everything later. Right now, just rest." She nods and closes her eyes. I can tell she is getting her sense of pain back. I hate that but it's for the best. We walk out and Dr. Davis meets us at the door. "I'm sorry you had to see her in that condition. Just keep your hopes up. Vanessa is a strong one." I smile and nod and we leave. When we get to the hallway Sloan speaks up.

"If you don't tell me everything right now I'm kicking your ass." I can't help but smile at that. He's so damn cute. "I'll do ya one better. I'll show you." I take his hand and walk us into my shadow. There we had a chat with the other me and put the stone back for safe keeping. The look of astonishment on Sloan's face of the whole situation and seeing the real Shade for the first time made me think he would actually pass out.

We head back to Earth so we can chat with Tristan. He lets us know that Vanessa is stable and healing. He also tells us he has agents working on some leads to track down Kevin, but for now we need to go get some rest. We decide to take his advice and head home and hug the shit out of our fur babies.

CHAPTER TWENTY-THREE

LYING HERE AWAKE in my puppy pile with Sloan snoring away and the pups breathing in my ear, I can't get my head to stop spinning trying to figure out how to get to Kevin and how to find Kain's body. How do we stop him? I can't think of anything at all and it's starting to piss me off. I think Sloan actually feels my frustration because he wakes up and rolls over to hold me.

"It's going to be ok Brandon. We will find him." I give an evil grin. "I can't wait until we find him. I'm going to make him suffer." Sloan chuckles. "I'm sure you will baby." He rolls over and I can see the sadness on his face. "You ok? What's wrong?" The smile on his face is sad as he says. "Yeah, I'm fine."

I roll over to get face to face with him. "Stop lying to me. You really do suck at it." He sighs and looks at me with those sad eyes. "I killed someone Brandon. I killed her." Shit. Yeah, I'm a selfish prick. "She was totally evil Sloan. She was trying to kill you and she would have killed everyone else." I look at him staring into space and it pains me.

"That doesn't matter Brandon. She was a person. A living person." I realize then that it was just me. All this time I tried to blame myself for feeling nothing when I killed someone for being a vampire. I tried to convince myself that vampire blood took that guilt away. I finally realize you can't take away what was never there. I've always known I was different from others. That death had a different effect on me than it did on everyone else. I've never felt bad about it. People die, people get hurt. It's a part of life. To be honest, the only person I've ever truly loved was Sloan.

I've always had problems forming attachments with anyone. Being with Sloan made that possible for me. I have friends now. I love my friends and I enjoy hanging out with them. Before I didn't care for most people, to be honest I still don't. Only the ones that I like. Sloan taught me how to be social. How to talk to people. Killing those two people didn't bother me in the least, but Sloan is in pain because of it and I can't do anything because I can't feel what he feels. I roll over and hug him tight.

"I'm sorry baby. I wish I knew what to say to make it all better for you." He looks at me and gives me a sad smile. "I know. I also know it doesn't affect you like it does me. You shouldn't feel guilty because of that. I just need to process it, I just need some time. I'll be ok." I nod in frustration. "I know nothing I say will make you feel any better. I'm sorry about that but just know I'm here if you need me." He kisses me and we sleep the rest of the day.

We wake up refreshed and frustrated as ever so we head back to HQ. When we get there, we run into Daniel and he informs us that there will be a meeting in the Main Hall for everyone on staff. It's one hundred percent mandatory for everyone to attend, no excuses will be tolerated.

We head up to Tristan's office and see that he is back at his desk doing paperwork as usual. He waves us in and I take a seat next to Sloan and Daniel. He looks up as soon as we take a seat then locks eyes with me. Oh shit, here it comes.

"We are still following up on a few leads to find Kevin. I am certain that we will find him eventually, but for now we have our own problems to deal with, don't we Brandon." I know that wasn't a question, and all I can do is give him a nod in shame.

He continues. "Don't get me wrong, I'm not angry, I know you did what you had to do to save the lives of our family. But people are starting to talk and I have to give them answers." He leans in propping himself on his elbows. "How much information do I need to reveal about you and your powers Brandon?"

I'm shocked. "You're asking for my permission?" He nods. "This is your life we are talking about Brandon and it should be your decision alone. I trust every member of this House completely but I totally understand if you don't. You barely know anyone here. This House is sworn to protect our own first and foremost. Unfortunately for the humans that work here they are in the process of having their memory wiped. Well, basically what you did is now being wiped from their memory.

Vampires are more resistant to that sort of thing so we can't actually rely on it working on everyone. I trust that every vampire in this House will protect your secret with their lives if I ask them to do so."

I can't help but feel the same pride he feels for his Guardians. It's amazing the love and respect he has for this House and every member in it. I sigh and lean back in my chair. "I'm not sure, I don't want to tell them everything. I mean, telling them that they weren't supposed to be vampires to begin with is cruel. How about we just focus on what they witnessed?"

He nods in agreement. "Thats a good point Brandon. Telling them everything could cause panic and fear. How about this. For now, we will just tell them your gift is strong because you are a life drinker. There have been vampires with that ability in the past and they were very powerful."

I nod. "I know and I have also heard that they were destroyed because of their gift." He looks me dead in the eye. "For good reason. They had no control of their power and many innocent souls died because of it." I give a nervous cough. "But I do." He nods. "Yes, yes you do and that's what I'll tell them. We won't be lying, but only giving them information that is needed." I can't help but know the smile on his face is because of the irony of the situation we are about to put ourselves in. Just like me keeping things from him when I first arrived.

I rub the back of my neck. Seems the stress is getting to me. "It sounds like the best plan we are going to get at the moment. Let's go with it." He gives me another nod and stands up. "Shall we then?" I jump "You mean right now?" He walks next to my chair looking down at me. "Yes, why do you think I called the meeting?" Shit, It's all about me. I totally hate being the center of attention. "Well damn. Guess I have no choice." He gives me a grin and we make our way to the Main Hall.

There we all stand. Tristan at the podium standing with pride and authority, Kristin and Daniel to his right and Sloan and I to his left. He stands with confidence as he begins to speak.

"My Guardians. We have been the victims of great horror and betrayal in our own House. I want to let you know that we will find and punish all those involved." Tristen looks around the room at each person and I know he's speaking to each and every single one of them as if they are family, because they are.

"Nobody betrays our family and gets away without the most severe punishment and they will pay dearly for what they have done." Everyone cheers at this decree. He smiles and holds out a hand to calm them. "We have witnessed great tragedy and betrayal, yes, but because of this we have witnessed an awakening of power from one of our own, and I know it's confusing for you. I've called this meeting to explain what you have witnessed and ease your fears."

He holds his hand out to me looking me right in the face with a prideful smile. "This amazing and strong young man is my newest Bloodborn, Brandon as I'm sure many of you have already met. We have just come to realize that he has received a very powerful gift from the blood. Many of you have witnessed that special gift firsthand and I understand it may be causing you to fear him. Rumors are starting to be spread about him and his power. I'm here to tell you they are all completely true." The room exhales a collective gasp.

"The rumor that he is a life drinker is true." Everyone starts to speak up all at once with concern. People are throwing out questions and concerns as if they are the only one in the room. Tristan holds out a hand to settle them. "It is true in the past there have been life drinkers who have had no control over their power and have had to be put down. But I'm here today to tell you with absolute certainty that this one, Bloodborne, is the first life drinker we have known to have full control of his gift.

With his gift, he has saved the lives of many of our Family and destroyed many of our enemies. If nothing else we owe him a chance because of that, do you not agree?" He looks over the crowd with stoic resolve while they look at each other with confusion and wonder. Some of them nod in agreement and some still seem scared. "I believe we owe him a chance. The loyalty to this House, to our Family alone earns him a place in this Family." To my surprise I notice the crowd is starting to nod in agreeance. "With that being said, I have a question for all of this House. We protect our Family from any threat we receive do we not?" The crowd lets out an enthusiastic cheer. "Yes Sir!"

Tristan continues. "Those outside this Family have no business knowing what happens within this Family do they?" In unison, they all cheer. "No Sir!" He smiles. "Knowing this and how you all feel about our Family I have new orders for everyone in this Family. Your orders are to protect our newest Family member by never revealing how powerful his gift is. All the public needs to know is what they have already witnessed themselves. They need not know what you have witnessed here on the day of our attack. It is not their place to know or be involved in our affairs, this is our House and our business is our own!"

The crowd screams in agreement. I can't help but feel the love of everyone here. Sloan takes my hand and they still cheer. I look down to the crowd and realize everyone is looking at me and actually smiling. Finally, in amazement I realize that they are actually starting to accept us. Tristan takes my hand and holds it high. "Welcome your brothers Brandon and his husband Sloan!" Nobody even flinched at the word husband. The only reaction we get is excited cheering welcoming us as brothers. My eyes start to tear up, I hold them back but it isn't easy.

CHAPTER TWENTY-FOUR

AFTER THE ANNOUNCEMENT from Tristan that made us official brothers of the House, we leave the Main Hall with hugs and handshakes and pats on the back from everyone. I've never felt so accepted in my life. I decide right then and there that I will protect this House with my life if need be. We get back to Tristan's office and I'm still high from the love shown to us. Sloan is smiling from ear to ear. It's good to see him smile again.

"Thank you, Tristan. I have to say I've never felt this accepted before." He smiles. "You're family. We protect family and accept family fully. There is nothing more to say about it." Sloan squeezes my hand and my face starts hurting because of how big my smile is. Tristan sits at his desk and getting back to his serious look he announces to all of us. "We have a lead on Kevin. It seems he was spotted at the Birmingham Shuttlesworth International Airport. He was seen boarding a Southwest flight to New Orleans." I smile.

"What, no magic portals for the little shitbag?" Tristan smiles. "I'm guessing you killed their Traveler when you killed that vampire with Ava." I laugh. "Good." I noticed Sloan's smile fade when I said that. I also notice that Tristan notices the same thing. "His flight lands in about ten minutes. We cannot attack him at the airport, too many witnesses." I nod in agreement.

Sloan speaks up. "How about I lay a bug on him, that way we can track him to the others and we can take them all at once." Tristan nods. "That's exactly what I was thinking, Sloan. We don't want to let him know we are onto him. We want him to feel safe and comfortable. We also want to get a visual on everyone involved. We need faces and names, that makes this a great opportunity." Daniel speaks up. "Agreed, we need information. Brandon, you can use your nifty shadow trick and let Sloan bug his stupid ass so he can lead us to the prize."

There is a voice behind us. "When you do, I want to be there to help take them down." We all look back. It's Janet. Tristan speaks up. "I'm not sure that's a good idea Janet. You are too personally involved." Kristin interrupts. "He's right. I hate to say it, but we are more than likely going to have to destroy your brother."

She looks angry. "I have no brother. My brother died the moment he decided to join that damn cult. He has lied to me for years and shamed my family name. He must be put down and I need to be the one to do it to bring honor back to my house." Tristan leans back and sighs. "I'll think about it Janet." Daniel looks shocked. Janet bows.

"Thank you Sir. If you allow it, I will make it right." She leaves the room and Daniel jumps up. "What the hell Tristan? Are you seriously considering her to help us?" He looks up at him. "Yes, actually I am. Daniel we are short on power here. We could use all the help we can get. She passed Kristin's interrogation. She had no idea at all, and her family line has a long history of defending their honor. I believe her when she says she will destroy him to bring honor back to her family."

I shake my head. To have to kill your own brother. That sucks. "I believe her too." Daniel looks at me and sighs. "Fine, I hope you're right. But if she shows any sign of betrayal I'm taking her down." Tristan nods. "I would expect nothing less."

A few minutes later I take Sloan into the Shade to find the shadow connected to the airport. While I'm sifting through shadows trying to locate Kevin, I have to get something off my mind. "Sloan, I don't want you to go with us when we find the cult."

Sloan responds like he was just slapped in the face. "Why the hell not?" I look back to him. "Because we will have to kill. Sloan and you are just not built to kill. It's tearing you apart inside that you killed Ava, I can tell." He looks pissed now. "You don't get to decide that Brandon. We take Kain down together, remember? We are the only ones who can!" I nod.

"Yes baby, I know we said that but that was before you actually killed someone. Can you honestly tell me you can take another life without thinking about it?" He shakes his head in anger. "I can and I will." I look him in the eyes. "Yes, but can you do it without thinking about the ways you can take them out without having to kill them?" He stares back.

"I, I don't know." I give him a nod. "That's the kind of uncertainty that can get you killed. I'm not proud that I can take a life without thinking about it, but I can, and it makes me perfect for this job. I'm not sure this is the right position for you." I grab his hand. "I want you to speak to Daniel about this. He has years of experience. He might be able to help you cope with killing Ava. Please? Do it for me?"

He looks sad. "I don't want to leave Brandon. I love it here." I smile. "I'm not saying you have to leave silly. You freaking kick ass at covert work. Just when it comes down to fighting to the death you step back." He seems less sad but still not his happy self. "Ok Brandon. I'll talk to Daniel. Just don't die on me. I'll never forgive myself." I hug him.

"That's not going to happen." He nods and smiles. And I get back to searching. It took about a minute to locate him. The piece of shit seems confident and smug as usual. As soon as I do, Sloan releases two bugs through the shadow. We didn't even need to enter the airport. The bug's land in Kevin's hair unnoticed and we head back to HQ.

When we return to HQ, we inform the crew and we get battle ready. Sloan walks up to Daniel and asks if he can speak with him for a minute and they walk off to get some privacy. Tristan decides to allow Janet to come along with us to New Orleans. Soon after, Sloan and Daniel come back from their pretty talk and Sloan seems slightly better. When we are all geared up and ready, I take everyone to the Shade. Time to end this.

CHAPTER TWENTY-FIVE

WHEN WE ENTER the Shade, I walk up to Sloan and take his hands so we can meld our powers again. Before we even get to start, Janet starts to freak out. "Holy shit! Where the hell are we? Did you do this Kristin? You didn't say anything about this!" She walks up to Kristin with murder in her eyes. "If you plan on leaving me here I promise you will regret it."

Kristin can't help but chuckle. I step in before we have a dead teammate on our hands before we even start the battle. "Calm down Janet, we're not leaving you here. We are just using this place to find your brother." She gives me her annoyed look. "Would have been nice if someone would have informed me about this first. Surprises don't help a mission."

I start to laugh. "Well lady, you might want to get used to it. We have too many surprises to even cover right now. Just go with the flow." She stands there with her mouth open With the amazing feat of shutting Janet up under my belt, Sloan and I fuse our powers again. It's pretty amazing being able to see through Sloan's eyes. He finds Kevin pretty quickly. He's in a cab on the outskirts of town pulling into an abandoned salt mine. Oh goody, more underground shit. Kevin gets out and pays the cabbie. After the cabbie leaves he pulls out his cell phone, sends a text and waits. I look back to the others.

"Seems we play the waiting game now." Sloan looks up to me with a smile. "Not necessarily." He takes a step back and pulls out a knife. "Um… what do you plan to do with that baby? I don't think we have time to practice." He giggles and slashes his wrist. "The hell man!?" He then puts the knife away and holds out his hand and lets the blood drip onto the ground. The puddle of blood gets bigger and starts to move. Janet looks on in terror.

"Holy shit…someone better explain this shit or I'm going to freak and start clawing people." The blood puddle begins to take form growing and forming four legs. A tail sprouts from its rear, then a little head appears. Its eyes open and before we know it there is a black cat standing in front of us. I stand there blinking in amazement at it with my jaw practically on the floor. Janet looks at him eyes wide.

"What the hell are you?" I gain the ability to speak again and smile. "He's the Chosen. My little Chosen hubby." I walk up and pick up the kitty and look at Sloan. "You have to find this hilarious. I mean, you used to be allergic to cats and now this." He laughs. Daniel takes a step forward. "That's amazing as shit and all but what's your plan?" Sloan looks at him.

"I'm taking a page from Brandon's nerd nights and I am going to do some scouting." Daniel looks at me and chuckles. "Nerds rule." I smile and nod back. "Damn right nerds rule." Sloan smiles and releases the cat into a shadow that's next to the mine entrance.

I'm still connected to Sloan, so everything that he sees I see. I'm actually looking through a cat's eyes. How freaking cool is that?! He sends the cat into the tunnel. I didn't think it would be able to get far because even though cats have damn good night vision, pitch black could still be an issue. For some reason the lights in the mine are illuminated. Sloan's cat made its way down as far in the tunnel as it could go. What we saw looked like a dead end. The path ends into a solid earthen wall. Looking down there is a giant hole with ropes draped over the edge going down into it.

I look to Sloan. "I'm not sure if even a cat could make a landing that far." He gives a nod. "You're probably right." I shrug "Good effort though baby. You tried your best." He smiles. "Do I look like I'm finished?" I grin with pride. "Show me."

He nods and I see through his eyes again. The cat sits down and starts to change. It starts with its legs shrinking to tiny mouse hands. Its tail went away into its body completely disappearing. The whole body shrinks and the next thing I know I'm looking through a bat's eyes.

"Hot damn Sloan!" The others were just looking at us like we were crazy. I forgot they can't see anything. We are basically just holding hands, eyes closed talking to each other. The bat takes off down into the hole. It is pretty dark down there but it looks like it isn't just a cave. It seems to be a room. A giant room with some kind of altar in the middle of it. No not and altar. It looks like a…. shit! "It's a coffin!" Kristin Jumps. "What?!" I look back at her.

"I think we found Kain's body!"

I jump up and disconnect with Sloan's hand. I saw Kevin waiting without noticing anything that we were doing. "Guys, this is it. That's got to be Kain's body in there."

Janet steps up more pissed off than ever. "What the hell are you talking about?!"

I realize she has no idea what we are doing. Anyone would think we were messing with them if they didn't know what we could do. So, I decide she needs to know what she's about to get herself into. "This Janet, this is what we are talking about." I point at a shadow and make it visible to her. Her eyes light up in amazement as she sees Kevin standing there with his stupid smug face on. Janet's face changes and I can see the rage flowing off her. She's pissed and ready to kill.

Kristin speaks up. "Janet, you might want to calm down." She doesn't move but says with anger in her voice. "What? You expect me to just run on in like a crazed bitch and take his heart? I'm pretty, not stupid. I know our objective."

I have to say I'm impressed. Daniel walks closer to the shadow. "Guys, we've got visitors." A car pulls up and three people step out. Two men and one woman. One of the men is Kain still in the Traveler's body, all dressed up in a suit and tie pale faced as ever. I'm guessing the rumor is true and that he is running out of time. The woman is a redhead all dressed in black leather. The outfit is very tight fitting. She has all kinds of sharp toys strapped to her looking like a deranged dominatrix.

Daniel breathes out. "Holy shit, No!" Kristin looks closer and speaks up. "Shit, Donovan?"

I look at their shocked faces. "Guys, who is Donovan?" Janet chuckles. "Looks like I'm not the only person here whose Master is a traitor." Daniel looks at me. "That's Donovan, he's the Master of Alabama." Well shit. How many crazy people are in power anyway. Sloan points to Donovan.

"Guys, look." Donovan opens his coat up pulling out a dagger and hands it to Kain. "Shit! That's why he said that he claimed the dagger and wouldn't give it to Ava, because it didn't matter, they were on the same team!" Daniel nods.

"Brandon, we need to let Tristan know right now." I nod and start pulling at the shadows, I find Tristan in his office and step halfway through the shadow coming out of a wall next to him. He jumps and almost punches me in the face. "Don't do that!" He looks around his empty office making sure nobody walks in. I don't hesitate.

"Donovan is a traitor. He's with Kain at an abandoned mine where Kain's body is buried. He just gave Traveler Kain the dagger!" He looks panicked. "You need to stop them Brandon. Do whatever it takes. I'll handle things on my end." I nod and head back in from the shadow. "I told him everything I could. He said we need to do everything we can to stop them."

Janet giggles and gives a hair flip. "Wasn't that the plan to begin with?" I shake my head at her. "Let's get ready to go." I look at Daniel. "What's the plan?" He smiles at me. "We probably need to take them out before they go in." Sloan speaks up. "I think it's too late for that. They just ported in!" Frickin sorcerers.

"Well guess we need to get our asses in there. What does your bat see?" He holds out a hand for me to take. As soon as I do I notice the room is lit up and Donovan is trying to open the sarcophagus. The little Miss Stabby Redhead joins in and helps along with Kevin. I still see no sign of Kain.

"I don't like not knowing where he is, but it might be easier to take those three out before he gets back." Sloan nods "I agree. I look back to the others. "Donovan and his lady friend are opening up the sarcophagus with Kevin but Wizard Kain isn't there." Daniel looks confused. "That's weird, I don't like it but I think you are right. Taking those three out before he gets back could be easier. Let's do it." I look to Sloan, he looks to me and nods.

"I'll be right here." I smile and give him a kiss. "You did freaking great. See you soon." I take a deep breath and as soon as everyone is in position we all go in. We go in surrounding them. Janet has her eyes on Kevin with the evilest look I've ever seen on her. Daniel is in front of Donovan with blades ready. Kristin has the redhead lady in her sights. I position myself next to the body of Kain in his sarcophagus. Looking down at him I notice that he's practically mummified probably from the salt mine keeping moisture and creepy crawlies at bay. His body isn't totally decayed, but it has no life in it at all. He looks like a raisin that has been left out in the sun too long, dusty and frail.

Donovan makes the first attack. From the palms of his hands something that looks like ropes with blades attached to the ends of them sling out toward us. Looking closer I notice they aren't ropes, they are actually alive and a part of him. One of the gross tentacle thingies launches itself straight towards Daniels face and the other springs right up to the ceiling.

Daniel is able to dodge his tentacle with ease. Leaping off the ground like on a bungee cord Donovan flies through the air swinging from his weird ass pointy tentacles from the ceiling and when he gets over Daniel he breathes out this nasty green spray down toward Daniel. Daniel immediately melds himself into the ground before the nasty shit hits him. As soon as the spray hits the rocks, it starts to sizzle. Freakin nasty.

Little Miss Redhead smiles an evil smile at Kristin. Suddenly all of the sharp things on her outfit begin to float up in the air. I thought Kristen was doing that but then I realize it's not her magic webbing doing this. Little Miss Redhead isn't a vamp. I should have noticed that, what's wrong with me?

The next thing I know she's breathing fire! Kristin looks to her left and right but blades are waiting on both sides. She is trapped. I try to use my power and slow down time and grab her from the shadows but as soon as I use my power I feel an awful low vibration deep within my body that just about makes me vomit and stops me in my tracks. I'm too late, there isn't enough time to save Kristin. The fire is all around her along with the blades. Shit, I'm too late. I start to panic. What the hell was that anyway?!

After the fire stops and I see that Kristin is still standing there. Her webbing is practically solid and it's formed an actual bubble around her protecting her from the fire and metal. Kristin gives an evil grin as all the blades that have just been launched at her start flying back toward their owner.

Miss Redhead dodges most of them, but takes one blade to the leg and another stabs her in the arm. I breathe a sigh of relief and see that Janet and Kevin are now going at it. He has transformed into a full on snake face now, but Janet is still the perfect Barbie we all know and love. Well that's what it looks like at first glance. With a closer look I notice her skin is reflecting the light around her somehow. I look closer and see that she has transparent scales covering her body.

Keven throws quick and precise attacks but she dodges them easily. She flips, dodges and spins out of the way of every attack like some kind of slithering contortionist super hero. Have to say she's damn amazing.

Suddenly a nasty tentacle blade comes flying by my face. I feel the wind as it passes within inches of me. Out of nowhere, Daniel pops up next to me with stone skin. He grabs the blade with his hand in midair and pulls it hard towards him bringing Donovan off the ground flying right into Daniel's stone fist.

I jump back and let Daniel do his thing to Donovan. I'm still trying to locate Wizard Kain. I can't see him anywhere. To be honest I can barely make out any energy signatures. I yell to Kristin. "I can't see any energy except ours and I can barely see that!" She looks back to me "There's a dampening field of some kind here! He's hiding himself!" She looks back to stabby redhead chuckling her evil face off

"You are all going to die here." The only thing I could think of is maybe she's the one who's doing it. I decide to take action. I focus through the low vibration and try not to vomit so I can slow time just enough to appear like I'm teleporting and pop right up in little Miss Stabbies face. The surprise on her face is delicious. I grab her arm and with my vamp strength I launch her across the room into the wall. She hits hard and I hear a crack, or six. I can't help but smile.

She hits the ground but is still alive. Before she could get back up Kristin was above her with her blade. She swings it quickly and the redhead's head rolls away. I have to tell ya, vamps are easier to take when you kill them. They turn to ash. Travelers do not, it's just a wee bit disturbing to me. Her body falls to the ground and her blood pools around it.

I really need to learn to pay more attention because suddenly one of Donovan's nasty rope tentacles comes close to stabbing me in the eye. I dodge it just in time and he tries to spray me but I think he realizes he could hit the dude he's trying to bring back laying in the sarcophagus next to me. Lucky me. I look down and see a few blades laying on the floor next to me and decide to make em float. Donovan's eyes look to the blades and

I see the panic set in on his face when he realizes I'm the one doing it.

I immediately send the blades flying at Donavan and his shocked face lets me know Tristan told him nothing of me and my powers. Two brownie points for Tristan. My level of trust for him just went up a few notches. I do love a good surprise. He smacks the blades easily away with his rope tentacles. He then looks down to the ground and he and I see a rock fist coming up from the floor in the direction of his face.

He jumps back a few steps and I can tell by the look on his smug face he's totally pissed off now. "I'm going to open your ribcage with my bare hands, and feed you your heart!" After his big baby tantrum, his suit suddenly starts to shred as bladed rope tentacles start coming out from every inch of his body. Six tentacles come out of his back and three more out of the front. His eyes start to change and his face transforms into some kind of hideous insect like a cross between a hornet and cockroach. He tries to attack us again and spits this rank acid at us, Daniel goes into the ground again.

I use my power and slow down time to get the hell out of the way. A smaller wave of nausea hits me this time. I guess I'm getting used to it. I end up behind him and decide to give my floaty blades another shot and let em fly again. He sees the attack coming and smacks them out of the way like he has eyes in the back of his head. Probably because he does. I'm not fast enough for his next attack.

He sends his tentacles at me. They do their job and wrap tightly around my arms. He gives me a clicky insect like chuckle and I feel a blade going through my back and then see it coming out of my chest. I start to panic and my body practically starts to work on its own. I start draining the life out of him as an instinctive reaction to what is happening. This is new. I didn't know that my body would be able to do this. He panics when he realizes what I am doing and what is happening to him.

He tries to let me go quickly to stop the draining, but I grab one of his tentacles tight and hold him pulling myself to his body and lapping up his life force like a thirsty beast while I make my way closer to his face. Even though his face looks like a deformed version of a mutated cockroach I can see the panic in his eye...eyes.

"Impossible, your kind is extinct." I grin. "You've never seen my kind, ass face." I laugh and stare into his eyes before I sink my teeth into his throat. He tenses up and screams as I drain every bit of life from him. Then I have tons of ash in my mouth. Gross. I spit and look over at Janet holding her blade at Kevin's throat.

He's crying. "You're my sister, you can't kill me." She looks back with cold eyes. "You killed your sister the day you betrayed your family. I'm nothing but death to you now." She grabs him by the hair then in one quick motion takes his head and turns him into ash. As she stands over the pile of ash I can see the tears start to pool in her eyes.

I start to make my way to her but out of nowhere a wave of power sends us both flying. It holds us to the walls of the room lifting us off the floor. The vibration is so intense it prevents us from moving and making me want to blow chunks. I can see but my vision is starting to go blurry off and on. And it finally happens, I see Kain walking in with the dagger in his hand tapping the blade against his leg as he walks and the bracelets in the other spinning them on his finger.

He's smiling. "It's good of you to show up for the party." Yeah. He's not very original I know. He looks down to the beheaded traveler on the floor. "Well that's a shame. You killed my blood bag." He then looks over to Janet and gives a bright smile. "Fantastic! I finally get to hurt you like I promised." He holds out the bracelets and starts to walk over to her. Janet speaks up.

"I'm a vampire you dumbass...we killed your Traveler remember?" His smile grows.

"Oh, you silly puppet. She was simply food when I took back my body. Human blood isn't what my body needs. I need my own blood. Haven't you heard? Vampire blood is my blood." He puts the bracelet on her wrist. It latches on and starts to grow. It looks alive as it starts to form legs like some kind of insect, then sprouts out a stinger, I realize it's taking the form of a scorpion. It sticks its stinger inside her wrist and she screams in agony. As she screams in pain Kains smile grows and he starts to laugh.

"You see my dear, these bracelets are special. They can be either painless or as painful as the one placing them wants them to be. I chose pain." I look to the floor and notice Daniels' blade laying there. I pick it up with my power and fling it at Kain's throat. It stops midair inches away from his throat and he looks in my direction.

"You are an interesting one aren't you. I'm going to save you for last. Your power will be perfect for me. Don't worry, I'll drain you dry soon enough, but first you need to learn your place."

Four blades come flying at me, one in each of my legs and one in each of my arms. The pain is so bad I almost pass out. He makes his way to his shrivelled up body in the sarcophagus. As he puts the bracelet on the decomposed wrist I thought it might snap off. Unfortunately it didn't. Janet screams louder as blood starts to flow out of the mouth of the bracelet on her wrist, it starts to float to the other on Kain's body filling his body with life.

The body starts to basically rehydrate. It's freaking gross. I see Janet starting to grow pale. I look back over to Kain's body and see Traveler Kain thrusting the dagger into his true body's chest. The black cloud of ash emerges from his mouth and starts floating into his true body that's lying there getting a nice fresh transfusion. After a minute I see the hand of Kain emerge from the sarcophagus trying to get the last of Janet's blood. His power evidently fades when he transfers bodies so thankfully we all fall to the ground.

I start to see spots in my vision because of the pain of being crushed and impaled but notice Janet fading fast. I pull one of the blades from my leg and with every ounce of power I have left

I launch it at Kain's hand. It flies through the air and makes a clean slice cutting the hand with the bracelet clean off his body.

Kain screams and starts to rise from the sarcophagus. Janet falls to the ground and the bracelet falls from her wrist. Kain makes his way to me getting up close and personal then takes his good hand grabbing my throat lifting me from the ground.

He's finally fully formed back to his beautiful self. And he is beautiful. I can see why Lilith fell for him so hard. He smiles at me. "Time to take my first gift. Thank you for your sacrifice." I can't help but think of how many times he has said this and to how many victims he's left behind without hesitation. He opens his mouth and sinks his fangs into me. As he starts to drink me down I can't move. I get a flashback to the parking deck where it all began. Here we go again. I start to fade fast. My vision goes in and out and I look down to my hand. I notice my skin starting to turn black. I'm about to turn to ash.

Suddenly he flinches back gasping, choking and coughing up blood. He holds his throat like he can't breathe. I start to chuckle weakly as my skin starts to burn. "Gotcha." I say knowing I'm taking his ass with me. He looks at me and growls. The next thing I know Sloan is in my face. I smile and look down to take his hands one last time. I realize that his hands are in the form of claws and can't help but smile at them. I do love that he can do that. Suddenly he thrusts them into my chest piercing my heart. The hell? Surprisingly I start to feel better for some reason. I feel his blood entering into my body. He's giving me a transfusion. I look up to his beautiful genius face and give him a bright smile.

"You came. My white knight." My skin stops burning and I'm able to move again. Sloan looks back to Kain. I've never seen this level of anger on his face, he's gone totally feral! His aura is massive and as red as blood. He jumps up and launches himself at Kain. I see Kain's smug face smiling like he's amused.

Big mistake. Sloan disappears and reappears behind him with a foot to the back of Kain's head. Kain goes flying back into the sarcophagus slamming into it and smashing it to bits and pieces. Sloan makes his way back over to me and I see a swarm of bugs come flying from the severed hand of Kain that was laying on the floor.

Sloan absorbs them and goes into a trance. Shit! He's vulnerable like this. I grab his hand and slow time trying my best to take him with me. It works. I look up and Kain is coming at us in slow motion. Sloan finally blinks and smiles at me. "I knew you would do that baby." That tricky little bastard. He looks at Kain coming at us in slow motion and I smile at him. "Do your thing baby." He chuckles. "On it."

He opens his mouth and a giant cloud of insects emerges. I'm still too weak to hold time and am about to pass out so I have let it go back to normal. As soon as I do, the cloud of insects swarm Kain and he starts to freak out swatting at them. It's useless. The insects go into every opening of his body, his ears, nose, mouth, eyes and the stub where his hand is severed and he screams.

All of the sudden a giant portal opens behind Kain and I see two well-manicured hands with long perfectly done red nails and a gaudy sapphire jeweled ring come out wrapping her arms around his body and pulling him in. Soon after the portal closes leaving us on the ground beaten, bleeding and out of breath. But alive. We sit there for a second not knowing what the hell happened.

"Is that it?" I say looking at Sloan. He shrugs. "I wasn't able to kill him." I take his hands.

"You did your best. And saved all of us." He turns to me. "No, I wasn't able to kill him because he didn't have a heart Brandon." My jaw must have dislodged from my face with the amount of shock I was in. "You're kidding." He shakes his head.

"No. but I did leave him a little gift." I see that fantastic evil grin on his face. I love that grin.

"I might have altered his DNA a bit. He won't be able to steal anyone else's gifts, ever. Vampire blood of any kind is now poison to him."

I can't help but laugh. "You rock baby." I realize he's here but I didn't bring him here.

"Um…not that I'm complaining but how the hell did you get here." He smiles. "You brought me here. The other you anyway." I lean my head back against the wall. "Go me."

I eventually get enough energy to get us all back to HQ through the shadows. We let Tristan know everything that transpired tonight. Letting him know about Donovan beforehand gave him time to send a unit to his house and capture a few more cult members that were trying to escape. Janet gets better after a few feedings and back to her old bitchy self.

When she leaves, for some reason she gives me a hug and thanks me. I know, I'm shocked as shit too. Word got out about the Masters of two states' betrayal and releasing Kain into the world. It also got out that they are now dead. That left two positions open. The vampire community decided to shift the position of Master of Alabama to Tuscaloosa from Mobile.

Yep, Tristan is now the Master of Alabama. The position for Master of Texas is still being discussed. Renovations on HQ are taking place as we speak. Our House is gonna kick ass when it's finished.

Kain has gone into hiding. Probably because he's not all powerful anymore thanks to my Sloan. Janet is keeping our secret especially after I tell her everything. She's the first one outside of our Family that knows the full truth. I trust her. Don't know why but I do. And of course, our House is keeping their mouth shut. That's what family does after all. They protect their own. Daniel and Kristin are getting ready to become Vampire and Bride.

I can't tell you just how excited they actually are. It's like they are getting married or something. Sloan and I decided to take a vacation, and by vacation I mean we go home and go back to our jobs. Gotta pay the bills. The House pays us, quite a bit actually, but Tristan says we need to make sure we don't lose our humanity and the best way to do that is to stay connected to humans. The House gave us an alibi for work, family, and friends by impersonating law enforcement saying we were witnesses of a major crime and our assistance was needed to solve it.

We still don't know who the woman was that pulled Kain into the portal but are keeping our eyes and ears open for any clues. For some reason Sloan doesn't have a connection to him even though he used his blood to make Kain not able to feed from vampires anymore. Either he has no connection or his connection is being blocked. Either way we are in the dark. Our family and friends of course freaked out when we returned wanting to know everything. I'm pretty good at keeping up the story, Sloan is getting used to it but it's going to take some time I think. He really does suck at lying, and I hate that I'm so good at it.

Laying here in our puppy pile, I can't help but smile. To think, not long ago, my life was a full on repeat of the same day to day events. Not saying I didn't love the life I had, I just didn't realize what my life was actually missing. Finally I know and have that thing I couldn't figure out I needed. I feel complete. I think I understand what Lilith was saying. "You are now complete". For so long I've felt useless. To be truthful the only person that made me want to keep going was Sloan. Now there's so much more. I have a family, friends, and finally, a purpose. Not to forget about the best part, Sloan and my furbabies. Truly the best part of my immortality. As I lay here with a smile on my face I can't wait to see what's to come in my new beautiful life. But for now, all I'm going to do is roll over and enjoy my puppy pile of love.

GLOSSARY

BLOODLINE - Lilith "Mother" {Chosen}
Turned
Bloodline Mother- Live human life. In death become undead.
{Requirement-The Chosen]

BLOODLINE - Kain "Father" {Cursed}
Turned
Bloodline Father- Instant undeath. Cursed blood. {Requirement-any Human}

Primogenitus
"Born-Turned"- {First-born of Lilith bloodline} Brandon King
"Father of the Chosen"

Travelers
"Born"- {Witches, Sorcerers} "Unknown"

Lilith {Mother, Goddess}
First created human female. Banished for not being submissive.
First Traveler. Can travel to any dimension "Reality" except Earth
because her blood runs through Kain's veins. Had an offspring
before being betrayed by Kain.

Power {alter reality of all dimensions except Earth.}

Kain {Father of the Cursed Vampires}
First love of Lilith. Betrayed her for her blood. Became the first vampire by stealing her blood and returning to Earth. Is the reason why Lilith can't travel to Earth any longer.
Power {His power comes from each of his offspring's gifts. Has to completely consume the offspring to retain the gift permanently.}

Brandon King {Primogenitus, Firstborn Chosen Vampire}
Only living human of Lilith's bloodline. Became Primogenitus after being murdered by a cursed vampire.
Power {Tribus Sanguinem} The only vampire to receive three gifts.
"Shade" = Power over the shadow dimension, a dead reality brought back to life by Brandon's very existence. The source of his undepletable energy.
"Energy Manipulation"= Power over all types of energy.
"Time Manipulation"= Power to slow and almost stop time. In truth he just speeds up his own body so greatly time seems to slow.

CPSIA information can be obtained
at www.ICGtesting.com
Printed in the USA
BVHW071540150720
583806BV00001B/117